FOUR CALLERS
IN RAZOR STREET

Borgo Press Books by S. Fowler Wright

Arresting Delia: An Inspector Cleveland Classic Crime Novel
The Attic Murder: An Inspector Combridge and Mr. Jellipot Classic Crime Novel
The Bell Street Murders: An Inspector Combridge and Mr. Jellipot Classic Crime Novel
Black Widow: A Classic Crime Novel
The Capone Caper: Mr. Jellipot vs. the King of Crime: A Classic Crime Novel
Crime & Co.: An Inspector Cleveland Classic Crime Novel
Dawn: A Novel of Global Warming
Dead by Saturday: An Inspector Cleveland Classic Crime Novel
The End of the Mildew Gang: An Inspector Cauldron Classic Crime Novel (Mildew Gang #3)
Four Callers in Razor Street: An Inspector Combridge and Mr. Jellipot Classic Crime Novel
The Hanging of Constance Hillier: An Inspector Cleveland Classic Crime Novel
The Jordans Murder: An Inspector Combridge and Mr. Jellipot Classic Crime Novel
The King Against Anne Bickerton: A Classic Crime Novel
The Mildew Gang: An Inspector Cauldron Classic Crime Novel (Mildew Gang #1)
Murder in Bethnal Square: An Inspector Combridge and Mr. Jellipot Classic Crime Novel
The Police and the Public
Post-Mortem Evidence: An Inspector Combridge and Mr. Jellipot Classic Crime Novel
The Return of the Mildew Gang: An Inspector Cauldron Classic Crime Novel (Mildew Gang #2)
The Rissole Mystery: An Inspector Combridge and Mr. Jellipot Classic Crime Novel
The Screaming Lake: A Lost Race Novel
The Secret of the Screen: An Inspector Combridge and Mr. Jellipot Classic Crime Novel
Three Witnesses: A Classic Crime Novel
Too Much for Mr. Jellipot: An Inspector Combridge and Mr. Jellipot Classic Crime Novel
The Vengeance of Gwa: A Fantasy of Prehistory
Was Murder Done? A Classic Crime Novel
Who Murdered Reynard? A Classic Crime Novel
The Wills of Jane Kanwhistle: An Inspector Combridge and Mr. Jellipot Classic Crime Novel
With Cause Enough?: An Inspector Combridge and Mr. Jellipot Classic Crime Novel

FOUR CALLERS IN RAZOR STREET

AN INSPECTOR COMBRIDGE AND MR. JELLIPOT CLASSIC CRIME NOVEL

by

S. FOWLER WRIGHT

WRITING AS "SYDNEY FOWLER"

The Borgo Press
An Imprint of Wildside Press LLC

MMVIII

CONTENTS

BOOK ONE: THE CRIME

BOOK TWO: THE TRIAL

BOOK ONE

THE CRIME

CHAPTER I.

MURDER OF ABEL MARKS

"IT looks," Inspector Combridge said, with excusable irritation, "as though I shall be late again. There ought to be a law against the discovery of murdered bodies after 2:30 P.M. on Saturday afternoons."

Superintendent Davis was sceptical of the utility of this proposal. "Considering," he said, "that we're dealing with people who break the law—"

"Not the discoverers. They're often quite decent folk. And, besides, they'd get fined if they did. There'd be some consolation in that.... Razor Street is in the Hatton Garden district, isn't it?"

"Yes. North side. Mostly manufacturing jewellers and allied trades about there."

"Nothing residential?"

"Am I a directory of London?"

"There's not much about it you don't know."

The superintendent, a large, slow man with a delusively sleepy manner, was not insensible to flattery, as few men are. He responded with the information that his subordinate sought. "Yes, more or less, I should say it is. Some of manufacturers still live on their premises in the old style, though not many, and there must be a number of caretakers, and houses which are occupied by private residents. What's the point?"

"Only, being Saturday afternoon, I wondered what they were doing there."

"It may have been morning when he was killed."

"Has the brilliant young constable expressed any opinion on that point?"

"I didn't say Decker was brilliant. I said he had acted with promptitude and discretion. All he said when he rang up was that he was called in by a woman who took him to an upstairs office, where she said she'd found her husband dead a few minutes before. The man had evidently been the subject of a murderous attack, and was quite dead, so he thought he'd better ring us up here at once, and stay on the spot to see that nothing was disturbed. He added that the woman said she knew nothing about it, and he saw no reason to doubt that she was telling the truth. But he told her she'd better stay till you should arrive, which she readily agreed to do."

"The dead man's the head of the firm?"

"So she said. Proprietor, I understood."

This conversation was interrupted by the entrance of the police-surgeon, Dr. Dillinger, for whom the inspector had been waiting. He ended it with: "Well, it's no good guessing. I shall know a bit more when I get on the spot." He went out with the doctor to the waiting car....

The streets between New Scotland Yard and the Hatton Garden district are congested with traffic during five and a half days of the week, but from the early afternoon of Saturday until Monday morning they are comparatively clear, and it was in little more than ten minutes that the police-car entered Razor Street, and drew up at the door of No. 33, the double-fronted premises of A. Rosenbaum & Co., a firm that specialised in the manufacture of rings, brooches and pendants, as its sign-board testified.

"It may be a murder," Dr. Dillinger commented as he got out of the car, "but it looks more like a hoax to me."

He glanced up at the premises that, like most of those in the street, appeared quiet and vacant, as though they had been abandoned for the weekend by their human occupants. He looked round on a pavement equally quiet and bare. He had expected, from numerous previous experiences, that there would be a curious crowd round the door: that people would be leaning out of open windows along the street.

"My instructions are…," Inspector Combridge smiled in reply, "that Constable Decker has the matter in hand, and that he is a discreet and capable man."

While they spoke, and ignorant of the good opinion of himself that Superintendent Davis had scattered abroad, P.C. Decker opened the door.

The discreet constable showed himself to be a lean man with an exceptionally long neck, and with a manner of solemnity suitable to the occasion. "I suppose," he said, as he led the way to the first floor, "you'll take a look at the body first; or will you see Mrs. Marks?"

"We'll see the murder first, if that's what you've got to show us," Dr. Dillinger, who was always willing to take the lead in conversation, replied.

The policeman opened the door of a large front room that was of the whole breadth of the premises. It was furnished well, if not sumptuously, as a business office. In the centre of the floor, facing the double windows, was a large mahogany desk. A swivel armchair stood before it that had been pushed slightly back at a slant, as though for its occupant to rise, and by its side on the floor, as though he had fallen from it, a man lay.

He was a thin, rather small man, bald, approaching middle age, rather carefully dressed. By the attitude in which he lay it was hardly necessary that Dr. Dillinger should give his expert opinion that he was dead. He lay somewhat on his left side, showing no evidence of violence until the police-surgeon turned him over and revealed a depressed wound on the left temple, from which a small jagged fragment of bone protruded whitely. There was a little dried blood going backward toward the ear, and on the carpet was a dark stain.

"Scarcely needs a post-mortem here to tell how the beggar died," Dr. Dillinger exclaimed, with his usual cheerfulness. I suppose this is just how he was found?"

"Unless Mrs. Marks interfered with him before she called me in," Decker replied with precision, "he hasn't been touched at all."

"And the murderer," Inspector Combridge remarked, "was kind enough to leave the weapon behind. A few finger marks from this, and there oughtn't to be much trouble in proving the case when we run him in."

"First catch your hare," the police-surgeon quoted. "But that's your business, not mine.... You've got the weapon, all right. There's no doubt of that."

The inspector had lifted, in a handkerchiefed hand, a round metal bar, small but heavy, from the carpet on which it appeared to have been carelessly dropped after the fatal blow had been struck. He looked round the room, and observed a safe that stood open. Its cash-drawer was pulled out.

"Looks like robbery," he commented. "Mr. Marks if that was the gentleman's name, stayed a bit too long after the staff had gone, and had his head bashed in when the thief saw him, and they both got a surprise."

"That's about it," the doctor agreed. "But that's your business. All I want is an ambulance. I suppose there no objection to using the telephone? A man's afraid to put his hands anywhere since this fin-gerprint business—"

"No. You can do that. I don't suppose the murder used it to ring up his friends; and, anyhow, the discreet Decker must have pawed it over already."

Inspector Combridge thought that if the murderer had been one of those careless amateurs who leave fingerprints for the assistance of the police, he would find them in a more probable place. He added: "And now I'll have a few words with the mourning widow."

The words had a callous sound, and Inspector Combridge was not an unfeeling man, but the fact was that Abel Marks was not of an appearance to suggest that his loss would be the cause of incon-solable grief.

CHAPTER II.

THE EVIDENCE OF THE BRIDE

INSPECTOR COMBRIDGE had a surprise. He had expected to meet an elderly Jewess, probably of the broadly full-blown variety, for his observation was that the meagre type of the male of that race will prefer weight in a wife. He saw a girl of about twenty, slimly built, and with no suggestion of Hebrew blood in her freckled face or her auburn hair. He had anticipated a woman expensively dressed, as the wives of wholesale jewellers are likely to be. He saw one who was clothed with a simplicity suggestive at once of good taste and an empty purse. He felt vaguely that something was wrong.

The incongruity suggested the unusual situation, from which is bred the unusual crime, and with this thought there came his first doubt that the murder might not be as commonplace in its occasion, nor its solution as simple as he had first been inclined to think. Not that he felt any suspicion of the girl who now faced him. There was nothing murderous in her appearance, and her ruddy hair alone would have disposed him to conclude her innocence in the absence of evidence of directly incriminating quality. Inspector Combridge himself had red hair. So had his five children. In common with all others who are similarly adorned, he had heard and resented the general aspersion that red-headed people are quick-tempered and prone to strife. He knew himself to be just, cool, and particularly slow to wrath. He was prepared, on any appropriate occasion to enter into a heated argument that most red-headed men are of this disposition, and that red-headed women have even more admirably angelic qualities

Now he saw a young girl who did not look as though Mrs. Marks was likely to be her name. In fact, but for a new wedding ring on her hand that he had been quick to observe, he would have called her Miss with no hesitation at all. In his own phrase, she had not "the married look."

Neither did she appear to be affected by grief, even to the extent that the widow of such a man as lay on the floor of the opposite room should be expected to feel, or at least display. Then why assume a relationship improbable on so many grounds? Even if Mrs. Marks were her name, she might be no more than a daughter-in-law, or a married niece. The assumption of the discreet Decker might have gone leaping beyond the fact. Inspector Combridge had learnt that the less you assume the less unlearning you have to do. He said cautiously: "You are Mrs. Marks, I believe?"

The girl who faced him was quiet in manner, but, though she showed no sign of grief, the inspector's experience was aware of bewilderment, perhaps anxiety, perhaps fear, which she was restraining with more success than all young women similarly placed would be able to do. Had she been a darkly passionate girl, or one of those notoriously dangerous blondes—! It was curious that she looked at him now for one blankly puzzled second as though not recognising the name. But after that she said: "Yes. I suppose there's no doubt he's dead? The policeman I called in said that there was no doubt about that." She added, as though her continued presence needed to be explained: "He asked me to wait here till you came."

"Yes," he answered, "I'm afraid there's no doubt he's dead. Do you live here, or are these premises only used for business?" The inspector looked round as he spoke at a scene that puzzled him. It was a living rather than an office-room, but singularly free from any aspect of femininity. It looked like a room where a single man of some means, but of no fineness of aesthetic taste, might live, and in which his meals would be served in a utilitarian manner. A bird, or a cut from a good joint, but the mustard might not always be freshly made.... The question did no more than approach the outskirts of the enquiry on which he was engaged, but he had found that central facts may often be reached more quickly by a quiet commencement some distance away. It appeared to be one which should be easy to answer, but he noticed that the girl hesitated again before she said: "Oh, they're the business premises. Mr. Marks lives here, as well. There's nowhere else, if you mean that."

"Was there anyone else, as far as you know, likely to have been in the house when the murder occurred?"

"No. I shouldn't think there would be. I don't really know. I came in, and came upstairs, and found him—like he is now."

"You mean you've no idea who did it, or how it occurred?"

There was again that curious, hardly perceptible half-second of hesitation before she answered: "No. Not the least. I can hardly believe it now." And yet when the words came Inspector Combridge felt that they sounded sincere—unless, of course, she were the one who had struck the blow, in which case the moment's hesitation, followed by denial in a woman's convincing tone, might be the natural reaction as courage or desperation roused itself to face the ordeal on which liberty or life itself might ultimately depend.

But Inspector Combridge knew the danger of speculating in advance of the facts he possessed. In the prosaic course of his investigations, he had found that a crime is most often what it appears to be. Here was a plain case of murder and robbery under such circumstances as were natural to such a crime. It was asking for trouble to look round for less probable solutions before the obvious one had been negatively probed. Yet there was a shade more of official distance, a shade less of natural friendly humanity in his manner, as he asked: "As there was no one else in the house, I suppose you were able to let yourself in?"

"Yes. Mr Marks—Abel—gave me a latch key this morning."

"This morning? For some special purpose today?"

"We were only married this morning."

Inspector Combridge paused upon this second surprising statement, though it might be an absolutely irrelevant fact. Actually, it explained some things which had seemed puzzling before. But it raised other questions that must be asked. The assumption that he was investigating a simple case of warehouse-breaking, with an incidental murder arising therefrom, lessened as he considered the girl before him in the light of a bride of a few hours.

He remembered having noticed that the dead man had been rather carefully dressed for one who was at the end of a business week. Well, that was explained now. But the girl who had married him, though it might be said that she was no worse dressed (or even better) in her way, had certainly not been hard to please in her choice of bridal attire. And married people usually remain together during their wedding-day. Violently bereaved brides must, he supposed, commonly show more emotion than this girl appeared to consider appropriate to the event. But he knew that the investigation of such a crime will often involve the exposure of awkward or unseemly matters which have no more than a fortuitous connection therewith. An innocent man may find an alibi impossible to establish without disclosing privacies of most unexpected kinds. It is as when a sudden earthquake rends away the side wall of a house, and the astonished occupants are exposed in instantaneous nakedness of love or quarrel, of sloth or prayer, of prying meanness or private grief....

"You'd better tell me about it," he said, "in your own way."

He left it to her to guess what he wished to know. There might be no little significance in what she took the question to mean.

She paused a moment, perhaps having her own doubt of the implications of what he asked, but when the answer came, it was brief and clear.

"We were married at the registrar's office this morning. After that I went home to fetch some things that I needed to have. I had arranged to get here at about half-past two, but it must have been later than that. About three I came straight upstairs, and into this room first. I waited here for a time—perhaps twenty minutes. The place seemed horribly quiet. I'm sure it must all have happened before then. I was waiting and listening. I should have heard every sound.... After that, I got restless. He told me to come straight up to this room, in case I got here first, but he'd expected me to be sooner than that, and I thought, suppose he hadn't heard me come in, and might be waiting in another room as quietly as I was here. So I went across the landing and looked into the next room—and when I saw him I thought that he was dead from the way he lay, and I ran downstairs to fetch someone at once. There was a policeman on the other side of the street, and—well, he came back with me, and then asked me to wait here. That's really all that I know about it."

"You came in a taxi, or your own car?"

"No. By bus. I didn't have much to bring." She glanced, as she spoke, at a suitcase, cheap, light, and small, which stood on a chair by the door. Certainly, if that were all, her personal property had not been difficult to convey. It occurred to Inspector Combridge that, if the dead man were the owner of a prosperous business, the two events of morning and afternoon might have made an enormous difference to her worldly prosperity. The question of a will could hardly arise. Wills are annulled by the ceremony of marriage. Abel Marks would not be likely to have made one in the two or three hours that had intervened between marriage and death. But if he had.... He asked: "Was the front door fastened when you came in?"

"Yes. I think so. I'm—well, practically sure. Of course, I wasn't noticing particularly. I just put the key in the lock, and the door opened."

Given with some hesitation, this yet had the sound of a truthful, and indeed natural reply. Yet the inspector saw that, if she were herself the criminal, it was clever, too. It did not risk the downright lie of the assertion that she had found the door open, which might be refuted, or discredited in ways she had no time to consider, but it left the possibility there. She had not said with precision: "I unlocked the door when I came in."

"May I see the key?"

"Yes, of course." She handed him a Yale key of ordinary pattern and size, which he did not return. He said: "I can judge better when I've had a look at the door.... I suppose you'll be staying here?"

"No. I shouldn't like to do that. I shall go back."

He saw it as a natural decision. She would hardly be likely to wish to stay alone in this place of death. But would it have been alone? Had Abel Marks meant to bring his bride to a servantless home? Or perhaps they would have been leaving together in the next hour?

"I suppose," he said, "you don't know this place very well? You can't tell me whether there's a caretaker or anyone who ought to be here?"

"No. I've only been here once—no, twice before. But one of those times was a good many years ago. I don't know it at all."

"You would have been going away together this afternoon?"

The answer hesitated again. "No.... Well, yes. I expect we should. There hadn't been anything arranged. I can't say what Mr. Marks intended to do."

"I'd better have a look round now. You can come with me, if you like, or wait here. I may want to ask you one or two questions after that."

"I'll come with you, if you don't mind. I've had enough of being alone here. I'm afraid I've not been very much help."

"You can't tell me what you don't know," Inspector Combridge answered reasonably. He was still disposed to regard her as an innocent woman, perhaps not the less because she had admitted freely that she had been in the house long enough to have committed the murder herself before calling P.C. Decker in. Yet that again might be no more than the calculated candour of a woman too shrewd to make any statement which might be disproved by the observation of others.

As he opened the door of the room, they heard the sound of the telephone bell in the front office, and a moment later Dr. Dillinger met them on the landing with the words: "There's someone on the phone wanting to speak to Mrs. Marks."

"I'll answer that," Inspector Combridge said quickly.

But, for the first time, and with a surprising sharpness, Mrs. Marks asserted herself against him. "I'll take my own calls, if you please."

As she spoke, anger, or some other emotion, gave a quick flush to her freckled cheeks. She stepped forward, entering the room where the dead man lay. To be first, the inspector must have used actual violence to push her aside.

He knew that he had no shadow of legal right to insist on taking the call, but that deficiency might not have deterred him had he felt assured that it would have assisted his investigation to do so. His trouble was that he was as yet quite unsure, like a hound on a doubtful scent. He might have wasted twenty minutes already talking to a woman who could give him no more help than she had done in the first sentences they had exchanged, and who was as innocent as himself of any responsibility for the crime, or connexion with it. Still there *was* a contrary possibility. She had been the one to announce the discovery of the death. She had been alone in the house with the murdered man. Violent and fatal blows have been struck before in the world's history by attractive young women of innocent appearances. Even, it is immensely probable, by some whose hair has been neither blonde nor black. And there had been those curious momentary hesitations before she spoke—Inspector Combridge remembered seeing a switchboard in the office below.

Doubtless, Mr. Marks would have the telephone switched through to his own office when the premises were otherwise vacated at midday. Doubtless, also, the conversation which was now to begin could, at that switchboard, be either interrupted or overheard. With this thought, the inspector descended the stairs with such celerity that by the time Mrs. Marks (taking the longer way round the desk to avoid the dead man, though the doctor observed that she looked down at him as she passed with unblinking eyes) had lifted the receiver to her ear, he was already in a position to overhear the conversation, and with a pencil poised over the operator's note-pd to take it down.

"Is that you, Carol?" a man's voice asked, rather thin and high-pitched. "I just wanted to let you know that I'm here, and—"

"Oh, Dad," the girl's voice interrupted. "I'm so glad you've rung up! I'm all right, but a dreadful thing's happened. Mr. Marks has been killed."

"*Killed*? Good God! Are you sure? It can't be much more than two or three hours since—what's happened?"

"He was dead when I got here, in the office upstairs. I didn't find out at first. He'd been shot, or hit on the head. It was a horrible sight. The safe was open, as though he'd caught someone clearing it out. The police are here now.... Where did you say you are?"

"Didn't I tell you? I'm at your Aunt Carol's. We—"

"I'll come to you," she interrupted again, "as soon as the police finish here. I don't see what they think they can do. The man who did it isn't likely to come back to be caught."

"No, he wouldn't do that. But I don't know what their procedure is. I don't think we'd better wait here for you. I'll come over at once. You'd better wait till I arrive. What a dreadful thing for you to find!"

"Yes, it was rather a shock. Well, good-bye, Dad. I'll wait here, of course."

Inspector Combridge made a full shorthand note of this conversation, and then frowned over it with a vexed conviction that he had been wasting his time. And yet—did not father and daughter take the bridegroom's sudden decease in an exceptionally heartless, almost casual way? It was a shock, of course! An unpleasant shock for a girl to come upon the body of a man violently slain. But that would be so without the important addition that it was the man to whom she had pledged herself till death did them part a few hours before. "What a dreadful thing!" her father had said, but it had been in no more than a flurried tone, as being the appropriate words which such an event required.... And yet might it not be argued that this absence of pretence, of aping grief or other emotions they did not feel, was an indication rather of innocence than of guilt? Would not a bad conscience have felt the need of demonstrating in a different way? Suppose that this young girl had married a much older and certainly unattractive man for the money which such a bargain brings, which was, in itself, the simplest, most probable explanation of such a union, was she (or her father either) likely to be overwhelmed with grief at such a tragedy as had occurred? Was the fact that they made no false parade of feelings that were not theirs to be counted against them as evidence that they were responsible for the crime? The law requires different proof from that—which is fortunate for innocent men.

But then again—when an older man of substantial income, if not of actual wealth, marries a girl who is young and poor, in an endeavour to buy her love, does he not seek to show her the advantages of the comfort that money gives? Does he leave her at the door of the registrar's office to fetch her suitcase herself, and bring it by bus to her new home?

It was more after the manner in which a new housemaid would be engaged and arrive.... Inspector Combridge, climbing the stairs in less haste than he had gone down, decided that there were still some things that he would like to know before he could put an attractive red-headed girl finally out of his mind as a candidate for the con-demned cell.

The red-headed one, whether or not she were responsible for her own bereavement, showed no disposition to linger beside the body of the husband she had lost so quickly. She was already cross-ing the landing as the inspector reached it. She said at once: "It was my father. When he heard what had happened, he said he'd come here at once."

Inspector Combridge must recognise this to be a frank and suf-ficient summary of the conversation he had overheard, but he re-solved that he would remain on the premises long enough to meet the father-in-law of the murdered man, and that he would occupy the intervening time in an examination of exits and entrances which had been too much delayed already. He said "I'm going to have the look round which I mentioned before, and which was interrupted by your telephone call." Mrs. Marks followed him down the stairs.

CHAPTER III.

THE EVIDENCE OF THE NEWS-VENDOR

INSPECTOR COMBRIDGE locked and unlocked the door several times, while Mrs. Marks looked silently on. He tried putting the key from the outside into the unlocked door, which opened before it could be turned. In fact, unless the heavy bolts on the inside were shot, or a larger key turned, the door, which had no other fastening, would not remain closed against the slightest outside pressure.

"I think," he said, "that it must have been locked when you came in."

"Yes," she agreed, with no apparent reluctance, "I should say it was."

She added a moment later: "It looks as though the man got in some other way."

"Unless Mr. Marks knew him, and let him in."

She made no comment on this suggestion, to which he silently added: "Him—if not her," and a sense of equity influenced him to add aloud, as though in rebuke of the unspoken thought: "Of course, he might have hidden on the premises before they were closed at midday."

He thought that she controlled relief at this suggestion to reply tonelessly: "Yes, it does sound rather more likely."

Its probability was not decreased as they went round the rear of workshops, the windows of which were strongly barred, and their outer sills coated with ancient dust. They found the yard door to be not only locked, but bolted and chained on the inside. They could observe no other means of entrance or exit. "However, he may have come in," Inspector Combridge concluded, "he must have gone out by the front door." Unless, of course, he—or she—were still there, which he did not say. But there was no reason that the murderer should not have walked out by the obvious exit. A Yale lock fastens itself when the catch is loose, and he would only have had to close the door quietly for Mrs. Marks to have found it locked when she arrived.

Still, the inspector felt that he had taken a first step forward along the slow path of investigation he knew so well. A man— probably a stranger—leaving business premises during Saturday afternoon when they are normally closed, is very likely to be observed. He remembered having noticed a newspaper-stand at the street corner, which was only four doors away. He decided that enquiry there should not be longer delayed. As he thought this, there was a sound of cars pulling up at the pavement outside. He said: "This will be the photographers, and the ambulance. You won't want to see them take him away. You'd better go back to the sitting-room upstairs, and wait there. I'll bring your father up to you, if he should come before they get off. By the way, what name will he give?"

"Merritt."

"Very well. I suppose he won't be long now? Had he far to come?"

"About half a mile. It was Isabel Street he spoke from Clan-ranald Mansions. He was at my aunt's flat."

She retired to the sitting-room, as he had proposed, and he turned his attention to giving instructions that there should be no avoidable disturbance of the scene of the crime. Being satisfied on this score, he ran rapidly downstairs, and out of the house. Arriving on the pavement, he strolled to the corner with the air of one to whom time was of no value at all, and paused before the wooden trestle on which were displayed the penultimate editions of the evening papers, together with a thin background of the residue of morning publications, and a few commercial and other journals for which there were customers in that business district.

The proprietor of this stall was so short and slender, and of so youthful a manner in his brisk alertness, that a casual observer might have taken him for a half-grown boy, unless a closer inspection had disclosed the greying hair, and the many wrinkles at the corners of the dark, quick eyes. He greeted Inspector Combridge in a way that showed that he was either able to recognise him personally, or was at the least aware of the profession to which he belonged. "Afternoon, Inspector. Anything I can do for you today?"

"Yes. You might tell me who you've seen going in and out of Rosenbaum's during the last three or four hours."

The dark eyes looked at him dubiously. "I might not have noticed particularly."

"Or again you might. I don't suppose you miss much that's going on round here."

"There isn't much going on to miss. Not on Saturday afternoons. It wouldn't be worth while to keep on if other days were the same."

"Which makes it easier to notice anything that does happen?"

"It might if you wasn't mostly looking the other way."

Inspector Combridge observed some reason in this reply. Upper Lot Street, at the corner of which they stood, is a much busier thoroughfare than Razor Street on any day of the week, and on Saturday afternoons this difference is at its highest point. It was reasonable that the man's eyes should be turned most often in the direction from which his customers came. But the inspector felt also that the replies he had received, though good-humoured in tone, might easily have been of a more helpful quality. He concluded that the newsvendor did not mean to tell him anything without knowing why he was asked, and that frankness concerning that which must soon be publicly known was the best card for him to play.

"Happen to know anyone on the press?" he asked, in his most casual tone. "I might know one or two."

"You might know one who'd give you something for the first tip of a murder not far from here?"

"Exclusive? I'd say he would."

"Very well. Give me what help you can, and in five minutes you can be ringing him up. By the way, what's your name?"

"I'm called Dick mostly round here."

"Very well. That'll do. How long have you had this stall?"

"Most of twelve years."

"And you must know the people by sight who go in and out of the places round?"

"I don't suppose there's over many I don't."

"Nor I. You know Rosenbaum's?"

"Yes. I know Mr. Marks. It's been his business the last six years."

"Do you know anything about his movements today?"

"I should say he's there now."

"So he is. What I want to know is whether you've seen anyone else going in or out there during the last three or four hours."

"You mean since the workpeople left at one?"

"Yes. Since then."

"Well, I've seen one or two."

Dick's reply seemed to be the prelude to information which must be important, and might be of vital quality. But, having said it, he paused, and stared at the inspector as though suddenly realising the significance of the questions he was asked.

"You mean," he said, "that Marks has killed someone this afternoon?"

"I didn't say so. Why do you suppose that?"

"If he'd killed them, they couldn't have come out."

"Obviously not. It's Marks who's been killed. He's been murdered, and most probably robbed. So you see why I look to you to give me all the help that you can."

"Well, I'll do that. There was a man who went in about one-thirty. I couldn't say to ten minutes one way or other. He stayed a good bit. Say half an hour."

"What sort of man was he?"

"Shabby. Not young. Fifty or more. Rather tall. Bowler hat. Not much to look at, if you know what I mean."

"You'd know him again?"

"Yes. I reckon I should. I should if I saw him walk."

"How did he come out? As though he didn't want to be seen?"

"Not to notice. Not special. I didn't look at him that careful."

"Naturally not. Which way did he go?"

"He came right past me, along here."

"So that you got a good look.... Anyone else go in?"

"Yes. A lady went in a few minutes after. She came out quicker."

"You mean she came out in a hurry?"

"No. I didn't mean that. I meant that she didn't stay long."

"A young lady was it?"

"No. More what you'd call middle-aged. About the same age as the man, but a bit different style. Not so much under the weather, as you might say."

"Know her again?"

"Yes. Anywhere."

"And after that?"

"That's the lot that I know of."

The reply was disconcerting. If he had seen nothing of Mrs. Marks either going in or coming out in agitation to summon P.C. Decker, it discounted the quality of his previous observation, though its value might not be entirely destroyed. Or if he had seen her and could describe her as an elderly lady of fifty-five, it made him even more unreliable in memory of what he saw. Apart from that discrepancy, his evidence was almost exactly what the inspector had hoped, though hardly expected to hear.

He would have proceeded at once to probe the defect in observations which seemed otherwise to have been so exactly made, and were stated so confidently. But even as he considered how best he could frame a further query which would test the value of the replies he had already received, a taxi came round the corner at which they stood, and pulled up as nearly before the front of Rosenbaum & Co.'s premises as the ambulance allowed. Guessing who it would most probably contain, he hurried back, intent upon having a few words with Mr. Merritt before he should meet his daughter, or, at the least, of making sure that it would be in his presence that that meeting would take place.

As he approached the taxi, two people descended from it. The man, who got out first, was thin and of somewhat nondescript appearance. He stooped slightly. By the way he peered at the dial, it might be inferred that he was short-sighted: by the way he fumbled and hesitated over paying the fare, that a taxi was not a vehicle that he was accustomed to use.

The woman who followed was as tall as he, and looked taller. She stood on the pavement, quiet and self-possessed, waiting for her companion to discharge the fare, and watching the detective's approach. Inspector Combridge, using his wits, observed a woman who, though of a generation older than that to which Mrs. Marks belonged, and nearly a head taller, was not without some resemblance to the younger woman. He remembered that Mrs. Marks had said that her father would be coming from her aunt's flat. Evidently this was the lady, who had decided to come to her niece's assistance. The inspector, who had been puzzling himself for two previous seconds as to why it should have taken Mr. Merritt such a considerable time to come half a mile by taxi, saw that there might be a sufficient explanation in the fact that he had had someone for whom to wait.

"Mr. Merritt, I expect?" he asked, in his more genial, less official manner. Even if Mrs. Marks must be under the vague suspicion attaching to one who has announced the finding of a murdered man until some other person can be indicated as responsible for the corpse—a suspicion which had been appreciably lessened by the news-vendor's evidence—that was no sufficient reason why her relatives should be treated with the reserve appropriate to those who are on the doubtful border of criminality. "And, I suppose—?" He looked at the lady, who announced herself without waiting for her companion's lagging introduction. "I am Miss Barman—Carol Barman—Miss Merritt's—I should say Mrs. Marks's aunt."

"I am Chief Inspector Combridge. I believe you have heard already that Mr. Marks has been murdered this afternoon. Mrs. Marks is upstairs. If you'll come in here, I'll give you a few details before you see her."

He had spoken to Miss Barman, rather than to her companion, as though recognising the stronger character, and while he did so he led them into the warehouse that was at the back of the ground floor. The offer to give them information was not one to which they would be likely to object, though it might be no more than a pretext for gaining it from themselves—information which might prove to have no importance beyond enabling him to eliminate Mrs. Marks from the case in a final, orderly way.

CHAPTER IV.

MISS BARMAN REMOVES THE BRIDE

INSPECTOR COMBRIDGE discovered a single chair, of the cane-seated variety, for Miss Barman's use, and a stool for Mr. Merritt. He decided that a table-corner would be sufficient for his own use. Miss Barman said: "You'd better take the chair, William," and seated herself on the high stool. Her brother-in-law obeyed her in a bewildered, preoccupied manner. He appeared to be overwhelmed by events which had passed either beyond his comprehension or his control.

Inspector Combridge was brief and lucid in description of the tragedy which he had been called in to investigate, but it was not his habit to distribute information with a promiscuous liberality, and he saw no reason to mention the conversation which their coming had broken off. He concluded: "That's how it is, and I expect you'll be prepared to take charge of Mrs. Marks, and probably get her to return to her own home. It couldn't be very pleasant for her to remain here, especially as I shall be leaving a constable on the premises. But I needn't tell you that everything will be safe with us.... What I wondered was whether either of you could tell me anything that would throw light on the crime."

Miss Barman answered for both: "No. I don't think either of us would be likely to do that. Perhaps I ought to tell you that we have never known much about Abel Marks' private affairs. And though, of course, you might call it a dreadful thing, happening in this sudden way, I don't want you to think that it's any great grief to us. We consider Mrs. Marks first, as you'd expect us to do, and there's no doubt that Carol's had a very lucky escape."

The inspector saw that he had met a lady who was prepared to talk, and in a downright manner. He still wished to hold an open mind between the more probable theory that Abel Marks had been killed by a warehouse-breaker, with no other incentives than fear of capture and greed of gain, and the alternative possibility that he had been struck down by a personal enemy (perhaps through jealousy of the morning's marriage?), on which theory it was possible that these people might be able to give him information of greater value than they would be aware. Anyway, a little further knowledge could not be harmful to have. "I gather," he said to Miss Barman, "that the marriage did not have your approval?"

She still answered for both: "We did all we could to prevent it, from first to last."

"Young people," he sympathised, "won't take much advice these days. They prefer to find out for themselves."

But Miss Barman wouldn't accept this explanation. "No," she said with emphasis. "It wouldn't be fair to her to put it like that. Carol thought first of her father all along. A bit too much, if you ask me. But we'd better tell you the whole tale now we've begun."

Inspector Combridge prepared himself to listen patiently, though in a fresh doubt of whether he might not be losing time during which the murderer would be making his traces harder to find. The talkative lady had already said that there was no information regarding the crime to be had from them, and his experience was that tales which the police are anxious to hear are usually those which others are slow to tell. Still, on the balance of doubt, he would have listened to the offered narrative, if Mr. Merritt had not obtruded himself for the first time.

"No, Carol," he said. "The Inspector won't want to be hindered with all that now. He's got this murder to investigate, and his hands must be full with that. Carol can come home now, and that's all that matters to us."

The inspector, only momentarily confused by the fact that aunt and niece had the same name, judged correctly that the offered tale would have contained particulars of Edward Merritt's actions or circumstances which he preferred should remain untold, but it did not follow that they would assist the enquiry he had on hand. Anyway, here was information which could be had, if it were required, at a later hour. It might be of far greater urgency to obtain a fuller description from the news-vendor of the man who had called upon Abel Marks during the afternoon, and to start it circulating through the usual channels. Mr. Merritt's interposition tipped a doubtful scale.

Inspector Combridge rose briskly from the table. "Yes," he said. "I don't want to be rude, but I have got my hands full at the moment, as Mr. Merritt is good enough to observe. You'd better take Mrs. Marks home with you, as you propose. You must let me have the address where she can be found—19 Clanranald Mansions? That's quite sufficient. I know where they are.... We shall want a short statement from her, but I'll arrange about that tomorrow."

Miss Barman said: "Oh, well!" and shut her mouth firmly upon the words. The exclamation was in a tone which made him vaguely uneasy, and inclined to wish that he had reached an opposite decision a moment before. But he must not blow hot and cold.

Five minutes later he saw William Merritt, with the two Carols, old and young, depart in a taxi which he had himself been obliging enough to stop for them in Upper Lot Street, and walked back himself to the street corner to complete the conversation which their arrival had interrupted.

The news-vendor was still there. "I tried to tell you," he said. "But you'd gone too quick. Them was the two that I saw going in before."

"You mean that those were the people who called on Mr. Marks separately during the afternoon? You are quite sure about that?"

"I'd take my Bible oath on the man."

"And the woman?"

"I'm about as sure."

"You're quite certain that the second wasn't a smaller woman a girl of about twenty?"

"You mean her that's gone off with them now? No, I can't say that I ever set eyes on her before."

"I'm not trying to trap you. I think you're telling me all you know, and as accurately as you can. But it's a fact that, whether she went in or not, that young woman came out and called a constable in from the other side of the street about an hour before I got here."

Dick Skimmer heard this without appearing to be either surprised or abashed. "Well," he said, "what of that? I didn't tell you nothing happened I didn't see. It might have been when I was away having some tea."

"You were away part of the time?"

"About ten minutes."

"Or more?"

"Not much."

"Did anyone take your place?"

"No. There's never anyone here except me."

"You just leave the papers?"

"Yes. If a customer takes one, he puts a penny down. It's too public for them to steal, even if they'd be mean enough for a try. I don't lose tuppence a month."

Inspector Combridge considered this. It was possible that Carol Marks might have entered, and come out to call the policeman, within the time that the man had been away from his stall. Possible, but no more. Her own account made the two events somewhat further apart, but he considered that time may go slowly while a woman waits in an empty room, and perhaps not least so when she is a nervous, if not an unwilling bride; and the man's absence, for all he knew, might easily have been for twenty minutes rather than ten. It was possible. But one thing was certain. It could not be stretched to leave a margin for another individual to have entered, murdered, robbed, and left before Mrs. Marks had arrived. If the man's evidence were to be relied on at all, it seemed to follow that Abel Marks had been killed either by William Merritt or Carol Barman, or that they had called, one after the other, gazed at a murdered man, and gone silently away, which was not an explanation easy to entertain.

Inspector Combridge cursed himself that he had not listened to the tale which Miss Barman had been so willing to tell. It was ten to one, or even much higher odds, that, if she had any guilty knowledge, she would have given herself away, either by statements the falsity of which would have been demonstrated subsequently, or by omission to mention some damning fact, such as that of her earlier call.

Well, it was useless to lament an error already made! It was through such inevitable blundering that the truth would often be reached by a patience that did not tire. He went back to give some instructions for the guarding of the premises during his absence, and for a brief telephone conversation with Scotland Yard, and then took a taxi to Clanranald Mansions with a determination to listen with greater patience to whatever Carol Barman might have to stay.

CHAPTER V.

THE VACANCY OF MISS BARMAN'S FLAT

INSPECTOR COMBRIDGE pressed a bell and had the satisfaction of hearing it ring. That, in fact, was all the satisfaction he had, for, though he rang more than once, no one opened the door.

He lifted the letter-box flap, and his temper was not improved by a vision of uncarpeted boards. It appeared that No. 19, Clanranald Mansions was not only empty of human life, but bare of the furnishings by which residence is probably, if not certainly, indicated. How great a fool had he been? It was a question on which speculation was unpleasant, and its answer was not easy to guess.

"Well," he thought, "there's the man in the lift. I suppose I shall soon know. I wonder what sort of fairy tale I should have heard if Merritt hadn't tipped her off to keep a shut mouth?" He remembered that he had first had this address, as her aunt's residence, from the younger woman. It appeared to indicate that she also was in the plot. Wholesale robbery, by marriage and murder, it seemed to be, with an audacity that he had seldom met. Doubtless it had been the younger woman's allotted part to give the alarm, after the major criminals had cleared off. The simulated plundering of the safe was calculated to be sufficient to put him on a false scent, which, but for the news-vendor's observation, it might have done.

Yet, if so, why give the address of an empty flat? Surely that was to invite a suspicion which might otherwise glance aside. It seemed so pointless a folly that the inspector recognised the possibility, even the certainty, that the explanation must be less simple than that which had suggested itself to his mind at his first instinctive resentment against the trick which appeared to have been played upon him; and which had been sharpened by the suspicion that he had had the actual murderers in his hands, and had allowed the whole party to escape together, leaving him with no better means of tracing them than a false address which they had combined to foist upon him. Why, it had actually been his own proposal that they should take the younger woman away!

Yet—if the whole tale of the marriage were not a hoax, the meaning of which was not easy to read—if there had been any hope that the bridegroom might be murdered without the guilt being traced to the bride or her accomplices (relatives or not, yet a relative he judged the elder woman to be)—what could be the object of the false address, of the unfurnished flat? Perhaps they had taken fright at something he had done or said, and fled suddenly in consequence of that panic fear? Had they seen him talking to the man at the corner, and been conscious of that sharp-eyed individual's observation when they had left the premises of the murdered man during the earlier afternoon?

Yet—if that were so, had they prepared the false address in advance, and why had the younger Carol used it when first she did? If it had been her aunt's legitimate home, there was the difficulty that it could not have been cleared in an hour, even if murderers in flight would be likely to burden themselves with the furniture of a four-roomed flat.

All these thoughts passed through the detective's mind as he waited at the door of the lift, with the whining noise of its approach in his ears.

The liftman, on his appearance, proved to be uncommunicative at first. No. 19 was occupied by Miss Barman. It was not to let. He would say no more until his tongue was relaxed by the sight of the detective's card, and the details which he then added did nothing to reduce the mystery. Miss Barman was a single lady of whom he spoke with respect. She had been a tenant for several years, possibly longer. In fact, longer than he had held the position of caretaker to the premises. She was quiet in her habits, and punctual in her payments.

But, two days before, Messrs. Loames & Prideaux, the second-hand furniture dealers in Easter Street, had sent a van and removed most of her effects, with her consent and assistance. He had informed the landlords by telephone of this event, as he was instructed to do under such circumstances, and they had replied that there was no rent outstanding and that they had no occasion to interfere. He had had no subsequent instructions from them to offer the flat for reletting, and, when he had asked Miss Barman whether she were leaving, he had received no more than a curt negative in reply. He believed (though he was only able to judge from what he had seen removed) that the contents of the kitchen, and probably a few other essential articles were still in the flat.

Miss Barman, he said, had been at home until about two hours earlier, when she had left with a gentleman. Mr. William Merritt? He could not say. He knew no one of that name. In fact, he had scarcely seen her visitor, who had come up the stairs, avoiding the lift. They had gone down together by the same way, but there was no singularity in that. Miss Barman was a lady who used the lift to come up, but would often descend by the stairs rather than ring for it to take her down.

Inspector Combridge found that he had to adjust his mind once again. It appeared that the address was genuine, and to that extent Mrs. Marks must be acquitted of any deception. So, perhaps, should the other two. The episode of the vanishing furniture, strange though it was, might have no connexion whatever with the murder of the Razor Street jeweller, nor was it a matter which Miss Barman would be likely to disclose to strangers whom it did not concern. Besides, he must not forget that he had rejected her offer to explain something to him, and what it was he might never know. But the death of the man whom she and her brother-in-law were said to have visited during the afternoon, and whom her niece had married earlier in the day, still awaited solution, and he must lose no time in the effort to retrieve whatever blunders he had already made.

How then was he to proceed? The essential question was whether Miss Barman were now in flight, or would shortly return to her empty flat. He decided that an inspection of it might go far toward answering that question. He asked the caretaker for permission to go over it, and received the reply that he must refer to his employers, who would not be normally at their offices at so late an hour on Saturday. Perhaps, if the inspector would look in again on Monday morning, he could obtain the necessary permission, or Miss Barman might then be in, and able to speak for herself.

It was a delay to which Inspector Combridge was not prepared to agree, though he recognised that he was proposing a trespass which, if Miss Barman were an innocent woman, might be very hard to defend. He said "Come now, Mr.—Mr. McAdam, is it? I knew you were Scotch at the first glance. So is my wife's sister-in-law. Born in Kirkcudbright. One of the nicest women I ever met.— You're not going to tell me that you don't know of any way of getting in touch with the owners or their agents during the weekend? Suppose the place were on fire?"

"I could get through to Mr. Ritchie, at his house," McAdam admitted, "but that would be a trunk-call."

"Well, I'm willing to pay."

"I'm not allowed to ring him up without something serious happens.

"I haven't asked you to. Give me the number, and I'll do that in the name of Scotland Yard, and you can hear his reply."

The caretaker wavered, but the three-fold influences of respect for the law, the personal magnetism of Inspector Combridge, and his somewhat nebulous connexion with Kirkcudbright, were too strong to resist. The Scotsman looked at his watch. "It's nigh a shilling," he said seriously, "up to two, seven pence from that time till seven, and five-pence after that hour. It's six-fifty-three now, so I suppose you'll—"

"No. I think not. As a matter of fact, there'll be no charge for this call. I'll get through at once, if you'll give me the number, and come with me to the box. I suppose you've got one where we can get through?"

They were on the ground floor, standing at the door of the open lift, as the conversation came to this point, and McAdam would have led the way across the hall to a telephone-box that was concealed by the foot of the curving stairs, had they not been interrupted by the approach of a white-aproned vanman, who held out a dirty envelope. "Mr. McAdam?" he said. "I suppose that'll be you?"

The liftman tore open the envelope, and glanced at the few lines that it contained. He said to the vanman: "Yes, that's right; you can bring it in."

He handed the note to the inspector. "I don't see," he said, "that you'll be wanting to make that call."

Inspector Combridge read a pencilled note:

> Please let the bearer have access to my flat to deliver some furniture. I shall be grateful if you will tell him where to put the things, as well as you can, if he isn't sure.
>
> Carol Barman

He followed the vanman, who was already moving toward the street, to ask: "When did you get this?"

The man looked puzzled. "It's all right," he asked, "isn't it? We're not wanting to clear anything out. The lady wrote it while we were loading up."

"How long ago?"

"Well, about two hours back, or it might be a bit more."

"You're not usually working at this hour?"

"No, we don't reckon to deliver at this time of day. Not on Saturdays, anyhow. The guv'nor wanted to put it off, but she said she needed some things special for the weekend, and she'd pay time-and-a-half rather than wait."

"She said this not more than two hours ago?"

The man showed some irritation at the pressure of these seemingly pointless questions, but did not refuse reply. "No, I didn't say that. She gave her orders when she came at three o'clock, more or less. She called to write the note while we were loading up, and she said she'd found she mightn't be here when we were bringing it in."

They were in the street before this explanation concluded. A tarpaulin-covered lorry stood at the pavement, showing the name of Loames & Prideaux along its side. The vanman said: "Right you are, Tom. Carry on," to his mate, who commenced to throw off the cover, disclosing a number of articles of domestic furniture. The inspector observed that though they were solidly made, and in reasonably good condition, they were not new. He remembered the name on the lorry as being that of the firm who were said to have removed the lady's furniture two days before. "Not the first time you've been here?" he suggested.

The man looked at him doubtfully, and his tone had become surly as he replied: "The guv'nor says if the lady likes to sell her things and then buy them back, it's no business of his."

The manner in which this was said suggested that there might be others who would do well to adopt the guv'nor's attitude of aloofness to a maiden lady's eccentric ways, but the man had already given the information that the inspector sought.

Two days before Miss Barman had been in such need of money that she had sold the furniture of her flat. The call had been so urgent that she had not been able to wait the advantages of a public auction, but had accepted whatever a firm of second-hand dealers could be persuaded to give; and the inspector had sufficient knowledge of such transactions to conclude that she must have received much less than the things were worth.

Today, she had bought them back, at whatever profit to Loames & Prideaux they had had conscience to ask, and she had been willing to pay. She must have called to arrange the transaction after her afternoon call upon Mr. Marks, and made the second visit when on her way to Razor Street with her brother-in-law, to fetch Carol Marks away.

That she had obtained the means of redeeming her furniture from Mr. Marks appeared to be a most probable guess. On the most innocent interpretation of her share in the events of the afternoon, she had lost no time in reaping advantage for herself from her niece's marriage. And the father appeared to have acted separately with an equal promptitude. And after that, when the father had telephoned to enquire concerning his daughter's welfare, and in professed ignorance of the tragedy which had occurred, the two had been together in the almost empty flat.

In its simplest, most innocent aspects, and even if (which was becoming increasingly difficult to believe) it had no connexion with the bridegroom's death, the conduct of the two older people appeared to furnish an extreme example of instant begging by the impecunious relatives of the young bride of an elderly, and presumably affluent man; but even this explanation did not clear the event of some very puzzling features. There was Miss Barman's gratuitous statement that they had both done their utmost to oppose the marriage. That might be no more than a bold lie: a denial hurriedly made before the accusation arose. But there was also the fact that the married pair had separated immediately, the bride of the wealthy man going off to fetch her clothes, and then travelling by bus, with the weight of her suitcase on her own arm as she came to her husband's door. This was not, perhaps, beyond some simple, reasonable explanation. But it was certainly queer. And when murder and queer events go hand-in-hand (as they often do) their relations to each other, in the inspector's experience, would prove to be of more than a casual kind.

So he wondered and thought, as he returned to Miss Barman's flat, not by the lift, but following the slower course of the stairs. For he was resolved to take the opportunity of entering it, and he had been quick to take the caretaker's hint that he might now do so by a method which would have no sanction from him, but with which he would not interfere.

He found that the flat consisted of a lounge, two bedrooms, a bathroom, and a small but sufficient kitchen. Clanranald Mansions is not one of the newest blocks of flats. It has no central heating. It cannot boast of hot-and-cold in its bedrooms. But the rooms are larger and better-proportioned than has been the more recent mode, and Miss Barman's lounge, when fully furnished, had been one into which no gentlewoman need have been ashamed to invite a guest. But now it contained little besides a fender, and some artistic but commercially valueless pictures upon the walls. One of the bedrooms was in a state of almost equal nudity. The other contained a bed, a chest, and a few minor articles upon its carpetless floor. The kitchen appeared to have retained its furniture and equipment undisturbed, and the debris of a meal for two, on its small deal table, revealed that it had been used as a living-room earlier in the day, when Mr. Merritt had received his sister-in-law's hospitality, presumably after their separate visits to the Razor Street premises.

Inspector Combridge concluded from what he saw that, whether Miss Barman had regarded the departure of the more valuable of her effects as being of a permanent character, or had foreseen how quickly they would return, she had intended to hold her ground in the flat she rented, for which purpose she had retained the first necessities of civilised existence, though its comforts had been removed.

The redeemed goods were now commencing to arrive, some by the lift and some by the stairs, and the vanman, seeing the inspector to be walking about the flat with the confidence of one who is conscious of his own right, very naturally concluded that he had spoken previously with an authority which he certainly did not possess, and when he asked: "You're not going to tell me that you've brought back all Miss Barman's furniture on that lorry?" the man answered readily: "No, sir. Only some things that she wanted particular. It's mostly bedroom stuff that we've brought now. The rest is to come on Tuesday. We're full up on Monday with other jobs."

"You seem to know where to put it without asking McAdam?"

"Well, sir, we get some practice in seeing where stuff is most like to be fitted in. And it's only two days since I took this lot away."

"You must have a good memory, all the same," Inspector Combridge replied genially, as he moved toward the door. He had decided to give Miss Barman a call at a later hour, when she would presumably have returned, and to use the interval for a much-needed meal. But before his eyes had come round to the entrance, he was greeted by the voice of the lady herself: "I'm sorry that I was out, Inspector; but you seem to be making yourself quite at home."

CHAPTER VI.

MISS BARMAN PREPARES TO TALK

"I BEG your pardon," Inspector Combridge said, in regrettably mendacious self-justification, "but I thought I'd better wait as you were out; and seeing these men bringing the things in—"

"I'm sure your professional curiosity was aroused."

It was not the way in which he had intended to complete the sentence, which was one of those which may be advantageously broken short, and he recognised that she had the better of this opening exchange. Yet he did not think she was quite at ease, and he had leisure himself for a thought that there might be self-exposure in the asperity which her words contained. Would it not have been wiser, more natural, to have greeted him in a more indifferent manner, if her own conscience were clear? But, against that, was not the condition of the flat itself a sufficient reason for her annoyance? Whatever explanation there may have been for the movements which her furniture had suffered she might resent the observation by one whom (unless it were of a criminal character) it certainly did not concern.

But whatever annoyance she may have felt appeared to have left her mind as she went on in a quieter voice: "I suppose you want to see me again about my niece's trouble?"

"I did want to have a few words with you."

"I'm afraid I can't ask you to sit down, except in the kitchen. I've been having some of my things moved." She added with a smile: "But I expect you've been able to deduce that for yourself."

He thought: "She's either an innocent woman, or one with an exceptionally good nerve." He said aloud: "I'm sorry to have to trouble you at an awkward time, but I shall be quite comfortable here."

They were in the kitchen as he concluded this sentence, and she offered him one of the two chairs which it contained, and then began to clear the table. "I don't know how you're feeling," she said hospitably, "but it's a long while since I had a meal. There's not much here, but I'm going to make myself a cup of tea, and you're welcome to anything I can dig up."

He hesitated in his reply, a feeling of satisfaction that she was evidently prepared to talk being complicated by another which required him to maintain some formality of distance between himself and a woman whom it might be his duty at any moment to take into custody on a capital charge. He was not one of those officers who will endeavour to establish friendly relations with suspected persons that they may entrap them the more easily. But he reminded himself of the doubtful axiom (which was not doubtful to him) that if she were innocent she would have nothing to fear from the justice of English law, and answered: "Well, just a cup, thanks. If you're sure it's no trouble to you." And then went on at once, while she continued to busy herself with the crockery and the electric kettle: "In a case of this kind, we always ask everyone who's been in immediate contact with it to make a statement of what they know. They're not legally obliged to comply, but it saves a lot of trouble to us if they do, and sometimes to them as well."

"I tried telling you once," she said, but with amusement rather than hostility in her voice, "and I understood that you were too busy to hear."

"Well, we all make mistakes sometimes. I didn't know then that you'd seen Marks during the afternoon."

She showed no surprise at this statement, nor did she attempt denial. She said simply: "And now I suppose you'd like to know what I was doing there."

"Yes, I should."

"I went to get back £80 17s. 10d., which I'd paid two days before."

"You mean paid to Abel Marks?"

"Not exactly. Though it was going to him."

"And he gave you the money?"

"Yes. He did that." Her voice as she said this was quiet and matter-of-fact, but he thought he detected an under-current of grimness, as though it would have gone ill with Abel Marks, had he declined to disburse the money.

"And do you know that Mr. Merritt also called on Mr. Marks during the afternoon?"

"Yes, I know that."

"And did he also call to collect an outstanding debt?"

"No. His account wasn't the kind that anyone would be able to pay.... If you'll just wait till the kettle boils, I'll tell you several

38

things that you don't know, and that it would take you some time to find out, if you ever could. But what it's got to do with you, or with Abel Marks' death—well, it wouldn't be any use for me to say it's just nothing at all. You'll say you've got to decide that for yourself, and don't want advice from me.... But I'll tell you one thing. I'm one who likes to talk straight, and I'm glad he's dead. And if you can find anyone who'd wish to see him alive again, you'll have done a harder thing than finding out how he died."

"I had understood already," Inspector Combridge concurred, "that you hadn't any strong affection for him."

"Not a shred. As a matter of fact, I met him this afternoon for the first time, though I'd heard talk enough about him during the last three years, and off and on before that."

"But your niece looked at the matter rather differently?"

"So you'd think, seeing what she's just done. But you'd better let me tell the tale from the start. If we don't get the beginning first, we shall be a long while reaching the end."

"Well, I'm ready to listen."

But Miss Barman said no more till the kettle boiled, and an improvised meal of the oddments the larder held, but with an unexpected daintiness of service, had been laid out. Then she sat down opposite her uninvited guest, and started her narrative.

CHAPTER VII.

MISS BARMAN HAS MUCH TO SAY

"WILLIAM MERRITT," Miss Barman commenced "married my sister Sylvia, about twenty-two years ago. He was a harmless worm of a man then, as he is now, and if you think he'd got the backbone to kill Abel Marks, for which you may see, before I've done, that he had cause enough, you'll save time if you begin making another guess.

"He was a traveller for Aaron Rosenbaum then—the old man's been dead these seven years—and Abel Marks was another. But Will had some money his uncle left coming to him when he was twenty-five, and he used it to go into the retail trade. I remember my sister saying some nasty things about Abel then. Nothing serious, but he used to call her Miss Barmaid, which he seemed to think a good joke, and she didn't agree. I don't suppose he'd have come on the scene again only that, after they were married, he used to call on William for orders, and William gave all the trade he could to his old firm.

"Carol was born when Sylvia had been married about two years, and three years later my sister died. William's business did well up to that time, and a good bit longer, but there came a time when it began to go down.

"I wouldn't say that was William's fault. He worked hard enough, and he didn't spend; but the fact was that people were moving away. The world was changing round him, and he went on as though things would always be just the same.

"Things had changed at Rosenbaum's too. Abel had given up travelling, and became general manager. Aaron Rosenbaum was an old man, and he was nearly blind in his last years. He used to trust everything to Abel, and when he died, Abel came forward with an offer to buy the business, and the money was in his hands.

"No one knew where it had come from, though it was easy to make a guess. Things were said, but nothing could be proved, and the end was that the business passed into Abel's hands, though he didn't alter its name.

"William was still buying from Rosenbaum's, and when he began to do badly, it was natural that he was slower to pay, so that the account grew bigger from year to year. Other firms pressed him if he got much behind, and so he dealt more and more where he could still get credit, having been on the books so long.

"By this time, Carol had left school. She hadn't gone on to college, as her father had first meant her to do. Times had got too bad for that. She went to serve in the shop.

"Of course Abel watched how William's debt was increasing from year to year, and though he didn't reckon to do the travelling now, he took to calling on William himself, and talking over his business with him. You can't blame him for that. There came a time when he wouldn't let William have more goods, beyond the amounts that he paid off. You can't blame him for that either. They'd done business for many years, but if William couldn't make the shop pay, he couldn't expect Abel to go on for ever filling the hole.

"But Abel Marks saw Carol when he called, and began to talk more about old times, in a friendly way, and less about the cheques that he didn't get. William found that if he made out his order, and then asked Abel to stay to tea, the fact that he hadn't paid anything for a week or two mightn't be mentioned at all, and of course it was clear that it wasn't William but Carol he stayed to talk to.

"That might have been well enough if she'd taken the fancy to him that he did to her. Of course, he was twice her age, and a good bit more, but I don't say there need have been overmuch trouble for that. It was a difference on the right side, and I've seen it work well enough. But Carol didn't look at it in that way. She said he made her feel sick, and if he touched her she wiped her hand.

"Of course, matters couldn't go on like that very long. Abel tried to get Carol to go out with him, and when her excuses got too many to be believed he stopped pressing her, and began pressing her father another way.

"If you think I'm going to tell you that Carol made up her mind to marry him just to save her father from going broke, it's because you don't know the girl, nor did her father ask her to in a straight-out way. I daresay he looked at her sometimes like a begging dog, but he wouldn't go beyond that, and when he saw how she felt he began to look round for another way of escape.

"This is where John Colvin comes in. John travels for Kohn & Auster in ladies' handbags, and he got to know Carol over the counter, in the same way as Abel, only she soon found time to meet him outside, and after a few weeks there wasn't much of the position he hadn't heard."

Miss Barman paused at this point, as though considering her words, or hesitating upon how much of the climax of these events it would be needful for her to tell. Inspector Combridge was aware of a sympathetic interest in the narrative which threatened to deviate perilously from the attitude of official aloofness which should be observed by those who represent the impartial implacable law. The importance of legal retribution for Abel Marks' violent end had receded before the problem of why Carol Merritt, with the disposition she had, and the loathing she had expressed, had become his wife; and of how John Colvin had resigned her to him. Yet he was not so negligent of his duty as to fail to observe an increasing probability that the fatal blow might have been struck by the hand of the younger woman. Well, if it were a fact! Even young, attractive, red-headed girls must not be permitted to marry men they dislike, and then free themselves with a hard blow from a metal rod.

"I don't know," he said, "that I have often heard a clearer statement than you have given me of what happened up to that point. But you're feeding me, and eating nothing yourself. There's no such hurry that you need to go on like that. That is, unless you're anxious for me to get away."

If Miss Barman had any guilty knowledge in her own mind, or had been fearful of the object which had caused the inspector to follow her so quickly, she must have felt some satisfaction at the implications of this remark. She may have felt that the deadly searchlight of the law, if it had paused ominously upon her, was now disposed to move on, to cast its penetrating light on other potential victims of the blind justice that it proposed. If she thought this, she may have recognised it as the consequence of the clear truthfulness of the narrative she had so far given, and this may, or may not, have encouraged her in concluding the tale to its more dramatic, or what might even be called its more tragic end. But a shadow of tragedy, she might have said, which the event of the afternoon had lifted away.

She showed no sign of such thoughts, or of anything beyond a mild and natural satisfaction in the praise that she had received, as she answered: "Oh, well, it's a good listener makes a good tale! It isn't often you meet anyone who'll just listen without asking questions that make you wander about. But there's no particular hurry for you to go. I've got no callers, and nothing more to do for tonight.

I thought I might be putting up Mr. Merritt when I hurried that bedroom furniture back, but now they've decided to go back home together—I mean Mrs. Marks and him. It seems queer calling her that!"

"I gathered," Inspector Combridge admitted, with the candour that candour breeds, "that there was a special reason for getting the second bedroom furnished tonight."

"Yes. I supposed you'd have got all you could out of the men. But it wasn't much they could tell. I've no doubt you've been puzzling over what I've been up to during the week, but it's all part of the same tale, and we'll have it in its place, if you don't mind."

"I'm quite willing for it to wait its turn."

"Well, where was I? I'd told you something about John Colvin, and how it was plain to see that Carol preferred him to Abel Marks, or anyone else, for that matter, and how Abel was pressing her father to find some means of discharging his debt, and hinting at bankruptcy as the best way out, which he knew that William hadn't the courage to face as a man should; and William's mind was going round and round like a trapped mouse, trying to find a way out.

"William knew that John Colvin had money, though it turned out to be less than he had hoped, and he must have got the idea into his head that John might buy the business, and enable him to pay Rosenbaum's off. The young people had the same idea, but John's got a cautious side, and he wasn't sure that he'd got enough capital to carry the deal through, and then to set the business up with the kind of stock that would give it a fresh start.

"But he was in love with Carol, and he was misled in two ways. In the first place, Carol knew that there was a large sum owing to Rosenbaum's, but she thought it was much less than the true figure. That was William's fault. If he had to tell the truth, he always did it in a mean way, as though he were giving away something he ought to sell. He'd had to own to her that he owed Abel a lot more than he was able to pay, and she thought she knew what the figure was, but she was miles out.

"Then, William began to talk in a mysterious way of a rumour that one of the multiple stores wanted the row of shops where his business is. I don't believe there was a word of truth in it from first to last. I believe it started in William's own talk, and was whispered from mouth to mouth till it came back to him, and he came to half believe it himself. Anyway John got to think there was something in it, more likely than not, and that may have influenced him. He knew that if he married Carol something had got to be done, or it would be the signal for her father's business to close in a i way that neither of them wished to see.

"So with one thing and another, John raised all the money he could, and they went to a lawyer together. The lawyer, a Mr. Jellipot—"

"Jellipot?" the inspector interposed. "In Basinghall Street? Yes, I know him. Well, they went to a good man."

"So it sounded to me. Anyway, he wouldn't do anything until proper accounts had been prepared, and when John saw them he had a shock, but I suppose he thought he'd gone too far to draw back. He bought the business for a lot more it was worth, and thought he'd given William enough money to clear his debts, which weren't much except the one big amount that was owing to Abel Marks.

"William was to go on managing the business on a weekly salary, but John took the buying and the financial management into his own hands. It was all done so quietly that there mayn't have been a dozen people who knew that there'd been any change at all.

"The best of it, from John's point of view, was that Carol thought she was free now to marry the man she chose, without any fear that her father would suffer, and her engagement to John was announced to their friends even before Abel got a cheque which must have been one of the biggest surprises he ever had. The worst of it was that John had cleared himself out so completely that they had to put off the idea of marriage for six months, which might seem all for the best, Carol being as young as she was, but she didn't see it in that way, and though she didn't say much to John, and let him think she agreed that it was the best way, I know from what she let out to me that a little less caution would have pleased her a lot more.

"This was about five months ago, and it's not many weeks since it's been known that they were taking a house, and were to be married about this time, though they'd have to furnish on the hire system, which John hated doing. But meanwhile things hadn't been going smoothly at all. There had been constant quarrelling between William and John, with Carol trying to make peace between them, and finding every week that it got harder to do.

"The fact was that William had got fixed in his ways, and didn't like the younger man interfering, as he felt it to be, and expecting to know all that went on, and saying that it must be done differently more likely than not. And John found that the business was going even worse than he had been told—and he'd thought that had been bad enough—and he saw he'd made himself responsible for its future debts, which he took in a very serious way, particularly as his own money had gone.

"I daresay it might have been different if there'd been fresh capital to put into it, but when Rosenbaum's had been paid there hadn't been much margin for that. Practically all the money that John had been able to find had gone into Abel's bank, and, apart from the fact that that debt was paid, everything was about the same as before, except that John's money was gone, which wasn't pleasant for him.

"Then the wholesale stores didn't show any sign of coming forward to buy them up, and altogether John Colvin felt that he had been rather badly let in, and that if William had been franker with him, or even with his own daughter (which would have come to the same thing), the whole matter would have been dealt with another way.

"It's necessary to explain all this because, if John hadn't been feeling rather bitter to William, it isn't likely that things would have happened quite as they did, but up to ten days ago it looked as though it would all end well enough.

"John was keeping on his job at Kohn's—he'd been too cautious to give that up for the risk of a business that didn't pay—and it had been agreed that if William's accounts showed a loss at the end of the year the shop should be closed down, or sold for anything it would fetch—and then Carol came round here in a dreadful state to say that her father had been arrested, and was in Brixton jail."

"You mean he'd been arrested for debt?"

"Yes. That was what it was. It turned out that there had been an old account of nearly £100 owing to Rosenbaum's that William hadn't disclosed, even when they'd had an accountant in to make up the books, as Mr. Jellipot had insisted they should."

"You mean he had concealed it deliberately? It sounds an almost impossibly silly thing to have done."

"He persists that he overlooked it completely. But he says that that was because it had been agreed with Abel some years before that if he kept up his payments on later accounts he wouldn't press him for that. There may have been truth in that, or he may have been afraid that John would back out altogether if he had disclosed more debt than he did, and just hoped for the best. He always did go along in that muddled way.

"But even if there had been an understanding that he wouldn't be pressed for the old amount if he kept later accounts paid up, I'm told that it wouldn't have been any good in law, and, anyway, William didn't try fighting it out. As soon as Abel Marks understood what the position was he had a writ issued, and when William got it he just kept it in his pocket, and said nothing to anyone.

"I suppose he'd got enough trouble with John by then, and he may have thought that Abel couldn't do him any more harm now that the business was sold, and he had accepted the position by taking John's money for the bulk of the debt.

"Anyway, that's what he did. I mean he didn't do any thing, and Marks went on—I expect you'll understand the legal proceedings better than I do—and in the end William had an order from the court to pay three pounds a month, which he did for two months without telling anyone, saving it out of the salary he got from the shop, so he says, but the third month he left it a bit too long, and next thing there were two men in the shop who'd been sent to take him to Brixton Prison.

"Well, Carol told me this—or as much of it as she knew then—and I said that if it was no more than a matter of three or four pounds I could manage that. So we got into a taxi together, and cashed a cheque at the bank, and then drove on to the jail.

"But when we got there we had a shock. They were very polite, and seemed sorry that Carol took it so much to heart, but they said William had got to stay there for six weeks unless the whole debt were paid.

"Then we went on to see Mr. Jellipot, and he was very kind too, but he said that William had been a fool, and if he'd brought the writ to him he could have dealt with it in a much better way. He explained to us that he wasn't being imprisoned for debt, but contempt of court, and there was no way of getting him out by then except paying the whole debt. Only, if Mr. Marks would take less, the court wouldn't mind the contempt, and William could come out at once. Perhaps you can make sense of that.

"So he got Abel's solicitors on the phone, and they said their instructions were that he wouldn't budge till the last penny was paid, which was just what we had expected to hear.

"Well, I'd done all I could, and Carol wired to John, who was away travelling for his firm, to come home at once. I don't say she was wrong, but he had to come back from Newcastle, and explain to his firm, which he didn't like doing, and they were rather nasty about it, which didn't improve his temper.

"Carol wanted to sell the stock anything—to get her father back home—you can understand how she felt—and John said point-blank that it shouldn't be done. He said they'd have to part with three hundred pounds' worth of stock at a forced sale of that kind to raise the needed amount, and how was the shop to be carried on, or the debts paid, after all the best of the stock were gone. As it was, he told me after, there was a quarter's rent due, and not nearly enough in the bank to pay it, so that he'd have to use part of his next month's salary cheque to make up the amount.

"He said that he'd about ruined himself helping her father already, and he wouldn't do any more. He'd got himself into the mess, and he must just stick it out like a man. After all, six weeks wasn't a year.

"The end of it was that they had a row. Carol said that if her feelings meant nothing to him, she was glad she'd found it out before it was too late, and she gave him back the engagement ring; and he told her that she only cared for her father, and didn't care that she ruined him, and she could sell the stock, and do what she liked with the money, but she needn't expect to see him again, and he walked out.

"Well, she came to me to know what she should do, and in the mood she was in then I think she'd have liked me to advise her to take John at his word, and sell the stock for anything it would fetch, but I told her that it was John's property, and as she was the one who had broken off the engagement she certainly couldn't go on robbing him any more. The fact was that I thought that there was a lot to be said for John's point of view, and that William had got about what he deserved. I told her the best thing she could do would be to make it up with John, and tell him she'd been in the wrong, but she wouldn't listen, and went off nearly as angry with me as she was with him."

"And so she decided to marry Marks, as the only way of getting her father free?"

"Yes. But I didn't know that. I never guessed she'd be such a fool till I got a letter from her today by the second post. If I'd had it two hours earlier, I reckon I could have stopped the marriage. But not thinking that her temper—or perhaps that and her love of her father together—would make her go so far, I worried over it after she was gone, and though I didn't think William had got more than he deserved, I didn't like the idea of Abel Marks thinking the family couldn't pay him off, nor of John Colvin looking at it in the same way. I felt very sorry for Carol, too, and I can't say I liked to think of William shut up where he was, especially during the nights.

"I don't know what motive was strongest to make me do it, and I felt that I was being silly all the time, but the end of it was that, after worrying for two or three days without being able to make up my mind, I decided to raise the money myself.

"I didn't think I should have much difficulty. I'd only got about seven pounds in the bank, but I have £45 quarterly from my trustees, and I thought, even without explaining more than I cared to do, that

I could get an advance from them. So I could have done if one of them hadn't been abroad, but, as it was, I found I should have to wait at least as long as the mail would take from Chicago and back, and there wasn't much use in that.

"I tried other ways that didn't succeed, and like a fool I didn't let Carol know what I was doing, meaning to give her a pleasant surprise, but the harder I found it to be, the more obstinate I got, and, in the end, I sold almost all the furniture here. But you'll have guessed that before now."

"Yes," Inspector Combridge admitted, "I thought you would be coming to that. So it was your money that got Merritt out?"

"I got Loames & Prideaux's cheque yesterday afternoon, and took it round to Mr. Jellipot, as I wasn't clear how I ought to proceed. Unfortunately, it was after banking hours before I could get to see him, and he said that the best he could do would be to get William released first thing this morning. When I got Carol's letter at about ten-thirty today, I thought of nothing at first but stopping the wedding, but she hadn't said where it would be and I was too late to catch her at her own home, and then too late when I got to the registrar's office.

"When I found that the marriage had actually taken place, I thought that at least I'd have that money back. If Carol had sold herself for £80, which was what she had, Abel Marks wasn't going to have it from me as well, while I ate on bare boards. I meant to have that money back from him, even though I—"

Miss Barman checked the half-spoken words, with an obvious realisation of the sinister implication which they might bear, in view of the condition in which the body of Abel Marks had been subsequently found.

The inspector had followed her graphic narrative with a trained perception of its straightforward sincerity, and a consequent sympathy which might hardly have observed her last exclamation as being more than the ordinary currency of indignant feeling, had she not checked it so abruptly. Did it indicate a temper which, if it were thwarted in that which it was determined to have, might express itself in a sudden murderous blow? Or might it be argued that only innocence would express itself so rashly, knowing what she did, and to whom she spoke?

Inspector Combridge asked himself these questions, and was unsure what the right answer should be. He looked at the woman who was now clearing away a meal of which she had taken no more than a perfunctory share, with light, firm, capable hands, and was uncertain again. She had courage, he had no doubt. Perhaps hardness—not normally, but when anger arose, or indignation was stirred. Physically, she was better fitted than her niece for a deed of violence such as that which had been fatal to Abel Marks.

He sat silent, reviewing the tale she had told, and reminding himself of the damning fact (if the news-vendor were to be believed) that she must almost inevitably have been the last to leave before Carol Marks arrived. Certainly there were questions that must be asked. But ought he to caution her first? He waited until the table was cleared, and she came and sat down again. "And now," she asked, "is there anything more you would like to know?"

CHAPTER VIII.

THE QUESTIONS OF INSPECTOR COMBRIDGE

"I WANT," Inspector Combridge answered, "to know a lot more than I do now, but whether the tale you've been telling me is a matter for further enquiry depends upon whether it had anything to do with the man's death."

"I thought," she said, "that you ought to know that I was there this afternoon, and why I called upon him, and I didn't see how I could explain it a shorter way."

"Yes, I see that. I am much obliged to you for explaining it so fully. It clears a number of matters that I might have had to check up. And I'll say this. I believe you've told me a lot of truth, which we don't always get. And I don't think you'd be the sort to kill anyone without more reason than you seem to have had.

"But there's the fact that, if one witness is to be believed, you were the last caller that Abel Marks had before his wife says that she found him dead. I don't say that's the case, and we don't accuse anyone of such a crime without enough evidence to make us feel sure that we're on the right track, but, on the other hand, we don't assume anyone's innocent till we're equally sure.

"There are some questions I should very much like to ask, but I think I ought to say first that you're not bound to answer them, if you'd rather not, and that any replies you give may be used in evidence if a charge should be made."

Miss Barman took this warning coolly, seeming, indeed, slightly amused. "You mean," she said, "that if I killed Abel Marks, and you ask me whether I did, I should be silly to give an affirmative answer? As if anyone would!"

But there was no reflection of that amusement in Inspector Combridge's eyes as he replied: "No. I shouldn't say you'd be silly at all. You'd be saving time. If you did it, we should find out in the end. It's a slow business at times, but we reckon to end up at the right address."

"And if I were to refuse to talk, after the way you've warned me, it would be almost like saying the same thing?"

"No. I couldn't go quite that far. You're not bound to talk. There's no getting over that. But it's a fact that innocent people don't often object."

"Well, I don't object at all. You can ask what you like and I'll answer you, unless it's something I don't know."

"Then I'll ask what time it was when you called on Marks this afternoon?"

"I didn't notice the time. But as nearly as I've been able to reckon since, I should say about two-thirty."

"And when you left?"

"About ten minutes later."

"He couldn't have made much difficulty about giving you the money back?"

"Oh, but he did! He refused altogether at first."

"But you were very quickly able to find a convincing argument?"

"I told him that he wouldn't like Carol to know that he hadn't been responsible for letting her father out—that I had already done it, before he got round to the jail."

"And you wouldn't tell her that, if he gave you the money back?"

"Yes. What good would it have been?"

"I suppose it had been his bargain with Mrs. Marks that he should arrange for her father's release as soon as the ceremony had been performed?"

"Yes. I believe he drove straight from the registrar's office to his lawyers to arrange that, and found that he was about two hours too late."

"In what form did he pay you the money? I suppose it would be a cheque for such an amount"

"No. It was all in cash from the safe."

"You mean in notes?

"Yes. One of £50, four of £5 each, and the rest in notes and small change."

"And you went straight on to the place where you'd sold your furniture to buy it back?"

"To buy as much of it back as they'd let me have."

"And I suppose you paid the notes over to them?"

"I paid them £70, and kept the £1 notes and the small change."

"And when you saw them you arranged for as much as possible to be delivered this evening?"

"Yes."

"Why did you do that?"

"Because I thought when William came out, and found what Carol had done, he might prefer to stay here with me rather than be alone. I didn't know quite what state he'd be in after being shut up where he was."

"And after that you saw them again?"

"I called a second time after Carol telephoned."

"You mean after her father had telephoned to her?"

"Yes. After she said that Abel was dead, and I decided to go back with him to Razor Street, to see if there were anything I could do. I thought they might get here while I was away, and take the things back, and, apart from whether I should want them or not, there'd be a second cartage to pay if they did that."

"When did you make the second call?"

"We stopped the taxi on the way to Razor Street."

"I should have thought that both you and her father would have wanted to go straight to Mrs. Marks when you heard what had happened."

"It didn't make many minutes' difference."

Well, Inspector Combridge reflected, that was true enough, and her answers had agreed with the vanman's tale. He had observed before that no two people placed in the same position will act exactly alike. But he asked himself whether it had not more the appearance of a plan already thought out than the natural reaction to so startling and tragic a call. The doubt prompted the apparent banality of his next question.

"Until Mrs. Marks told her father on your telephone, you had no idea that anything was wrong?"

"I thought that things were about as wrong as they could be. I should have said a good bit worse than they are now. I didn't know that Abel was dead, if you mean that."

"You say that he paid you the exact amount that it cost you to get Mr. Merritt out of jail?"

"Yes. I wouldn't have taken a penny less, nor accepted a penny more."

"Yes. I see how you felt.... You know that Mr. Merritt called on him before he came on to you?"

"Yes. He went home first, and when he found what Carol had done he went to find Abel, and have it out with him, and after that he came on to see me. I found him here when I got back."

"Do you know with what object he called on Marks?"

"I never know why William does anything. I doubt whether he knows himself more often than not. I expect he'd got worked up while he was in Brixton (I suppose you know they treat men like cattle there?) and wanted to let off steam, so to speak. And he wasn't likely to feel any better about it when he heard what Carol had done. He went to quarrel, of course. He says he gave him a father's curse. It sounded silly, but it certainly seems to have worked faster than most curses do."

"There's just one other question. When Marks gave you the money, I suppose he went to the safe to get it?"

"Yes."

"Then do you remember whether it was unlocked, or did he unlock it, and—more particularly—did you see him lock it again?"

Miss Barman did not reply to this question with the promptitude that she had shown previously. Inspector Combridge hesitated between the idea that she was making a genuine effort to recall something she had not noticed, or that she was considering what reply could be safely made without the danger of incriminating herself. But after that moment's pause she answered with apparent frankness: "I'm sure he opened, and I'm almost sure he unlocked it. I remember how the door swung back. But if you remember how the safe stands in relation to his desk and the chair by it, where I was sitting, you'll see that he would have had his back to me when he opened it, and I shouldn't have seen clearly what he did—not if I wasn't noticing very particularly.

"But as to closing it afterwards—well, I can't remember! I can only say that I think I should have noticed if he had. I think he took the money out of the drawer, and counted it, and came straight over to me. But of course he might have closed it as I was going out. It would have been a sensible thing to have done."

Inspector Combridge did not dispute that. He said: "I should be glad if you would hold yourself in readiness to come to New Scotland Yard on Monday morning, when we may send for you, and ask you to make a statement of what you have told me, in a more formal manner."

Miss Barman received this request with a moment of rather grim silence, and Inspector Combridge would not have been greatly surprised had she refused. She may have heard before then that people are sometimes "invited" to the headquarters of the metropolitan police who find themselves unable to leave when they have finished the statements which they have been so politely encouraged to sign.

But she said at last: "You won't need to trouble to send. I'll be there at ten-thirty, if that will do."

She said good-night with a recovered cordiality, and Inspector Combridge went thoughtfully away.

CHAPTER IX.

INSPECTOR COMBRIDGE
COLLECTS STATEMENTS

INSPECTOR COMBRIDGE collected statements. By the Saturday following the abrupt exit of Abel Marks from the human life which he had not greatly adorned, the inspector had a total of nine, and his trouble was that they were so straightforward in themselves, and so consistent with one another that he was constrained to the belief that they were substantially true. Truth is not often present to excess in such documents, nor is it an ingredient normally likely to irritate the mind of a conscientious detective, which the inspector certainly was. The trouble with these statements was that they explained everything except the one fact that he was determined to get—the cause and culprit of the killing of Abel Marks.

In addition to the collection of these nine documents of varying length and importance, there had been a great deal of systematic enquiry which may be dismissed briefly, as its results were of an entirely negative character. A number of professional warehouse breakers who happened to be out of jail at the time were invited to explain their movements between 1:00 and 4:00 P.M. on the Saturday afternoon, which they did with an alacrity and thoroughness more satisfactory to themselves than to the inspector. It may seem unreasonable that men against whom there was no charge whatever should be subjected to such inquisition, and improbable that they would respond to enquiries which they well knew to be made without legal right, but the fact was that they were too well aware both of the importance of maintaining friendly relations with the police, and of clearing themselves of a suspicion which (if the actual criminal should not be discovered) might otherwise remain a black shadow upon their names, concentrating upon themselves from that day the unwelcome watchfulness of the police, and probably (or so they believed) increasing the severity of the sentences they would be likely to receive at their next convictions.

But while these enquiries appeared to establish that the crime had not been committed by any of the likely professionals, a minute examination of the premises failed to discover any traces such as a bungling amateur would be expected to leave. An exhaustive search for fingerprints had discovered none which could not be identified as belonging to those who had legitimate access. These included some which had been made by William Merritt, by Carol Barman, and by Carol Marks, but these were not inconsistent either with their innocence or the statements which they had signed. The weapon with which the blow had evidently been dealt bore no marks whatever, which proved no more than that the murderer had had sufficient coolness and forethought either to protect his hand or to wipe it clean.

A similarly exhaustive examination of doors and windows had established beyond reasonable doubt that whoever had entered or left during the afternoon must have done so by the front door.

From another angle, the idea that the crime was one in which robbery had been the primary intention was reduced from its original plausibility to the extremely improbable by the fact that the cash was short by no more nor less than the exact amount which Miss Barman said that the dead man had handed over to her. But this, while discounting the probability that the crime had been the work of one who had entered with the intention of robbery, also supported the veracity of Miss Barman's story in an essential particular. The banknotes which she had paid to Loames & Prideaux that afternoon were also identified as having come from Rosenbaum & Co.'s safe, and while these facts did not amount to proof that she had not murdered Abel Marks, they did conclusively demonstrate the truth of the account she had given of the object of her call upon him.

It remained a conceivable explanation that an intending thief, after striking the fatal blow (perhaps in a sudden panic at finding himself discovered) had been so appalled in the next moment at what he had done that his first motive had left his mind. But was this theory consistent with the coolness that must have paused to clean a weapon hastily snatched up on the unexpected entrance of Abel Marks? Banknotes of substantial value, of which there had been some still left in the safe, he might have felt that it would be too dangerous to touch, but there were also a quantity of £1 notes, and a bag of silver which was plainly visible in the open drawer.

Systematically checking every possibility, the inspector went over the list of the firm's employees, considering the possibility that one of them might have secreted himself on the premises with the intention of pilfering from the safe, after the departure of the rest of the staff, and then been interrupted by his employer's unexpected return. But here again he drew in an empty net. One by one, he was obliged to eliminate them, as being outside suspicion, or on obtaining conclusive evidence of their movements during the afternoon. A young foreman of aggressive personality, and extreme and militant communistic opinions, against whom a conviction had been recorded for violence in a street brawl, might have received more particular consideration had his virile activities not included that of centre-halfback for the Clerkenwell Wanderers, and had there not been about three thousand potential witnesses to the fact that he had left a Gravesend football field at 3:17 P.M. after a difference of opinion with the referee.

So on the following Saturday morning Inspector Combridge found himself reduced to his nine statements, three possible criminals, and a remote alternative which he expected to be able to probe before the end of the day, when he would have the pleasure of putting a few questions to John Colvin, whom he had not yet interviewed.

Against John Colvin there was only the argument that he had as much cause for quarrelling with Abel Marks as the other three—if not more, and the fact that, while he was said by his landlady to have an established habit of returning to his weekend lodgings on Saturdays at 1:30 P.M., at which hour she would have a hot lunch ready to be dished up, he had not appeared on the last occasion until nearly nine, and had then been in a state of agitation which she thought he had endeavoured to conceal when she made some comment upon it.

Reserving that shadowy possibility, Inspector Combridge had first to decide in his own mind between three potential culprits, and then to face what might prove to be the harder task of arraying the evidence in a form which would satisfy the requirements of the criminal law, and the scruples of an average jury, by whom a unanimous verdict of guilty on the capital charge is not always readily given. The second might be the harder task, but at present the first was giving him a most tiresome difficulty.

Taking the three in the order in which they had called at Razor Street, he considered William Merritt first. He had, perhaps, more bitter causes of enmity than either his sister-in-law or his daughter, and he had admitted that his visit to Abel Marks had been with the sole object of quarrelling of expressing himself in words to which blows might seem an almost natural sequel. He had admitted, in his signed statement, that he had denounced the offender in phrases of concentrated bitterness on which he had brooded in the enforced solitude of his Brixton cell. It might be argued that such a crime was more likely to be a man's than a woman's work. And against this solution there was only the fact that Carol Barman said that she had found Marks to be alive when she had called subsequently.

But was this conclusive? Suppose that she had found him dead, and guessed—or even known—that it was by William Merritt's hand that he must have died? Would she have roused alarm at a moment when it must have given her brother-in-law to the hangman's rope? Would not a woman of her character and coolness have decided to leave as quietly as she had come, and would she not have had the wit to see that she would both be constructing a stronger defence of her brother, and a better tale for her own use, if she should take the money to obtain which had been the object with which she came, and which she had been determined to have?

There was, of course, the difficulty here that if Abel Marks were already dead he could not have come downstairs to open the door, but the importance of this point largely disappeared not only from the statements of William Merritt and herself, but on the supporting witness of Miss Miriam Aaronson, Mr. Marks's personal secretary, from whose statement the following relevant abstract may be conveniently given:

> I left at about twenty minutes past one, Mr. Marks having come in a few minutes before. It is the custom to close at 1:00 P.M. on Saturdays, and the workpeople and the office staff, excepting myself, had left at or immediately after that hour, but I stayed until Mr. Marks returned, as I had to report to him on various matters, and there were letters requiring his signature.
>
> When he came in I noticed that his manner was unusual. He appeared to be rather excited. He was hurried and preoccupied. He signed the letters I had ready, but I noticed that he did not read them with his usual care. When I tried to make my reports to him, he said: "Never mind now. Tell me on Monday. You need not stay." I left him seated at his desk in the front office on the first floor. To the best of my knowledge and belief, there was no one on the premises when I left.

I have a duplicate key of the safe, but I did not lock it before leaving. Mr. Marks would do that when he put the cash book away, which, after I had balanced it, I had placed on his desk for inspection, this being the usual routine. I cannot say certainly, but I believe that the door of the safe was open. I am sure that the cash drawer was closed, though it may not have been locked.

When I left, I did not close the front door, as Mr. Marks was still there. It frequently stood open under such circumstances after the staff had left. I do not see that there is anything surprising in that, in view of the fact that there is a counter in the hall, the flap of which must be lifted and the half-door unbolted to enter.

I know that Mr. Marks lived on the premises, but it was generally believed that he was often away at night, and almost invariably so during the weekends, but Mrs. Wibble, who waited upon him, would know more about that.

I had no idea that he had been married that morning, which he did not mention. He certainly spoke of being at the office on Monday. There was nothing unusual in his staying after I left.

I recognise the metal rod which I have been shown. It had lain on the desk for several years. I believe Mr. Rosenbaum used it as a ruler. I do not remember Mr. Marks using it in that way. I did not use it myself, as it was inconveniently heavy.

In view of this evidence, which Mrs. Wibble corroborated in the particulars of which she was cognisant, there was little force in the argument that if the murder had been committed by William Merritt, Miss Barman would have been unable to enter; and even if the statement of Carol Marks that she had found the door locked on her arrival were accepted as true, it showed no more than that Miss Barman must have pulled it shut when she left, which, if she were leaving a murdered man on the floor above, whether he had died by her own or her brother-in-law's hand, was a very natural thing for her to have done.

Considering these circumstances, Inspector Combridge had concluded that the evidence in his possession, though it might not point to William Merritt, was not such as could relieve him of all suspicion. It was true that Miss Barman had shown the manner of a downright and truthful witness, and that all she had told him on matters antecedent to the actual afternoon of the crime had proved to be true But if he were to exonerate her from having invented her interview with Abel Marks for the sake of concealing the guilt of William Merritt, must he not consider her in the role of the actual criminal, with an equal mendacity and a far heavier guilt?

That she had either been paid by Abel Marks, or herself taken the money which she considered to be due to her, had been finally proved when the banknotes which she had paid over to Loames & Prideaux had been identified as being part of a payment received by Rosenbaum & Co. from a customer on the morning of the crime. But suppose and it was at least not an improbable supposition—that Abel Marks had refused to make a refund which he could have been subject to no legal compulsion to do? Suppose he had made a jest of the payment which had been at such heavy sacrifice and so abortively made? Suppose she had struck him in sudden anger with the heavy rod which must have lain so close to her hand? Suppose she had then taken the money, and gone out, closing the door behind her, and probably without knowing at that time either that her brother-in-law had called earlier, or that her niece might be the next to arrive? Surely, in view of the time of her own call, and the discovery which Mrs. Marks was to make when she arrived, this was the simplest, most probable solution?

And yet—what *had* Mrs. Marks encountered when she entered the building, which contained only herself and a bridegroom whom it was certain she did not love? What proof was there that, perhaps in a revulsion against the bond she had undertaken a few hours before, he had not died by her frantic hand?

Inspector Combridge was glad to feel that he could defer his choice among these conflicting theories, which, to those concerned, might be literally an issue of life and death—he had still to meet John Colvin and hear what he had to say.

CHAPTER X.

THE ATTITUDE OF MR. JOHN COLVIN

JOHN COLVIN had been travelling during the week in the Eastern Counties, but he had not passed beyond the unobtrusive watchfulness of the police. Inspector Combridge knew that he had arranged to return from Ipswich by an early train on Saturday morning, and that he would be calling at the offices of his firm to make his report and draw expenses for the next week. There was nothing, at present, to connect him with the crime beyond the fact that the rivalry between the two men appeared to have resulted in a decisive victory for Abel Marks—and that the news of this victory must have come to him on the morning of the day on which the murder had been committed, in a letter which Carol Merritt had written to him the night before.

As Inspector Combridge considered this in the light of the fact that he knew nothing of Colvin's movements during the afternoon, except that they had not conformed to his usual routine, the desire to interview him became very strong. Indeed, he saw that, had there been no others on whom suspicion more nearly fell, he would have been disposed to think that he need look no further for the criminal, and that his only trouble would be to build up a case against him.

He determined to surprise him by a call without previous appointment, and on the assumption that he would follow his habitual course of lunching at his own lodgings after leaving Kohn & Auster's offices, he resolved to see him there before he would have had time to finish the meal and go out again.

At intervals during the morning he had been informed, first that Mr Colvin had joined the train at Ipswich, then that he had taken a taxi to the offices of his firm in Clerkenwell Road, and finally that he had boarded a Hampstead bus, on receipt of which last information he allowed himself no more than ten minutes for his own refreshment, and proceeded in the same direction.

On arriving at Thurlow Road he was informed by a man who lounged past him that his quarry was in the house, and he went on to press the bell of a detached semi-bungalow residence, faced by a neat lawn, and bright with bordering flowers. He knew the place, having called there to interview the landlady during the week, and had already admired the surroundings in which the traveller in ladies' handbags spent his weekend leisure.

"Good afternoon, Mrs. Nichols," he said pleasantly, as the door opened, "I should like a few words with Mr. Colvin if you would please show me in to him."

Mrs. Nichols, a small frail elderly woman, with pale eyes, and pale sandy hair drawn tightly back in a fashion of her own youth, had answered his questions willingly enough when he had called previously, and he had expected no difficulty from her. He had intended to be shown straight in, so that he could watch the demeanour of a surprised man, and that was what he supposed was happening as she opened the nearest door, and introduced him to an empty room. "Mr. Colvin," she said, "is at lunch. I'll let him know you are here."

He sat down irresolutely, but it was no more than a minute before she returned. "Mr. Colvin says he hasn't much time, so he'll see you now."

She led him to an adjoining room, where a young man, sitting with his back to the light, was engaged in serving himself with a goodly portion of apple tart.

"Good afternoon, Inspector," he said, without rising or offering his hand, "take a seat. You'll excuse me going on with my lunch? I haven't very much time, and my last meal was at eight-fifteen. What can I do for you? It's something about the Marks murder, of course?"

Inspector Combridge sat down with no cause for offence, but a vague feeling that the interview was not proceeding according to plan. The tone in which he had been addressed was neither hostile nor rude, but it had an aloof and business-like quality very different from that which he would have chosen to hear. It was such as an insurance canvasser, or a collector for some charitable object must become accustomed to meeting. He saw at once that he must put away any hope that he had come to the baiting of a nervous criminal, or the pumping of a garrulous fool.

The man at whom he looked was of no strongly marked characteristics. He was of medium height, of medium build, and his hair was of a medium brown. He was neatly, unobtrusively dressed. His character was in his voice, in the brisk precision of his manner, and

in a scrutiny which made the inspector feel that he was being criti-
cised rather than feared. It was as though Mr. Colvin felt confident
of his own ability to sustain correctly the part of one who is interviewed respecting the murder of an acquaintance, but less sure of, or
more interested to observe the behaviour of a police officer conduct-
ing such an investigation.

"Yes," he replied, "it's the Marks murder. I understand that
you'd known him for some years, and I wondered whether you
could help us in a rather difficult case."

"Not in the least. I've known him, as you say. But I don't see
any help for you in that. I could have identified him for you, but no
doubt that was done at the time. I'm sorry to hear that you're finding
it a difficult case. From what I've heard, and what I've read in the
press, it sounded simple to me. You either catch the man, or you
don't."

"I'll be frank with you, Mr. Colvin. We're not satisfied that it
was a robbery-with-violence kind of affair. I've got an open mind,
but at present I don't think it was.... There are three people who are
known to have been on the premises round about the time when the
murder must have been committed."

"And they can't help you? Then is it likely that I should be able
to, as I wasn't there?"

The inspector did not reply to this question. He went on, ignoring the interruption: "And these three naturally lie under varying
degrees of suspicion unless the case can be cleared up in another
way." This remark appeared to arouse Mr. Colvin to a more alert
interest than he had shown previously. "Suspicion?" he exclaimed
sharply. "What three do you mean?"

"Mr. Merritt, Miss Barman, and Mrs. Marks."

"I don't see what right you have to say that. It's not a crime to
be near a place where a man's killed. You want a lot more than that.
But I suppose you know that these people are friends of mine?"

"In a matter of this kind, it is the first duty of every citizen to
assist the law."

"Perhaps it is. But I can't. I've told you already I wasn't there."

"I haven't suggested yet that you were."

"No, but if you don't suggest that, I don't see why you think
you can get any help from me.... As a matter of fact," Mr. Colvin
added with deliberation, "I've heard what happened from the three
people you mention, and I don't see how you can get any help from
them either."

"Not if you believe all that they say."

"In such a matter most people prefer to believe their friends."

"You wouldn't call William Merritt a special friend?"

John Colvin considered this, and replied in the same deliberate manner. "No. I shouldn't call him a friend at all."

"You have found him to be a rather unreliable character?"

"He is a muddle-headed old fool. He isn't the sort to go about murdering people he doesn't like."

"No. But a sudden fit of rage— He seems to have had a good deal of cause."

"If you're going to accuse him of murdering Abel Marks, I'll only say that I think you're wrong. And beyond that I can't assist you, and would prefer to have nothing to do with the matter."

"I didn't say that I was. Abel Marks seems to have had a good many enemies. You didn't have much cause to love him yourself."

"You think not? I'm not grumbling. Things seem to be turning out well enough. I wouldn't say that I don't prefer him dead to alive."

"So I understood you would be likely to feel. Of course you know that we have to check up on every possibility, and that there's no reason to take offence if I ask you how you were occupied last Saturday afternoon?"

Mr. Colvin regarded the inspector with a cool amused interrogative glance before he replied: "So we come to the point at last! Are you suggesting that I might have killed him myself?"

"I am not suggesting anything of the kind. I quite expect to hear that you were occupied elsewhere."

"Well, so I was."

The inspector waited for a fuller answer, which did not come. Mr. Colvin had now finished his meal. He rose, as though considering the interview ended, and inviting his guest to leave. Inspector Combridge made no corresponding movement. He said: "You can, of course, refuse to give me the information for which I ask, but it will come to the same thing in the end. You will be putting us to needless trouble, and, if you are innocent, as I suppose to be the case, drawing a needless suspicion upon yourself."

Mr. Colvin listened with attention, but did not appear to be impressed by this argument. "Do I understand," he asked, "that the position is this? You have so far been unable to discover the murderer of Abel Marks, and you are therefore disposed to suspect any of three people who are known to have been on the premises during the afternoon, and you have added my name to the list for no better reason than that you think I had cause to dislike the man. So that, if I give you an account of my movements during that afternoon, I shall do it with the knowledge that I am either drawing suspicion upon myself or enabling you to eliminate the sole remaining doubt that hinders you from selecting a victim among my friends?"

The inspector did not like this manner of stating the case, nor could he fail to recognise that it held a large measure of truth, but he stood up to the argument stoutly enough. "I don't think," he said, "that you are adopting a very wise attitude, nor that you have put the position fairly. We don't want to charge anyone who is innocent, nor to put them to inconvenience of any kind. But we are determined to find out who committed the crime, and innocent people who are under unavoidable suspicion cannot do better for themselves than by giving us all the information that they possess. If you don't do that, you can't blame us for any trouble that comes your way."

"I'm not aware that I blamed you at all. And if you wish to accuse me of murdering Abel Marks—"

"I've told you already that I don't accuse you of the murder, or any connexion with it. Had I done so, I should have cautioned you before inviting you to treat me frankly. The position is that Marks was murdered by some person unknown, and that you are one— there may have been others who had serious causes of enmity against him, of which the principal one came to a head when he married Miss Merritt on the morning of the day he was killed. It was a Saturday afternoon when that happened, and it is a fact that you are in London during the weekends. I am told that it is your habit to come here to lunch at midday, but last week you omitted to do so, and did not come in till a late hour, when, if I am correctly informed, you showed some signs of unusual agitation. You cannot be surprised, under these circumstances, that I ask you to account for your movements during the afternoon, so that any element of suspicion should be removed."

"You put it so plausibly," Mr. Colvin retorted, "that when I listen to you I almost suspect myself, and I will concede that I always commit my London murders during the weekends, reserving the early-closing afternoons in mid-week for my provincial enemies. But as to what you are asking now, I won't say that I am surprised that you should put the question, but I should be surprised at myself if I were to gratify your curiosity.... I am afraid that I must go now, so that if you wish to continue the conversation, I must ask you to walk with me to the nearest bus-stop."

Inspector Combridge heard this definite refusal of a request which he felt that he had a right to make with an annoyance which was not lessened by the fact that the sarcasm came with a smile, and even the final words were said in a pleasant way. It seemed that Mr. Colvin gained in good-humour as he came to the point at which his decision was definitely made. The inspector, recalling the narrative of past events which Miss Barman had given him, had a thought of sympathy for William Merritt, reduced by financial exigency to explain and defend the conduct of his business to the self-confidence of the younger man. He could imagine that, faced with the prospect of the loss of his own money, and even the possibility that he might be involved in further liabilities that he could not meet, through William Merritt's muddling inefficiency, his sarcasms might have a bitterer, more incisive tone.

But he did not allow this feeling to deflect his judgment, and he could not recognise this as the common attitude of a guilty man. Rather, it was puzzling, and the case had already been puzzling enough. He said, rather sourly: "Well, it's for you to decide, but I think you are taking a decision which will do no good either to yourself or your friends."

Mr. Colvin did not appear to resent this. It seemed rather that he gave it a pause of serious consideration before he replied: "Well, I think differently. But I don't want to put you to any needless trouble. You may like to know that I am going to see Miss Merritt—I suppose I should say Mrs. Marks now."

The inspector expressed no gratitude for information that, if not actually sarcastic, might be considered contemptuous in itself, if not in the tone in which it was spoken. They went out together, but parted at the end of the street, with no pretence of cordiality. Inspector Combridge had come with no great hope, but he had not expected to be so absolutely rebuffed. If he had received a clear statement of John Colvin's movements during the afternoon, such as would have established an impregnable alibi, he would have been content to eliminate him. He might even have persuaded himself that there are advantages in reducing a list of four possible criminals to a smaller number. Had he heard a few unsustainable lies, it would have been better still, and his work would have been largely done. But he knew that, in the absence of any statement from John Colvin himself, he had not at present even the flimsiest foundation on which to build up a case against him. He turned his mind again to consider the three who must at least admit that they had been on the scene of the crime. He could do no better now than to prepare a report for the consideration of his superior officers, and for the final decision of the Assistant-Commissioner.... There came a time when this report lay on the Home Secretary's desk. It went on from there to that of the Attorney-General, whose opinion Mr. Hudson had requested upon it.

CHAPTER XI.

THE OPINION OF THE ATTORNEY-GENERAL

ABSTRACT from the opinion of the Attorney-General in re the murder of Abel Marks:

There is, therefore, in my opinion, no case against William Merritt. There is no shred of evidence to confute his own account of his interview with Abel Marks, and it is supported by the testimony of Carol Barman that the murdered man was alive at a later time.

Neither, in my opinion, is there a case against Carol Marks. There appears to be no circumstance which has been discovered which is inconsistent with her statement that her husband was dead when she found him.

But the position of Carol Barman is widely different. There is the evidence of William Merritt that Marks was alive almost immediately before she entered the building, and of Carol Marks that he was dead very soon afterwards. Against this, there is only her own statement that she did not kill him, which is no more than a natural denial for her to make. The two witnesses against her are reputable, and her own relatives. They are certainly not hostile to her, and their testimony can only be impugned on the ground that one of them is guilty, which there is no evidence to support, and it is to be observed that if the murder were committed by William Merritt she must be at least an accessory after the event, as she denies that Marks was dead when she arrived.

The only remaining alternative to the guilt of Carol Barman would be that the crime was committed by some other person in the interval that elapsed between her departure and the arrival of Carol Marks. This interval must have been very short, and the improbability, on that and other grounds, is extreme.

A prosecution either of William Merritt or Carol Marks would probably be misdirected, and almost certainly fail.

And it is to be observed that while, in the improbable event of the murder having been committed by either of these last-mentioned persons, there is, as the case now stands, no sufficient evidence against them on which a prosecution could be sustained, a prosecution of Carol Barman would result in their examination in the witness-box, where either of them, if guilty, would be likely to break down under that ordeal, even if they should not voluntarily confess their guilt, either then, or in the event of a conviction against Carol Barman being obtained, so that the ends of justice would have been reached, not in an ideal manner, but by the only possible path.

But, in my considered opinion, the murder was committed by Carol Barman, and the last-mentioned possibilities will not therefore arise.

* * * * * * *

The Home Secretary, Mr. Hudson, read this opinion, which was less equivocal than he had expected that it would be. Well, the Attorney-General had the legal mind, which he did not claim to possess! He recognised it to be the kind of case by which reputations are marred or made, and from which resignations will sometimes result. It was, he knew, from such consciousness that the Commissioner of Police had referred the matter to him. But he did not lack courage, and a legal opinion which the Attorney-General expressed so definitely was one which he should not hesitate to endorse. Yet his pen paused for a moment before he wrote: "I agree. E.H.H." in a firm rapid hand at the foot of the final sheet, and sent the document where it would become potent to start the slow inexorable machinery of the law.

BOOK TWO

THE TRIAL

CHAPTER XII.

THE ARREST OF CAROL BARMAN

INSPECTOR COMBRIDGE pressed the bell of Miss Barman's flat, and Carol Marks opened the door. She looked at him with a paling of freckled cheeks, having an instinctive perception of why he came. For the last ten days there had been no sign that the attention of the police was directed upon Abel Marks' three-hour bride, or her father, or aunt, or friend; but the two women had been too fearful to take much courage from this delay. They had felt that the storm was overhead, though it did not break. They had known the feelings of the partridge that crouches motionless in the stubble, while the hawk circles slowly above.

When the four had met in the little living-room over the shop which still bore the name of William Merritt, though it had passed out of his legal possession, Miss Barman had been decided in her opinion that she herself was the one who would have to face the inquisition of the criminal law, and John Colvin, to whom she had appealed, had reluctantly agreed, with some qualifications, that the police might be disposed to the conclusion that they could most easily construct a case against her, but had argued, perhaps rather from a disposition to give encouragement than deliberate judgment, that they would not proceed at all on vague suspicions, from which no jury would be persuaded to a verdict of condemnation.

"Well," Miss Barman had replied, with a cheerful grimness rather than any sign of abated courage, "we shall soon see," and turned the conversation aside to the changes which the death of Abel Marks would bring in varying degrees to the other three.

For if motive, or, particularly, advantage arising from the man's death, were to be the basis on which suspicion built, she should surely have been the last of the four on whom its sinister searchlight would be directed.

To John Colvin, and the dead man's nominal wife, the event had brought reconciliation, with a cessation of all their troubles, and the prospect of speedy union.

To William Merritt, as he was certainly not too muddle-headed to see, it meant relief at once from the weight of obligation, and the pressure of debt. It might be no more than a reasonable presumption (for Abel was known to have stated that he had no living relatives) that his daughter had become a wealthy woman, able from her own resources to stock the shop as it had never been supplied since he had opened it more than twenty years before.

Acting on his advice, Carol Marks had gone at once to Mr. Jellipot's office, and instructed him to act for her in claiming whatever her legal rights might be; and that astute though cautious lawyer, silently aware of the vague suspicion from which, until the responsibility for the murder should be legally settled, his client would not be wholly free, had seen that any show of diffidence or delay in that direction might be interpreted as the hesitation of guilt, and had applied for Letters of Administration, and taken steps for securing control of her deceased husband's estate, with an energetic promptitude not entirely appreciated by the legal gentlemen who had previously had the lucrative honour of handling Rosenbaum & Co.'s affairs.

To these three, the death of Abel Marks had brought new hopes and larger opportunities, darkened only by the fear that accusation might yet halt at their own doors, but to Carol Barman there had come no change, beyond that she had learnt the familiar difference between the experiences of those who sell and buy, in the fact that Messrs. Loames & Prideaux had considered that the return of about two-thirds of the articles which they had purchased a few days earlier erred on the side of generosity, if at all, when (as they had explained with almost apologetic courtesy) they had taken their overhead charges into account. It was from a mixture of sympathy with the older woman, facing in loneliness what they might regard as a common peril, and a desire for companionship with the one of her own sex who was so placed, that Carol Marks had come to stay with her aunt some days before that on which Inspector Combridge appeared at the door.

"Is Miss Barman in?" he asked, in no more than a perfunctory manner, for the time was 9:30 on Monday morning, and (even if the flat had not been under constant observation for the last fortnight) his knowledge of the lady's movements was sufficient to assure him that she would not have gone out at that comparatively early hour.

"Do you want to see her?" Carol Marks replied fatuously, without stepping back sufficiently for him to enter.

71

"Yes, I must see her, if you please." The formal courtesy of the words was discounted by the curtly official tone in which they were spoken. Inspector Combridge hated these inevitable incidents of a detective officer's life, even when, as now, it was a murderess whom he gathered into the cruel walls from which she might not escape, if at all, until the best years of her life would be done; and his assurance that Carol Barman was such a one was rather that of conformity to the decision of his superior officers, than an opinion freely and independently reached. In fact, he was watching the demeanour of the younger woman even now, in an active doubt of what it might imply, either of innocence or guilt.

She said: "You had better come in," and her voice sounded strange to herself. She was aware at once of an instinct of protection which would have delayed him further, and of the essential futility of such an attitude.

As he entered, Miss Barman came out to the narrow hall of the flat. If she guessed his errand, which she could hardly avoid, having heard him ask for her at the door, she gave no sign as she said: "Good morning, Inspector. You're calling early this morning."

"I'm sorry, Miss Barman," he answered, "but I have a warrant for your arrest for the murder of Abel Marks."

She stepped back into the room from which she had come, into which he followed her, with Carol Marks at his side. "I suppose," she answered, "that that means that you want me to come with you now?"

"Yes," he said. "It is my duty to warn you that anything you say may be used in evidence."

She made no comment upon a cautionary formula typical of the parade of impartiality which is one of the deadliest weapons of English law, and may be compared to the space that the hare is allowed before the hounds will be loosed upon it. Enough to ensure a good run, but not enough to enable it to escape.

She stood for one thoughtful moment pondering what, under such circumstances, it would be wisest to say, or whether silence might not be best. Forgetting some careful resolutions already formed in anticipation of the half-expected event, she almost said: "I suppose it is useless to say that I am not guilty?" but checked herself with a realisation of the ambiguity that the words might bear, should they be accented in a different way. "I say that I am not guilty," she said firmly, "and I am confident that it is a charge that you cannot prove."

Inspector Combridge drew out his notebook. He wrote down the words with careful exactness. He said: "I have a car waiting below."

72

"I suppose I can come with you?" Carol Marks asked.

"Better not, ma'am," the inspector answered, before her aunt could reply. "You couldn't stay if you did."

Carol Barman looked at her niece, and saw shaking hands, and eyes in which the tears shone. "It wouldn't be any use coming with me," she said. "You can do better than that. You can get Mr. Jellipot to see me as soon as possible at—at the police station, I suppose."

"Yes, Bow Street," Inspector Combridge supplied.

"And," Miss Barman added, "you can let John know, if he hasn't gone." She hesitated a moment as she stood at the side of the table, on which her handbag lay. She had a vague idea that, if she should lay a hand upon it, it would become part of that which Inspector Combridge would be entitled to remove, and that it would pass, for the time if not for ever, from her control. It seemed unjust. Till she were convicted by a jury of her peers she was innocent by English law, and what was her handbag to do with him? But she let it lie where it was. She said to Carol: "I'll leave everything in your charge here. I don't suppose it will be for long." (Why didn't the inspector's pocket-book come out again to record that cheerful prophecy?) "There's the butcher's bill for last week. There's nothing else owing. You'll find money enough."

"Never mind that," Carol said. "If I don't come now, how shall I—"

"Mr. Jellipot will arrange all that for you," the inspector interposed again. He had become just a shade harder, more impatient, in his manner, since he had heard the solicitor's name. Not that he was a lawyer of bad repute, or out of favour with the police. In fact, he and the inspector had long been personal friends, and had acted together in one criminal case of international importance. But he had also had Mr. Jellipot against him, and the experience had not been pleasant, nor its result satisfactory to his department. And this case had appeared difficult enough without the brains of a particularly astute lawyer becoming active to make it worse.

Apart from that, he knew from past experience that while decency forbids too great abruptness in such an arrest, scenes of hysteria are the likely penalty of prolonged delay. His hand was on Miss Barman's arm as he spoke.

"Yes," Carol Marks said. "I'll get on to Mr. Jellipot. And I'll ring you up at once." There was relief in the thought of action. She had an impulse to step forward and embrace the elder woman, but Inspector Combridge was now in the doorway between them.

"Don't worry, Carol," Miss Barman called. "See you soon." She hardly knew what she said.

Inspector Combridge pulled the door shut. He had observed Carol Marks' forward movement. Was it a kiss of Judas she would have offered? He wished he knew!

Left alone, Carol Marks went to the telephone at once. She rang up Kohn & Auster. Being Monday, John might be there. He might not yet have left for his week's journey. In two minutes she heard his voice.

"Oh, John," she said, "Inspector Combridge has just been here. He's arrested Aunt Carol."

She heard a low intense "Damn," and then a more audible voice. "Where has he taken her? Bow Street...? I'll see Mr. Jellipot at once."

"She asked me to do that."

"Well, leave it to me.... Don't worry, we'll get her clear."

He rang off rather abruptly. Probably, she thought, he was over-heard. But he was evidently prepared to postpone his journey. What would his firm say to that? They had been awkward before when he had returned in the middle week. Well, she must be thankful he had not left!

She had sufficient coolness to look in her aunt's handbag for the key of the flat, before letting herself out. She signalled a passing taxi when she reached the street, and went home to tell her father what had happened.

CHAPTER XIII.

THE RETICENCE OF MR. JOHN COLVIN

MR. JELLIPOT had been heard to say that he disliked practising in the criminal courts, and since his dramatically successful conduct of the Hammerton case[1] and of another which was less publicly known, he had had numerous opportunities of demonstrating the genuine nature of this antipathy. More than one notorious criminal, and several of their anxious or indignant relatives, had sat waiting patiently in his outer office for interviews which had been unpleasantly decisive and unexpectedly brief.

He was not young. Being single, he was not greedy for wealth. In his civil practice, he had abundance of remunerative and congenial work He had no intention of exercising his brains, for whatever fees, to assist wrongdoers to escape the consequences of crime, and he had a well-grounded opinion that an enormous majority of those who are prosecuted by the police are guilty men. Was it likely that only those who were innocent would continue to come to him? It was much more satisfactory to recommend them to Cyril Barnes. Cyril liked criminal business, and Barnes, Cockshott, and Barnes was an excellent firm.

In the Francis Hammerton case, he had really had no option, the Hammertons having been clients of his for three generations; and it was Inspector Combridge himself, in a spirit which he had never quite understood, who had caused him to capitulate to the trouble in Ada Hamilton's eyes.[2] But this matter of the Marks murder— He had seen the probability that it would settle down on his doorstep, and it was a prospect he did not like....

There was no question of obligation to old clients here. He had done some legal business recently for Kohn & Auster, on the rec-

---

[1] See *The Attic Murder.*
[2] See *Post-Mortem Evidence.*

ommendation of the London and Northern Bank, and the firm had recommended their traveller, John Colvin, to him. So it was that he had come to deal with the little matter of the Merritt business. And that had naturally led to his acting for Mrs. Marks in regard to her husband's estate. That was congenial—even important—business, for Marks was proving to have been an unexpectedly wealthy man.

Having her financial interests already in his hands, he did not see how he could decently have refused to undertake Carol Marks' defence if she should have been prosecuted for the murder of her husband, which, on his knowledge of the case, he had thought to be a very probable development. But he hoped that she would have the sense to prefer one of the well-known firms that specialise in the conduct of such trials.

He actually had the case in his mind, and was doubtfully wondering whether the police inaction of the last ten days indicated that it was to be dropped, "which," he said to himself, "isn't Inspector Combridge's usual way," when John Colvin was announced.

Being shown in, he came to the point at once. "I have just heard," he said, "that Inspector Combridge has arrested Miss Barman for the murder of Abel Marks."

"Miss Barman," Mr Jellipot announced, "is not a client of mine."

"She asked me—that is, she asked Mrs. Marks, who phoned me—to get in touch with you at once."

Mr. Jellipot was thoughtful, and slow to respond. "The prosecution of Miss Barman," he said, "must tend to relieve Mrs. Marks of any suspicion—baseless suspicion, of course—which may have attached to her as the one who discovered her husband's body, and who was alone with him at the time, and who has benefited by his death."

"We don't look at it like that."

"No?" Mr. Jellipot became thoughtful again. "The vital point," he said at last, "is how long an interval there can have been between Miss Barman's departure, and the arrival of Mrs. Marks."

Mr. Colvin received this in silence, showing no enthusiasm for the idea, nor disposition to discuss it. Mr. Jellipot regarded him speculatively. It seemed that the two men were engaged in a duel of unspoken thoughts. He asked: "It is not a matter on which you can help me at all?"

Mr. Colvin did not appear surprised at this question. But, after a short pause, he replied: "No. I think it may be better that I say nothing."

Mr. Jellipot replied with gravity: "I cannot press you to do so." He relapsed into silence, and when he spoke again it was evident that he was considering the problem from a different angle. "The fact that the metal ruler was used," he said, "indicates that it was not a premeditated crime. One who intended to murder would have brought a weapon."

This time Mr. Colvin responded more readily. "Unless," he replied, "he had known that the ruler was there."

Mr. Jellipot gave a doubtful assent. He looked at his visitor in a keenly questioning way as he asked: "You wish me to undertake Miss Barman's defence?"

Mr. Colvin was decided in his reply: "Yes, I certainly do."

Mr. Jellipot sighed, but the reply appeared to have resolved his own mind. "Very well," he said, in no very hopeful tone, "I will do what I can."

"You will want me to stay in town?"

"No. Nothing will happen this week. It will be better for you to keep to your usual business routine. Better in several ways. It is really not your matter at all."

"Then if you really mean that—I've just got time to catch the eleven-five. But I'm more than willing—"

"Yes, of course. But you'd better go."

Mr. Jellipot shook hands with Mr. Colvin with no less than his usual cordiality. Having seen him go, he had a few busy moments on the telephone, and then ordered a taxi for the police-court. He had learned that his client was to be brought before the magistrate at noon for no more than a formal remand.

CHAPTER XIV.

A CONFERENCE WITH MISS BARMAN

MR. JELLIPOT had a ten minutes' conversation with his client before the case was called. The time was not long, but it was sufficient for much to be said, for it was a meeting of two people who were not given to the wasting of words.

"I understand that we shall not be in court for more than a few minutes this morning. The police do not propose to take the matter further than to make their charge (to which we shall, of course, plead not guilty), and to offer formal evidence of arrest. But they tell me that they will be ready to go straight on tomorrow until they have concluded their case. It will be important, therefore, that I should be fully instructed this afternoon, so that I may be prepared both for the cross-examination of the witnesses for the prosecution, and to decide whether we shall seriously resist a committal, or reserve our defence."

"I saw Abel Marks alone," Miss Barman replied bluntly. "I don't see what witnesses I can be expected to have. And Carol found him dead when she got there. She can't help saying that."

"She must say that, if it be true," Mr. Jellipot replied cautiously, the fact that he had undertaken Miss Barman's defence already inclining him to accept nothing from the others concerned as beyond doubt, "but I don't think we shall have to call her. Both Mrs. Marks and her father will be subpoenaed by the prosecution. That will be unavoidable, though, in some ways, the procedure may be an advantage to us."

"You'll find William will get muddled, more likely than not."

"Well, he's their witness," Mr. Jellipot replied cheerfully. "But I suppose there's no doubt that he'll say that he left Abel Marks alive?"

"Oh, yes. He'll say that."

The conversation was interrupted at this point by the summons into court, where the proceedings, as Mr. Jellipot had foretold, were of a brief though formidable formality. At 3:00 P.M., after having returned for a short time to his office, and relieved his mind from other matters of business which he could not defer, he met his client again for a more leisurely conference.

He found Miss Barman to be composed in mind, though obviously realising the gravity of her position. He had already observed that he had to deal with a woman who was exceptional both in courage and character, though whether these qualities rendered it more likely or less that she had struck a fatal blow at the head of Mr. Abel Marks was not easy to judge.

"I understand," he commenced, "that the police have taken statements from yourself, and also, among others, from William Merritt and Mrs. Marks. I have not yet had an opportunity of inspecting these documents, but, regarding your own, may I ask whether it contains anything which you may have wished subsequently to modify or correct?"

"No," she answered, "I meant what I said. It is not in my words; but it was set down fairly enough."

"So I expect it would be. Then I may take it that it will give me the facts as you wish me to establish them in your defence?"

"Yes," she said slowly, "I think—" And then with more decision, "Yes, certainly."

"Very well. And are you sufficiently familiar with the contents of the other two documents to say whether they contain anything which you will wish to challenge?"

"No. How should I, not having seen them? But it isn't likely."

"Well, I must accept your instructions. But you will recognise that if we are not to question either your brother-in-law's statement that he left Abel Marks alive, or that of your niece that she found him dead, we are caught in a narrow space, and it may be difficult to formulate a theory which will be satisfactory both to an average jury and to ourselves."

"Yes, I see that. But what else would anyone expect them to say? The police surely didn't think that either of them would have said: 'I gave Abel Marks's head a hard whack, and if it killed him so much the better.' Even if they'd done it, they wouldn't be likely to give themselves away in that fashion."

"No. But the value of these statements to the police is often less in the truth than in the falsehoods that they contain."

"You mean that it's silly to be persuaded to make them at all?"

"Scarcely that. They often assist justice. They are sometimes to the advantage of innocent persons. In the present instance, looking at it from what I may call a family standpoint, it might have been wiser for you to have maintained a general silence, though that is much less than certain. It might, for instance, have led to the arrest of Mrs. Marks, instead of your own."

"You mean that I ought to plead guilty?"

Mr. Jellipot allowed himself to look slightly surprised. "No," he answered, "I certainly didn't mean to imply that. On your own statement, you are an innocent woman; and, in any case, a plea of guilty in a capital charge is one which the court is always reluctant to accept. Why should you suppose that I meant that?"

Miss Barman became silent. If, as Mr. Jellipot was inclined to think, she had asked that surprising question on an impulse which she regretted next instant, it was evident that she did not intend to repeat her error, and he showed no disposition to hasten her reply.

When she did speak, it was as though she thought aloud, and the connexion between the solicitor's question and what she said was not easy to see. But Mr. Jellipot was content to wait. The more freely she spoke, the more she disclosed her mind, the better would he be able to judge what the strongest line of defence, and more particularly what the dangers of putting her in the witness-box, would be likely to be.

"It seems a monstrous thing," she said, "that there's no legal distinction between the killing of a bad man or a good."

"I don't think," Mr. Jellipot replied, as though discussing a question of a purely academic kind, "that it would be a distinction which would be simple of definition, and it would certainly place a proportion of the population in a continual and lively peril. But I should be disposed to agree that as the crime of theft is legally subdivided into a score of offences of various descriptions and different penalties, so that of homicide might be more variously and more intelligently differentiated than it is now. But," he was careful to add, "it is only just to observe that the single penalty which the law provides for all homicides which come within the legal definition of murder, is subject to such a system of reprieve and subsequent gradation that the practical injustice, if it exist at all, is much less than might be inferred from a study of our legal code.

"For instance," he went on, as Miss Barman showed no disposition to interrupt or challenge his carefully qualified observations, "the extreme penalty of the law is scarcely ever remitted in the case of a convicted poisoner, while in crimes of unpremeditated violence it frequently is, and I may say invariably so in the case of women, excepting perhaps (as in the Bywaters murder) when it is against her own husband that—"

Miss Barman interrupted him with a sudden exclamation. "That is just it! That is what I meant. It would be so much worse for Mrs. Marks than for me."

"You mean," Mr. Jellipot said, "that, in the event of your own acquittal, you fear that Mrs. Marks may be charged, and that, if she were convicted, her position might be worse than your own under similar circumstances, owing to the fact that she had married the man a few hours before?"

"That," she said, "is what I have thought, and what I understood you to say."

"There might be qualifications. The circumstances of the marriage, and other possibly relevant facts— But do I understand that you instruct me—of course, in the closest professional confidence—that that is what actually occurred?"

But this time her reply came definitely, and at once. "No. When she found him, she says that he was quite dead. I don't see why anyone should doubt that. Only, if you can convince a jury that I didn't do it, won't it have the effect of throwing suspicion upon her, to which she might find it hard to reply? The time, as you say, couldn't have been very long."

"It must have been very short. But if you know that you left the man alive, and Mrs. Marks found him dead, then something *must* have happened in the meantime, and it's our business to find out what it was, if the police can't; or otherwise to put forward a plausible theory, such as will show the jury that it wouldn't be safe to convict on what can be no more than a proofless doubt."

"Yes, of course. If you can do that! I don't want to plead guilty. Nobody would. I only thought that if they mean to go through the family, one by one, it might be best to end it the shortest way."

"I shouldn't say they'll do that. If we can resist the present prosecution successfully—about which," he added, with the optimism which his position required, "I am not without confidence—I think they would be very cautious in commencing a second. The best result, if you are seriously concerned for the positions of either William Merritt or Carol Marks, might be to secure an acquittal in which the police would not believe. I mean that, if you were still guilty in the official mind, they would do no more to reopen the case."

"You think," she asked seriously, "that we might be able to manage that?"

Mr. Jellipot became equally serious in his reply.

"I think," he said, "you must put all such ideas—such remotely possible and almost fantastic aims—out of your mind. I can assure you that we shall have enough to do to resist the charge in the simplest and most unequivocal manner. It would be tempting Providence to plan out the defence in a subtler form. It is true that an acquittal might be regarded by the police in that light—it is more than possible—but to deliberately aim at such a result! I could neither draw such a brief, nor would it be one which any reputable counsel would be likely to accept. We should be looking for trouble which we should be almost certain to find."

Miss Barman accepted this decision without protest. "I've no doubt," she said, "you can judge that much better than I. And, after all, it is I who am in the mess now, and not they."

"That is the sensible view to take. When you endeavour to guess what may have actually occurred, had you considered the position of John Colvin?"

The question was asked with an intentional abruptness, but Miss Barman's reaction was merely one of apparently genuine surprise. "No," she exclaimed. "Why on earth should I do that?"

"There is the fact that he had very strong reasons for feeling ill-will towards the dead man—reasons both financial and sentimental. Indirectly, it was through the action of Abel Marks, and into his pocket, that Mr. Colvin's money had disappeared, and that he was burdened with a business of insufficient capital and precarious solvency. The arrest of William Merritt may not have disturbed his mind very seriously. It is clear that he was either unwilling or unable to take any effective steps to secure his release. But it cannot have improved his feelings towards Abel Marks to know that it was through his vindictive action that his prospective father-in-law was in Brixton jail.

"Yet until he returned to London on the Saturday morning he may have regarded his difference with Miss Merritt as being no more than a lovers' quarrel, that time would heal. He may have thought of himself as having won the game, though at a cost that he did not like. It was he, not Marks, whom Carol Merritt had preferred, and his marriage to her was to take place at an early date. That day he learnt that Marks had defeated him even in this. He was too late to prevent the marriage. His money was beyond legal recovery. May he not have thought that only revenge remained? And in the afternoon Abel Marks was dead."

The case against John Colvin, as Mr. Jellipot put it thus, was of an undeniable strength, which Miss Barman did not lack the wit to see. It was, in fact, stronger than Mr. Jellipot had felt free to state, he having knowledge of another fact, which, as he had learnt it from John Colvin in professional confidence, before the present position arose, he did not feel free to mention even to Miss Barman, without his client's authority being obtained. Being ignorant of this, she refused the suggestion with energy, striking the chain at its weakest link.

"That," she said, "may be true enough, but all the same I don't see that they've got anything against him at all. If a man gets killed, they can't collect all the people who might have cause to feel pleased, and put them in the dock together."

"No," Mr. Jellipot agreed, "they certainly couldn't do that."

"I suppose," she asked, "John isn't staying in London because of this?"

"No. He went away on his usual business on my advice. But I ought to say that I told him that little or nothing would occur during the present week. I anticipated that the police would have asked for a longer remand—for a week at least—on which point I made a bad guess."

Miss Barman displayed little interest in this scrupulous admission by Mr. Jellipot of the fallibility of his legal forecasts. She said: "Well, it was the only sensible thing for him to do," in a tone that dismissed John Colvin from the field of discussion.

Mr. Jellipot saw that she was not disposed to consider him in the light of a possible murderer, and changed the subject again to ask: "What should you say Abel Marks' character really was?"

"Putrid, if you ask me. But it doesn't follow that I knocked him down because I've no doubt of that."

Mr. Jellipot agreed again. He proceeded to go over the events of the afternoon, and others precedent thereto, in a careful detail which it would be tedious to recount, as Miss Barman gave them without essential difference from the narrative which she had supplied verbally to Inspector Combridge, and afterwards in a written statement at Scotland Yard.

Having completed this survey, he put forward a doubt which had been growing in his mind as it proceeded, and on which he felt that he could not take the responsibility of decision without assurance that his client understood and confirmed his action.

"I do not know," he began, "how far you may be already familiar with the legal procedure governing such a prosecution as this, but I may explain briefly that the magistrate before whom we shall now be appearing has no power to decide it. His discretionary power is limited to dismissing it, or sending it for trial in the higher court.

"There are, therefore, three different attitudes which we may adopt. We may contest the prosecution's evidence at all points, and the arguments based upon them, with the intention of convincing the magistrate that there is no case to answer, so that he will decline to send it for trial, which would be in every way most satisfactory for us; or we may resign ourselves to the case being fought out in a higher court, and aim at no more than to discredit the witnesses for the prosecution as far as possible in cross-examination, and to develop our own defence in such a manner that it will be set out fairly on the depositions which will be the basis of the actual trial. There is a third course open to us, which is to say that we reserve our defence, and to go on to the higher court with only the case for the prosecution set out, to which we shall, until the final hearing, make no reply.

"I should add, that, in such a case as this, it is most usual to fight at every minute and every stage, but I cannot say that the results of that method of procedure, although they may prolong the hearings, and increase their dramatic and spectacular effects, are always satisfactory in their results to those who are most concerned."

Miss Barman had listened without interrupting this lucid but somewhat lengthy explanation. She had already noticed that Mr. Jellipot was a man who must have all his statements exactly made, but that a careful attention would observe that they were neither discursive nor pointless. Having so much at stake, she had good reason to listen well. Now she asked: "What course do you advise?"

"I am not yet clear in my own mind. If I thought that there were any reasonable prospect that the magistrate could be persuaded to dismiss the case, I should advise fighting it with the utmost energy, so that, apart from other considerations, we could avoid the expense and anxiety of a further hearing. But I cannot honestly say, on the information we now have, that that possibility should be regarded seriously.

"There is, I am sorry to say, a strong tendency among magistrates to commit cases for trial when the Home Office is directly concerned in the prosecution (as it is now, we being in the metropolitan area), almost with indifference to the strength of the evidence which is put forward for the defence. I cannot actually recall a case where a metropolitan magistrate has declined to order a committal on a capital charge, though there has been more than one prosecution for murder within recent years which has been so obviously ill-founded that the judge has not allowed it to go to trial, or the grand jury have thrown out the bill."

"So it seems that we shall have to go over the whole course?"

"I am afraid that it does. But the advantage of setting out our defence at this stage in further detail than we have already done is more problematical, and my present inclination is in the contrary direction."

"Well," Miss Barman said, in the tone of one who is not going to worry about that which is in more capable hands, "of course I leave that to you."

CHAPTER XV.

MR. JELLIPOT WILL NOT FIGHT

IT was the end of the afternoon of the following day when Inspector Combridge met Mr. Jellipot, as the solicitor withdrew from the court. They came face to face amid the jostling, leaving crowd of lawyers, witnesses, and spectators, who had been drawn together by duty or curiosity to watch the opening stages of one of those dramas of life and death which are the nearest approach to the bullfight of the Spanish arena that is provided for the excitement of English citizens.

The intimacy of past acquaintance had been sufficient to explain the abruptness of the inspector's manner, and the nature of the question he addressed to the solicitor of the accused woman. He asked curtly: "What's the game?"

Mr. Jellipot gazed mildly upon an irritated and puzzled man. It was an irritation and bewilderment to which he knew that he must not attach too great a significance, but which he was not displeased to observe. He said: "If you are enquiring as to the nature, or criticising my conduct, of Miss Barman's defence, I must reply that it is an act of doubtful propriety, at a place and time singularly inopportune, and conveyed in an expression particularly unsuitable—I might even say unseemly—for a charge of the gravity of that with which we are now concerned?"

Inspector Combridge answered: "Oh, well, if you're going to take it like that!" He walked on in a worse mood than before. Yet what cause had he either of dissatisfaction or for complaint? The day had been occupied first with evidence of the nature of the injury of the murdered man. Mr. Jellipot had listened to this with interest, but said, at its conclusion, that he had no question to ask. There had been no cause for astonishment in that, though it was more usual for a defending solicitor in such a case to challenge almost everything that came from the mouths of the witnesses for the prosecution, wor-

86

rying for minute inconsistencies, or some clumsiness of reply which could be brought up for their confusion at the later trial. Then there had been the evidence of Constable Decker, and when he had narrated how he had been called in from the street by a distracted woman, whom he had afterwards learnt to be Mrs. Marks, and of how he had discovered the body of Abel Marks, Mr. Jellipot had received it in the same indifferent silence, rejecting the invitation of Mr. Walsham, the presiding magistrate, to cross-examination, such as, while seeking to discredit the witnesses' testimony, will often result in fixing it upon the depositions in a more deadly and tested form.

After that, there had been the evidence of the news-vendor, whose name now appeared as Richard Skimmer, and his statements, far more contentious, and coming much closer to the actual issue as it affected Carol Barman's guilt or innocence, had been accepted by Mr. Jellipot with the same refusal either to challenge what he had said, or to emphasize that which he had been so inconsistently unable to see.

Mr. Walsham, watching the performance with an acute legal perception of the importance of this unchallenged evidence, and a substantial doubt of how far it would endure the rigour of cross-examination, had raised puzzled eyebrows as Mr. Jellipot refused again to rise when his opportunity came.

Mr. Walsham had no doubt in his mind that, in due course, he would commit the accused woman for trial: no substantial doubt, as the police were prosecuting, that she had committed the crime: and little more that the eminent lawyers engaged for the Crown would handle the case with sufficient ability to secure her conviction. But there is a seemliness to be observed in these matters, a tradition of conflict which the prisoner is entitled to have waged on her behalf. If we return to the metaphor of the Spanish arena, we may say that the bull is allowed, is indeed expected to fight, though it is intended that it shall die.

And by this time Mr. Jellipot's silence had become an actual embarrassment to the prosecution, and had upset the time-schedule which experienced solicitors had carefully calculated.

The examination of the witnesses (of Richard Skimmer particularly) would have been fuller, and would have taken a somewhat different course, had it not been assumed that they would be subjected subsequently to a severe and possibly damaging cross-examination, and had it not been nicely calculated that some explanations would come out best in the course of that later questioning, or in the re-examination which would afterwards be permitted; and the time allotted to each of these witnesses had proved to be far more than the occasions required.

The fact is that, in a case of this kind, where the accusation is not merely of a circumstantial, but of an inferential character, it takes shape more definitely, perhaps more formidably, when each point that it attempts to make is challenged and contested in turn by an opposition which, though with an opposite purpose, will continue to follow the road it leads. Link by link, the chain of evidence is tested by the defence, which, if it does not break them in so doing, confirms their strength. But if the defence, at this stage, will not be provoked to reply, the prosecution must be left in a great doubt. Is it faced by the silence of impotence, or of a concealed strength which, in its ignorance, it can make no preparation to meet when the day of the final battle will dawn? It has deployed and exposed itself, and the opposite forces are still hidden in mist, from which they can attack at last at what point they will.

Now the afternoon was not done, though the witnesses had all been heard who had been intended for this day, and Miss Aaronson had to be called to the box, it being the course chosen for the prosecution to show first the surrounding circumstances of the crime, culminating in the witness of William Merritt and Carol Marks by which the accused would be hemmed in, as it were, both before and behind, and might find it too close a place to allow her to wriggle free. So they drew the net, while their victim, as expressed by her legal advocate, appeared indifferent or resigned to the closing meshes.

Miss Aaronson gave her evidence simply, clearly, and competently, and in a manner which Mr. Jellipot saw cause to approve. When, at its conclusion, Mr. Walsham's eyes were directed upon him, with slightly lifted interrogative brows, and he heard the customary query: "Any questions, Mr. Jellipot?" he surprised the court, and showed the detachment of his observation, by replying: "No. I thought Miss Aaronson gave her evidence in a particularly intelligent manner," at which the magistrate had looked at him in a moment of puzzled silence, opened his mouth as though to speak, checked himself, and then said only: "I think it will be convenient to adjourn at this point. Ten-thirty tomorrow, if you please, gentlemen." And so the court had risen.

It may have been that last remark of Mr. Jellipot which had edged, if it had not solely prompted, Inspector Combridge's protest. A prosecution has no cause for annoyance in the fact that its witnesses are clear in memory and exact in diction, but it is disconcerting to find the solicitor for the defence disposed to congratulate them upon it; and the evening press, with its unfailing flair for the unusual, which is the essence of the news that its readers crave, seized upon this episode for the front-page headlines which such a trial is sure to have.

"Prosecution Witness Praised by Accused's Solicitor," said the *Evening News*. "Carol Barman's Solicitor Compliments Miss Aaronson," announced the *Star*. "Mr. Jellipot Pleased," the *Evening Standard* proclaimed, with an emphatic brevity suitable to its heaviest type.

Mr. Jellipot read the three reports while enjoying his after-dinner cigar. He did not mind being thought a fool, if his client's interests could be served thereby. His anxiety came from a doubt of the wisdom of what he did. He felt somewhat at sea in these criminal cases which he so rarely touched. He had come to a good end once or twice before, but in each case he had been left with a realisation of how near the edge of the pit of failure he had stumbled along, and where (he thought) a more experienced advocate might have walked secure. It would be terrible if an innocent woman should be condemned through his own incompetence; and even a guilty one has a right to the protection the law provides, and to rely upon the skill of the advocate who accepts her fee.

Yet his judgment, stubbornly opposing his fears, continued to assert the prudence of what he did, or rather of what he declined to do. All these witnesses could be challenged when the real trial came, when the whole case for the prosecution would have been exposed, and after there had been time to examine it with the minute care it required, and to decide on the best line of defence with more assurance than he had yet been able to find.

He was interrupted in these reflections by a telephone call from his managing clerk. It was an expected call, for he had instructed him, when leaving the office that morning, that he should probably come straight home after the court adjourned, and that he was to ring him up at nine-fifteen, to report anything which had occurred in his absence. Now he heard, after a number of lesser matters had been discussed, that both William Merritt and Carol Marks had been to see him during the day. They had been persistent in this desire, and after waiting from 4:30 to 6:30 P.M. in the vain hope that he might return, had said that they would be at his office again at nine on the following morning, in the hope of seeing him before their subpoenas obliged them to be in attendance at the court again.

Mr. Jellipot considered this information in a brief silence, and then said: "I shan't be coming to the office tomorrow morning. Tell them I can't see them. They're the Crown's witnesses, not mine."

"Mrs. Marks is our client, sir," came the rather hesitating reply. "I'm not to imply that we're ceasing to act for her, am I?"

"You're not to imply anything more than I have said. As a matter of fact, she's our client in connexion with her husband's estate, but his murder's a separate matter. She's not consulted us about that, and I don't know why she should. But I don't intend to have any responsibility for anything either of them chooses to say in the witness-box tomorrow, nor for anyone to think I have…. And look here, Newman," he added, "if you can make them understand without saying it that I want Inspector Combridge to know that I've refused to see them—"

"Yes, sir, I can do that. I couldn't trust the man not to mess it up, but Mrs. Marks is quick enough at a hint."

Mr. Jellipot rang off, feeling, though he scarcely knew why, in a more buoyant mood than before. The fact that Mrs. Marks was already his client would have given him legitimate opportunity of talking over the evidence that she would give on the following day, and perhaps (for instance) stressing the importance of her not making the time of her appearance at Razor Street earlier than the admitted facts and her naturally fallible recollection required. The attitude which he had preferred was one of an immaculate propriety, at which he hoped that the prosecution would be additionally perturbed, as in fact they were destined to be.

Inspector Combridge, marshalling his witnesses in the waiting-room next morning, and giving an emphatic negative to a request from Carol Marks that she might see her aunt for a few minutes before the opening of the court, heard from her lips that Mr. Jellipot had cold-shouldered both her father and herself, and was led to an uneasy wonder as to what this attitude might portend. Suppose that the astute lawyer knew that one or other of these two had committed the crime, and that Miss Barman had supplied him with some convincing evidence which would be brought out at the dramatic moment that he preferred? Well, the ends of justice might be served, but the Criminal Investigation Department would not be pleased. It shared the common human weakness of preferring that its blunders shall not be publicly known.

A prosecution is in an uncomfortable position when it has no reliance upon the veracity of its own witnesses. Inspector Combridge's major doubt, until that moment, had been centred upon John Colvin, whose movements on the afternoon of the murder he had still been unable to trace, but now he looked with an increased suspicion upon the two on whose evidence the prosecution was so largely based. His feelings found no relief when the court opened, and Mr. Jellipot rose in his usual diffident manner to say: "If I may ask the indulgence of the court for a word of explanation in regard to the attitude of the defence toward the evidence already called—and possibly toward that which is still to come—I would say this: my client made a voluntary statement to the police, in which she explained her reason for calling upon Abel Marks on the afternoon of his violent death, and of what transpired at that interview. There her contention is that personal knowledge ends. She therefore welcomes any impartial testimony bearing on the events of that afternoon, as assisting us toward the truth, which we should all be anxious to reach."

The words were slowly, deliberately spoken, and more than one pencil was busy to take them down. Mr. Walsham said: "Very well, Mr. Jellipot," in a toneless voice. He thought the statement to be less than a sufficient explanation of the solicitor's stubborn refusal to cross-examine, as perhaps it was, and as it may have been intended to be.

But Inspector Combridge, digesting it as he best could, observed some careful qualifications which it contained, and which he knew its author well enough to take as signals which it would be perilous to disregard. "*Impartial* testimony.... *Possibly* toward that which is still to come." He watched William Merritt and then Carol Marks go into the box. He heard their tales as they had already been given to the police. He did not fail to realise that they might both have had awkward half-hours to follow, had they been subjected, say, to the hectoring tones of Ridgeway Ware, or the deadly suavity of Sir Henry Blackett. But Mr. Jellipot only shook his head. He had nothing to ask.

When the case for the prosecution closed, he rose to say no more than: "As I have listened to the evidence, I have been disposed to submit a plea that there is really no case to answer, but if you should be already decided that it is one that should be sent to the higher court, I do not wish to—"

"I am certainly of opinion that, as it stands, the case is one for a jury to determine," Mr. Walsham interrupted, "although, as I need not tell you, it is open to you to put your client into the witness-box, or to call any other evidence that you have."

"In view of that expression of opinion," Mr. Jellipot answered diffidently, "my client reserves her defence."

Miss Barman, who had listened to the day's proceedings with an undisturbed gravity, heard that she was committed to stand her trial at the Central Criminal Court, and was conducted back to the cells as the stir of movement rose in the crowded court.

CHAPTER XVI.

SIR HENRY BLACKETT TAKES A LEAN BRIEF

MR. JELLIPOT looked at his managing clerk, as though for an inspiration that did not come. He had had the inevitable conversation regarding costs with his client, and subsequently with her trustees, with the result that he was assured of a sum of £500 which could be expended on her defence—that, and no more. He was not greedy for personal gain, though he had no objection to drawing a bill of costs with the liberality which the law allows, but there was the question of counsels' fees, and in such a case—

"It's no use thinking of any of the best men, sir. They'd want that on the brief, and expect a good junior. And there'd be refreshers, and—to say nothing of ourselves. If I might suggest, sir, I'd tell her it can't be done."

Mr. Newman looked stubbornly irresponsive to his principal's more sanguine mood. He would disclaim any suggestion of Hebrew origin with emphasis, but he had sufficient of that sagacious blood in his veins to feel that questions of money should be treated with more solemnity than Mr. Jellipot would always show. Now the solicitor surprised his subordinate by saying: "But I am not sure that she is wrong."

"I should have thought Mrs. Marks—"

"Miss Barman's instructions are that she is not to be asked, nor indeed, allowed to contribute toward the costs of the case."

"Then I should say that she'd better try defending herself."

"Newman, I'm afraid you've not got a very high opinion of the English Bar."

"I don't know about that, sir. I know about how most of them expect their briefs marked."

"That's why I thought you might be able to help me with a suggestion now."

"I'm afraid I can't, if that's all she's prepared to shell out. We could do with that ourselves without being overpaid."

Mr. Jellipot did not rebuke a zeal which he recognised to be less for the speaker's interests than his own, though it was true that a good many extra fivers would pass into the clerk's pocket-book during the year as a percentage on more considerable items of profit that came to the firm's account.

"I was thinking," Mr. Jellipot said, almost in as diffident a manner as he would show to a presiding magistrate, "that perhaps Blackett—"

Mr. Newman stared. He controlled himself to the respect that his position required as he answered: "I can tell you that it wouldn't be any use to approach him, sir. He was asked to lead for the prosecution only last Tuesday, and he sent back the brief. Perkins—that's his clerk, sir—said he wouldn't look at it with all the work he'd got on for this term already."

Mr. Jellipot considered this. Unexpectedly, to Newman, he looked pleased. "Get through to him now," he said, "and ask him if he can spare me a few minutes if I come over at once."

It was not Edward Newman's habit to question his employer's decisions, or to offer counsel unless he were invited to do so. Now he went silently out of Mr. Jellipot's private office, to which he returned in a few moments to say: "Sir Henry says he'll be pleased to see you, sir, if you can be at his chambers within the next half-hour."

"Very well. Get a taxi for me at once."

It was no more than ten minutes later that Sir Henry Blackett, K.C., rose from a heavily littered desk to shake hands with Mr. Jellipot, and to forestall his intended opening with the words: "You needn't tell me that it's the Marks murder trial that brings you here."

"Yes. I heard that you had returned the brief for the prosecution."

"Which hardly sounds a good reason for taking yours."

"Well, I just wondered," Mr. Jellipot said diffidently. "I ought to tell you that there's nothing much in it financially."

Sir Henry looked surprised, but put that aspect of the matter lightly aside: "Never mind that. Is there any real defence?"

"I'm not sure that there is. I wanted to talk that over with you."

"Well, neither am I.... But I'll tell you this. I refused the brief because I didn't want to run the risk that I might be using what brains I've got to secure the condemnation of an innocent woman. And if I had another reason, it was that I thought you might have something up your sleeve to make the prosecution look silly, and I didn't care for the part."

Mr. Jellipot accepted the implied compliment of this declaration with some complaisance, but disclaimed the ability which was attributed to him.

"No," he said, "I've got no mine ready to spring. I wish I had. I may say that's why I didn't challenge the evidence in the lower court. I wasn't sure how far we might have to go in attacking any of the witnesses, or how far they might be useful to us. It didn't seem much use testing everything the prosecution alleged just to show up any weak spots, and set them tightening the nuts before they come into court again. Besides, I wanted to leave counsel as free a hand as I could."

"Well, it's not every solicitor who has the sense to do that. If I can trust what I hear (it didn't come from the brief, which I didn't read), you've rattled the prosecution more than a bit. It's always easier for them when they know what the defence means to set up."

Sir Henry spoke with a cordial sincerity pleasant to hear. He knew how greatly a solicitor may be tempted in such a case to show his own ability in cross-examination before a newspaper audience a thousand times larger than he has ever had, or will be likely to have again, and before the case reaches a stage at which he must retire to a less conspicuous position. And, even for counsel, silence is always the harder choice; and far more cases are lost by a word too many than one too few.

Mr. Jellipot felt that the interview had commenced well. He knew Sir Henry Blackett both by reputation and personally, having given him briefs in the civil actions in which the larger part of his practice lay. Suave in manner, seldom raising his voice, never showing sign of annoyance or satisfaction in victory or defeat, Mr. Jellipot judged him to be controlled by a strong pride, and more easily to be moved by the hope of a spectacular triumph than the certainty of a liberal fee. He was not of the temperament to make passionate appeal to a jury's emotions. But Mr. Jellipot held that such appeals are of doubtful value, and what effect they may have is unlikely to survive the cold logic of a summing-up which may be deferred to the next day.

It was to the jury's reason that Sir Henry Blackett would make insistent appeal. It was the tiny flaw in the logical structure of the prosecution on which he would be sure to seize, and which he could be relied upon to expose to the dullest mind. But it was rather to influence judge than jury that Sir Henry would direct his efforts. Mr. Jellipot remembered a dictum which he had once heard from Sir

Henry's lips, which he thought sound. "I don't bother much," he had said, "about the jury, one way or other, unless I've got such a rotten case that I know making fools of them is the only chance. Get the judge on your side, and he'll see that they don't go far up the wrong road, and they'll always listen a lot quicker to him."

Mr. Jellipot was following the line of attack which had been developed previously in his mind as he went on: "I don't say it's a simple case. It's one of those that may seem fairly so at first, but the more you think them over the more puzzling they get. I'm not going to tell you that I've got any settled opinions as to what really happened, but it's very much in Miss Barman's favour that she gave the police a statement at once, from which she has never moved. And it seems to me that there's no point on which they can prove it wrong. It can only be upset, if at all, on the broad general argument that Marks was alive when she went up the stairs, and dead when she came down, and that nobody else was there."

Sir Henry Blackett considered this. A statement of such a nature which is not found on enquiry to be inexact on some provable point is unusual, even from innocent lips. Made by a guilty person it would be a document of exceptional rarity. He decided that, if he should defend Miss Barman, whether innocent or guilty, he would be fortunate both in his client and the solicitor whom she employed. He said aloud: "The fact is that each side will be challenging the other to prove a negative, which is seldom easy to do."

In his heart he knew that he had already decided to take the brief. He asked, as Mr. Jellipot, who had already come to the same conclusion, remained contentedly silent: "Will she stand up to the court?"

"I suppose that she will make an exceptionally good witness. She strikes me as a woman who has an unusually good idea of the meaning of words, and when to stop talking. The danger is that she will be too cool and composed."

"You must warn her against that.... What's the trouble about finance?"

"It's her own obstinacy, really. She has some money settled on her, from which her trustees pay her a few pounds a week. They have full discretion, but she can't anticipate it without their consent.... There's no difficulty with them. They'll find anything she requires, but she says if she's a free woman when the case is over she doesn't mean to have to live substantially differently from how she did before. She'll ask them to find £500, neither more nor less, and if that isn't enough to provide legal assistance at the trial, she'll defend herself the best way she can."

"What about the press? There's usually plenty to come from that source."

"She won't deal with them at all. She says she can't help it if her relatives make themselves into public fools, but the reporters will get nothing from her."

Sir Henry Blackett considered this attitude without resentment. "She seems," he said, "to be an unusually prudent woman."

A doubt even crossed his mind as to whether she might not do as well for herself as he would be able to do for her. His mind moved forward to visualise the scene in the court when it should be announced that the prisoner was not legally represented.

He knew it to be a position which no judge will willingly permit, when there is a charge of murder to meet. He would question the prisoner as to her means. What would the effect on public sympathy be, if she should bluntly say that which Mr. Jellipot had just told—that she had offered to find £500, but had refused to be ruined in her own defence? What course would the judge take? He could not provide counsel for her under the Poor Prisoners Act, for that merciful legislative provision is for men and women only whose pockets have been already emptied. Probably he would appeal to some barrister present to take the case without fee, which few would refuse to do. But the incident would expose that which it is usual to veil in a discreet way. It would be as unseemly as for a butcher to kill in his front shop.

Mr. Jellipot, seeing victory achieved, was disposed to his own share of generosity. "I don't think," he said, "that my own costs need be very high."

Sir Henry recovered himself from a wandering mind. "Send me along the brief, and as soon as I've read it over, we'll have a conference with Miss Barman together. Don't worry about the cash. If you help me to get an acquittal, we shan't fall out over that."

Mr. Jellipot rose. He thanked Sir Henry, as he had some reason to do. He hesitated a moment, and said: "There's one thing that won't be in the brief, that you ought to know. The police have been enquiring respecting the movements of John Colvin, the young man who—"

"Yes. You needn't explain. I know about him."

"—on the afternoon in question, but I have some reason to think that they have learnt nothing. I have been aware all along that he was actually in Razor Street about the time of the murder, for which he can give a quite natural explanation. I had learnt this in professional confidence before I was acting for Miss Barman in any way. But I now have Mr. Colvin's permission to disclose this circumstance, if it should appear to be essential to Miss Barman's defence."

"He was in Razor Street at the time! And he is, in other respects, the most likely—I might say far the most likely—person to have killed the man. It is certainly a most interesting circumstance."

"You will appreciate that he had a quite separate and indisputably genuine reason for being there."

"I must believe what you say. And he will, of course, have denied this to the police?"

"Not at all. He refused to discuss his movements with them. To use his own expression, when he subsequently related his conversation with Inspector Combridge to me, he told him to 'go to hell'."

"So I am to compliment you on another client of unusual discretion? But it isn't easy to see how we can bring it in at all, unless we propose to put him forward as one who probably committed the crime."

"It is a suspicion which he appears to be willing to face."

"Well, if we can find some excuse for getting him into the box—! I suppose he didn't happen to meet Miss Barman going in or out?"

"No. He says he didn't see her at all."

"That's a pity in more ways than one. Well, send me on the brief, and we'll see what can be done."

CHAPTER XVII.

INSPECTOR COMBRIDGE HAS A NEW WITNESS

IT was only three days before that on which Carol Barman must stand her trial for the murder of Abel Marks that Inspector Combridge called at Mr. Jellipot's office.

"It's about the Marks case," he said, "I've looked in. We've got some fresh evidence, and though of course you'll hear from us about that in a more formal manner—"

"As long," Mr. Jellipot interrupted placidly, "as you've come to tell me that you've seen the wisdom of dropping a prosecution that you can't hope to sustain—"

"Not at all. It's the other way. We've got just one of those odd bits of extra evidence that are so useful to turn the scale when it's a bit wobbly."

As he heard this, the idea that he was about to be told that suspicion was lifting from Miss Barman to settle upon John Colvin in an even darker cloud, passed from Mr. Jellipot's mind. "Well," he said, "whatever it is, I shall be interested to hear."

"It's from a man named Gurtner, a diamond merchant who's just come back from abroad. That's why he hasn't been to us sooner with what he knows. He has his office almost opposite Rosenbaum & Co.'s premises, and on the afternoon that Marks was killed he was there till about three o'clock—he says he can't be definite to half an hour one way or other—and he happened to look out of his window and saw a lady leaving Rosenbaum's. From his description of her, there's no doubt that it was Miss Barman he saw. Indeed, for a description from memory, it was singularly good."

"I suppose," Mr. Jellipot suggested, "that, with the aid of the newspaper photographs that have appeared, the singularly good description would not be a matter of singular difficulty?"

"Of course," Inspector Combridge replied, with the good humour of one who has just drawn a good card from the pack, "you would be bound to suggest that. But Gurtner says that he hadn't seen any, nor, in fact, heard or read anything about the case, until he returned last Tuesday, and the woman who cleans his office began to talk about it, which was a very natural thing for her to do."

"That," Mr. Jellipot conceded, "is a point on which we shall be unlikely to take opposite sides.... I suppose the lady was not, by any chance, Mrs. Wibble herself?"

This time Inspector Combridge looked distinctly annoyed. It was true that the woman was the same who had ministered to the comfort of Abel Marks, and true therefore that she might have furnished Mr. Gurtner with Miss Barman's description. It did not follow that she had done so, or that he had required such aid to his own memory, but the inspector felt that Mr. Jellipot had invested the point of the woman's identity with a false and irritating importance by having guessed it before her name had been communicated to him.

"Yes," he said, "that's who it was. She cleans several buildings about there. Has two or three assistants, and is in quite a large way of business, so I am told."

Mr. Jellipot, who was already aware of this, as part of the result of exhaustive and unprofitable enquiries which he had no intention of mentioning, made no comment. He said: "It may be unfortunate that Mr. Gurtner's memory isn't more exact concerning the time."

"Well, he says he can't be. He says he stayed at his office, after his assistant left at midday, to clear some correspondence and other matters before he went abroad. When he finished, he took a bus to his club. He says it was about the middle of the afternoon, but he can't be more exact than that.

"One of the last things he did before leaving was to lock his safe, to do which he would pass between the front window of the room and a desk where his assistant works, and it was then that he noticed Miss Barman coming out."

"Why should he have noticed her so particularly?"

"Because he knew Marks. He had business transactions with him, and they belonged to the same club. He says he quite expected to see him there that afternoon, and would probably have chaffed him about his lady visitor. He knew Marks was usually alone there during Saturday afternoons, and he knew his staff by sight, and no doubt looked at Miss Barman more particularly because he hadn't seen her before."

"That's natural enough," Mr. Jellipot conceded easily, "but I am still unable to see that Mr. Gurtner's evidence will be any help to you, or any trouble for us, especially as he's so hazy about the time.

As to seeing Miss Barman leave, it does no more than confirm her own statement to you. She says she called on Abel Marks during the afternoon, and it seems a reasonable deduction that she came out. Unless, of course, you are going to suggest that she is still there?"

"I suppose that seems funny to you," Inspector Combridge answered, with the satisfaction of one whose ace has still to appear, "but it was what she did when she came out that impressed the incident on Mr. Gurtner's mind. He noticed that she closed the outer door."

"Wasn't that a very natural thing for her to do?"

"No. I don't think it was.... He says that the door always stood open till Mr. Marks left himself, and seeing a strange lady come out and close it, made him wonder what her position might be. He even wondered, making a guess that was curiously correct, though it was also entirely wrong, whether Marks had taken a wife."

"If we accept the accuracy of Mr. Gurtner's memory and observation," Mr. Jellipot replied, with a determination not to admit the importance of the diamond merchant's contribution to his already sufficient difficulties, "it only shows that Miss Barman left without haste or appearance of perturbation, which is exactly what I should have expected to hear."

Inspector Combridge rose. "I'm not going to argue with you about that," he said, "I've only told you what new evidence we're proposing to call."

Mr. Jellipot observed the tone of annoyance in this reply, and was disposed to blame himself for a defect of manner toward an old friend, and one who had just shown a courtesy, either personal or official, toward himself, which he might have received in a different way. It was the duty of the prosecution to serve notice upon him of any evidence they proposed to call which was not on the depositions of the hearing in the magistrate's court. But the inspector need not have given him this extra half-day's notice by making it the subject of a personal communication. He said frankly: "Sorry, Combridge. You've done me a good turn looking in like this, and I'm afraid I didn't take it quite in the right way. I suppose the fact is that neither of us feels entirely happy about this case, and it's making us inclined to be rather irritable. But we've been good friends before, and I've no doubt we shall be after Miss Barman's released, and we've forgotten that Abel Marks ever got a knock on the head."

The inspector's face showed that this apology was all, or indeed more than was required to remove any passing annoyance he had felt at Mr. Jellipot's reluctance to admit the importance of Gurtner's testimony. But he was uncompromising in the substance of his reply. "That's all right, Mr. Jellipot. I can understand how you feel. And when you say 'after Miss Barman's released'—well, you can't put it much higher than that. I reckon we shall both be a bit older before that happens, if it ever does. And if you think over the significance of that door, I reckon you'll come to the same conclusion."

With these words, Inspector Combridge departed, and Mr. Jellipot continued to "think over that door" with no satisfaction to himself, or seeing more than he had done already, though he declined to recognise it in the presence of his legal enemy.

Whether it was a natural action or not for Miss Barman to close an outer door which had been open when she entered, and after she had let herself out through a counter-flap, might be a subject of inconclusive argument. There might be nothing more in that than a counsel as adroit as Sir Henry Blackett might be equal to turn aside, or even convert to his own gain. But, if she had closed the door, who, before Mrs. Marks arrived, could have opened it again?

Mr. Marks might, of course, have come down in response to a ring of the street-bell. The murderer might have closed the door, when he left, as Miss Barman had been observed to do. It was not conclusive, therefore, but it slightly and yet definitely reduced the already slight possibility that another visitor might have come and gone in the short interval after she left and before Mrs. Marks had put her key in the lock. Mrs. Marks had found the door closed. Mr. Gurtner had observed Miss Barman close it. There was no satisfaction in that. Mr. Jellipot telephoned Sir Henry Blackett for a further conference.

CHAPTER XVIII.

THE ATTORNEY-GENERAL STATES THE CASE

MR. JUSTICE SUMNERS slightly adjusted his pince-nez, and looked at the prisoner. He had already read the depositions with care, and had observed the absence of any show of fight from the defending solicitor. It did not occur to him to doubt the guilt of the accused, his experience being that the metropolitan police are of a reliable efficiency in these matters. If they said that Carol Barman had committed the crime, he was quite prepared to accept their opinion in preference to that which a jury might ultimately be persuaded to bring in. But, guilty or innocent, the prisoner was entitled to be arraigned according to the strict rules of the game, and he was there as the referee to see that they were duly observed.

He liked to think of himself, in these criminal cases, by that word rather than that of judge. It was really more accurate, as it was the jury, not he, from whom the word of release or condemnation would come. In a capital charge, he had not even any power of decision as to what penalty should be imposed. And it assisted him to the attitude of aloof impartiality that the occasion required. He was there as referee in a game that was for others to play.

He observed that the Attorney-General appeared for the Crown. He had heard talk that this had been decided after Sir Henry Blackett had refused the brief. Evidently, it was a case in which some intellectual subtlety would be required to secure that Justice should not be denied her prey.

And now Blackett was appearing for the accused! If the prisoner had been poorly defended before Johnnie Walsham, she would have no cause for further complaint on that score. Mr. Justice Sumners foresaw a good fight, such as it would be a pleasure to watch and to referee.

He did not suppose that the hare would outpace the hounds, but, should it happen, he would not care. He might, indeed, be rather pleased. In these cases of sudden, perhaps provoked violence, it was often easier to sympathise with the criminal than his victim, and the joyous stir when a prisoner is released and legal advocates and friends make a happy congratulatory group round the opening dock is a pleasanter sight on which to look down than that of one who stands up, with what courage she has, to face the black cap, and the dreadful sentence of death.

No, Mr. Justice Sumners would have no objection if his friend Blackett could persuade the jury to let the prisoner go—always providing that it did not spring from any failure in himself as a referee, and in particular from no partiality or defect in his own summing-up, in which his own reputation, and his judicial honour were most concerned....

He said that the prisoner could sit down, and there was a kindly gravity in his voice that Miss Barman was glad to hear. It seemed that there was no enmity in the sound, and a friend was more than she could have expected to find.... Mr. Justice Sumners leaned back in his seat. He let his pince-nez fall. He half-closed his eyes. The vigilance of his mind had not relaxed, but he had settled down to listen to the opening speech of the Attorney-General.

Sir Hugh Wrexham was one whom it was always a pleasure to hear. Sir Hugh Wrexham was a man who had a great confidence in himself, and that confidence had been justified in so far that it had brought him to the high place which he now held. He had never been addicted to the expression of hasty opinions, nor to their adoption without deliberate thought. He had pondered long before he had chosen the political party to which he now belonged. But, having done so, he had shown an unswerving loyalty to his political chiefs: an unhesitating orthodoxy in defence of the principles which he now professed. He had given careful thought to the solution of the murder of Abel Marks, and there had been a time when he was in a great doubt. There had been a time after that when he had inclined to the opinion that the man had died at the hand of his four-hour wife. But finally he had decided that Carol Barman had struck the blow, and, having resolved thus, and put his signature to this deliberate opinion, the doubt was done. He knew that there is a time for hesitation, and a time when it should be put firmly aside. He did not under-estimate the abilities of his legal opponents, and he expected that the fight would be hard to win, but he did not doubt that it was the cause of truth and justice that he had undertaken, nor that his own capacity would be equal to secure that they would be vindicated when the verdict should be delivered.

He was less suave in manner than Sir Henry Blackett perhaps incapable of the finer subtleties of that adroit and ductile advocate, but his inflexible energy and the attitude of assured conviction with which his cases would be fought to the last ditch, were justly feared by those who were cast to oppose him in these deadly duels of wit where the ancient principles of championship were reversed, so that those who fought incurred no danger at all, and success or failure would be paid with an equal purse. The hazard would be for the one who must sit silent to watch the thrust and parry of legal wits, knowing that it was her own life that would pay, should her champion have the worse of the verbal war.

Now Sir Hugh was putting the case against Carol Barman in a clear, temperate style which Mr. Justice Sumners might have good cause to admire, but which she who was most concerned could not be expected to appreciate in a similarly impartial manner. She heard him glide lightly over the finding of the murdered man, and the cause of death, on which he assured the jury that the evidence would be such as to place beyond reasonable doubts both the fact that Abel Marks had died by homicidal violence, and the manner and instrument of the act. He went on with more particularity as he approached the point at which the prosecution sought to establish the identity of the hand by which the fatal blow had been struck.

"It is an undisputed fact," he said, "that Carol Barman called at these premises—premises which by all probabilities, and according to all available evidence, were vacant except for the presence of Abel Marks waiting there for his coming bride, a short time—I shall invite you to conclude that it was a very short time—before the arrival of Mrs. Marks, who will tell you how, after sitting for some time in the strange silence of the house where she had expected that her husband would be waiting to greet her, she at length commenced a search which resulted in the discovery of the body of the murdered man, upon seeing which she did the natural—and very proper—thing, by running into the street to call for the assistance of the police.

"If her evidence be true—and when you have heard her in the box I venture to forecast that you will have little doubt on that point—and if any credit whatever is to be given to Carol Barman's own statement of what occurred, then it is a certain fact that Abel Marks was struck down between the time when Carol Barman entered the premises, and that at which her niece, Carol Marks, entered by the same door.

"I have mentioned the statement made by the accused, which will be brought before you in due course. Your attention will no doubt be directed to the fact that this statement was voluntarily and promptly made, and that Carol Barman has not subsequently deviated from it. That is a legitimate point which the defence are entitled to make, and if the whole of that statement is to be believed—if it be not merely true, but the entire truth without the suppression of any material fact—then Carol Barman is an innocent woman. The difficulty of accepting that, is that Abel Marks was alive—that is her own witness—when she entered his office, where he must have lain dead immediately after she left, carefully closing the outer door as she went.

"But it is not with the purpose of argument—for which the time is not yet—that I have mentioned the statement made by the accused. It is because she naturally—indeed, unavoidably gave an explanation of her visit to the dead man. That explanation is consistent with the known facts of the case, and you will probably accept it without difficulty as substantially true. And to appreciate that explanation it becomes necessary to understand the past relations of the murdered man, not only with Carol Barman herself, but with the bride he had taken a few hours before, and the man who had become his father-in-law by the same act.

"To understand the cause of her call upon Abel Marks you have to consider a number of antecedent facts which constitute the background of the tragedy, and from which—I think you will have no difficulty in concluding—from which it came.

"From these antecedent facts, which I think you will find to be substantially undisputed, it will become apparent that there was sufficient cause for bitterness of feeling on the part, not only of Carol Barman but of William Merritt, the father of the bride, to whom I have alluded already. William Merritt had also called on Abel Marks on the afternoon of the murder. He called—there is no possible dispute about that—a short time before the visit of Carol Barman. He had come from a debtors' prison where he had been confined at the instance of Abel Marks. He had just learnt that his daughter had married his financial enemy as a means—though in fact it had not been the means—of securing his release. He went there to quarrel. Had it not been known that Carol Barman had called subsequently, he would have been under a grave and undeserved suspicion. But you will hear his own account of his interview with Abel Marks. You will see him in the box, and judge whether he is of the stuff of which murderers are made. His account is one which, as heard from his own lips, would probably have been accepted for true, even though the mystery had remained unsolved. But he is, as it fortunately happens, entirely exonerated by the admission of the accused herself that she met Abel Marks alive at a later hour."

The learned counsel went on from this point to give an account of the financial and other relations of Abel Marks with the Merritt family, which was mainly in accordance with the facts as they have been narrated, and which it would therefore be redundant to repeat. He concluded: "It is not necessary for the prosecution to discover the motive that may prompt the wickedness or weakness of human nature to the extremity of homicidal crime. Neither is it necessary to reconstruct the exact events of an interview at which only two were present, and one is dead. Nor, perhaps, may it be possible to do more than guess at what point the narrative of the accused fails in the veracity which must have involved her in self-confession of such a crime. Whether Abel Marks actually consented to repay the money which Carol Barman had found, whether he did actually so repay it, at what point the bitter hostility which Carol Barman must have felt prompted the snatching up of that fatally handy weapon, and the murderous blow which the threatened man appears to have been rising from his chair to avoid—these are matters of conjecture only, which you are fortunately not required to decide. It is the fact of the murderous blow with which you have to deal, and the hand that dealt it that you have to determine. And I submit that, when the evidence has been heard, the conclusion that that was the hand of Carol Barman will be one to which you will be irresistibly led."

With these words the Attorney-General sat down, and Mr. Justice Sumners stirred himself from the attentive immobility with which he had heard them. He recognised that the case against the prisoner had been lucidly and not unfairly put, nor with greater prolixity than was usual when the issue was a capital charge, though he had wished once or twice that Wrexham would control his tendency to argue the case before the evidence had been called, which was a weakness to which he was always inclined, and he recognised that the concluding peroration had not been beyond challenge in more than one of its legal assumptions. (Not that that would make any difference, one way or other, in the end.) And he observed that his friend Blackett seemed undisturbed. He thought he saw now what the course of the trial would be likely to be. Probably Blackett meant to put the prisoner in the box, when she would admit the act, but with an account of provocation, perhaps threats of violence, which would mitigate, if it could not excuse the nature of what she had done. She could say that she had not realised the weight of the weapon which had been so unfortunately near her hand.... Manslaughter would be the proper verdict. If Blackett hoped to sway the jury to a sympathy which would let her off, he would find that he was in the wrong court. Mr. Justice Sumners put the law first, and in his court it should be respected. He would know how to instruct the jury on that.... But it might be an offence which a term of penal servitude would fairly meet. Seven years...five...even possibly three. But the question of public policy must be paramount in such matters. Five years would be best, with a hint in the proper quarter which might mean a somewhat earlier release, even beyond the reduction good conduct earns. (Grounds of health, in all probability, would be the pretext allowed.).... So his mind moved ahead, approving, on this supposition, the reticence of the defence. Doubtless they wished to see what was alleged, or how far proof would go, before their own account could be staged in its final form.

But, to whatever end, the slow formal processes of the English law must not be hurried or set aside. Mr. Justice Sumners picked up his pen, as the first witness for the prosecution entered the box.

CHAPTER XIX.

WILLIAM MERRITT ENTERS THE BOX

TO Carol Barman, the first two hours after the luncheon adjournment were dull, and they seemed pointless to her. What did the medical evidence matter, and this other formal proving of that which was not in dispute at all? Why not come to the point? No one doubted that the man was dead. There was no question of how he died. Her own attention wandered at times. She even looked at the high clock on the wall, wondering at what time the court would rise to break the monotony of the slow hours through which she must sit waiting for them to really begin. Even the jury looked listless, bored; and one of them, a heavy man, of the beer-and-beef variety, with the appearance of a bookmaker or a prosperous publican, had an evident difficulty in keeping awake.

Yet she had intelligence enough to see that the battle was already joined. The legal gentlemen below her were alert to the implications of every word. The judge was vigilant to interpose in the elucidation of any possible ambiguity. His watchfulness never relaxed. He held up the proceedings at times while he wrote down a careful note. English justice may be inexorable in its conclusions, but its victims may observe that they are always butchered in the best way.... She was roused to sharper attention when the name of William Merritt was called, and her brother-in-law entered the court, and was guided to the witness-box in a state of nervous agitation evident to all in the crowded, expectant court.

The Attorney-General had the reputation of a skilful and relentless cross-examiner, and his handling of his own witnesses seldom failed to produce the required evidence in the form in which he wished to present it; but he lacked the friendly suavity of address by which some advocates will put a nervous witness at ease, and lead him easily along the path that the brief requires. His nearest approach to this attitude would be one of an impersonal matter-of-course tone such as might incline a witness of normal self-possession to forget himself in the narrative he had to give, and with a feeling that his counsel was in partnership with him to lay it clearly before the court.

In dealing with William Merritt, Sir Hugh had decided to be as brief as possible, and he did not anticipate difficulty. The only essential points in his evidence were that he had left Abel Marks alive (on which no ambiguity was to be anticipated) and the time at which his call had been made. All further detail—the object of the call, and the conversation which took place—Sir Hugh had resolved to leave. They were no part of his case. Let his learned friend bring them out, if he were willing to take the risk of their effect on the minds of the jury. What result could it have except to emphasise the bitterness of feeling between the murdered man and the relatives of his just-won bride?

But even on the two points to which his examination was confined William Merritt was not proving a satisfactory witness. He had no more to do than to repeat answers that he had given before in the magistrate's court, and which had been rehearsed on the previous day. But now he hesitated and qualified what he had said, looking not at the counsel by whom the questions were put, nor to jury or judge, but either down in a shamefaced way, or at the prisoner, as though asking forgiveness for what he said. It was an attitude which could be variously interpreted, but gave Sir Hugh Wrexham a well-grounded apprehension of what would be likely to follow when the time for cross-examination should come.

The fact was that, since he had given his previous evidence, Mr. Merritt had had opportunity for reflection, and he had seen how easily he could have made the time of his call (which was a matter of deduction rather than of memory) half an hour earlier than he had said, and though the importance of this, one way or other, was largely discounted by Miss Barman's admission that she had found Abel alive, yet he need not (as his daughter subsequently pointed out in very forcible words) have made it appear that he *must* have been in that condition when Aunt Carol had entered; suppose that her aunt had found him dead, and had lied in an effort not to convict her own relative? Might not his foolish, needless accuracy, if such it were (on which she had known her father too long to have any confident opinion), be construed into the deadliest evidence against the woman whose position might be entirely due to her chivalry toward himself?

So she had spoken, with what degree of sincerity might be hard to judge, among three people of whom (unless they held to the difficult opinion that the blow had been struck by an unknown hand) two at least must be in a vague doubt of the other two, and the argument had impressed an extra sense of folly and guilt upon a mind which had been burdened enough before.

Now, when Sir Hugh Wrexham asked, in the casual voice of one who required no more than formal statement of a fact which is neither of importance nor in dispute: "And the time which you made this call was—?" William Merritt hesitated, and said half-audibly: "I don't know for sure. It might have been one, or a bit later than that."

The Attorney-General looked at the witness sharply.

"I didn't ask you," he said, "what it might be, but what it was. Please think carefully before you reply. You must remember that you have sworn to this time already."

"I might," the hesitating reply came slowly, "have remembered a bit better then, but I won't say I was oversure."

Mr. Justice Sumners intervened: "Try to do yourself justice, Mr. Merritt. I must tell you that you are doing neither your sister-in-law nor yourself any good by this intransigent attitude. What was the time to which you swore when you remembered better than you do now?"

"I think I said half-past one, your honour."

Mr. Justice Sumners ignored the derogation of his judicial dignity implied in this style of address. He said sternly: "You know you said half-past one.... Go on, Sir Hugh, if you please."

"And you were with Mr. Marks for a period which you have already sworn to have been not less than from twenty to thirty minutes?"

William Merritt muttered and mumbled again, and was more reasonable in the substance than the manner of his reply when he became audible with: "I couldn't say, really. I wasn't taking any notice of that."

Miss Barman had so far conducted herself with the restrained propriety which Mr. Jellipot had enjoined. She had been warned of the danger of too great composure, of too great manifestations of excitement, even of too great display of intelligence, any of which might impress the jury in an unfavourable and fatal manner. The correct attitude would be subdued and rather plaintive patience.

She had set her lips rather grimly as the urgency of such appearance had been impressed upon her, but the intelligence which she was not to show to excess had been sufficient to lead her to regard it seriously. She realised the critical danger of her position, and, having no wish to lose either life or liberty, or to continue to endure the gross indignities which are considered suitable for accused persons for one avoidable hour, she had made a sustained effort to comport herself in accordance with the expert advice she had received.

She realised, also, the etiquette of extreme respect which is paid to the abstract Deity of English Law, and which is a manifestation of one of the basic qualities of national character, without parallel in the procedures of Continental or American justice, and far exceeding the attitude of awe which the same persons will consider sufficient for the temples of their religious devotions. But William Merritt was not the court. He was a brother-in-law, held for the last twenty years in moderate liking and much contempt, and now uselessly making himself a public fool, as she had expected that he would do.

As he gave his mumbled, non-committal response, her voice broke sharply on the decorum of the startled court: "Speak up, William, and don't be such a ninny. You know well enough when you were there. It's I'm in the hole, not you."

Mr. Justice Sumners turned a sternly expostulatory frown upon the occupant of the dock. Etiquette must be observed, but a prisoner cannot be ordered to leave the court, neither is a committal for contempt to be greatly dreaded by one who is already threatened with the extreme penalty of the law. Before he had time to speak, Sir Henry Blackett was on his feet, with a quick word of apology on his client's behalf, after which he turned to lean backward upon the rail of the dock in admonition less audible than were the closing words of Miss Barman's reply: "But it seems a bit hard that the one who is most concerned is the only one who can't open her mouth."

The Attorney-General was perhaps the only man in that crowded court who was really annoyed by the interruption. Even Mr. Rodney Westwood, his learned junior, had the satisfaction of remembering that he had advised against putting William Merritt into the box. But Sir Hugh Wrexham was not one to be turned from his course by the suggestions of his legal subordinates. He had interviewed William Merritt himself, and his decision had been that the jury had better see him, and judge for themselves whether he would be likely to murder anything larger than a good-sized mouse. Now he knew that he had not merely produced an unsatisfactory witness. He had established for himself the disadvantage that the personality of the prisoner, by that exclamation, had broken through the legal barrier which would have held her back, less as an individual than as an exhibit in the case. It was illogical enough, but no less true, that the foolish sympathy of the crowd might be stirred to take her side with a ten-fold conviction, a ten-fold energy, for no better reason than that she had admonished her brother-in-law in the open court for his deficiencies of mind and manner.

Worse than that—far worse—Sir Hugh Wrexham's experienced glance, moving rapidly along the two rows of jurors, while the prisoner's advocate had turned to expostulate with his client, had paused upon a woman at the far end of the rearward row—a schoolmistress, in fact, with alert intelligent eyes in a rather tired face and had seen a slight smile on thin mobile lips, a look of sympathetic appreciation in those lively eyes, which were danger-signals to him that he could not miss. His determination hardened to confront a more difficult struggle than he had expected to have to meet. When his time came for the final speech he saw that it was that woman he must convince: that he must marshal such arguments as would be potent with her. Duty to the state—the suppression of personal feelings—the sanctity of the oath she had taken—yes, he should be equal to deal with her. But he wished that he had not put Merritt into the box—and there was the cross-examination to come.

He saw his learned friend rise in a leisurely manner, and settled himself to watch for the chance that might recover the ground that had been so provokingly lost.

CHAPTER XX.

THE HESITATIONS OF MR. MERRITT

SIR HENRY BLACKETT began in an easy, leisurely conventional tone. He was feeling at ease himself, the pleasant anticipation of a surgeon about to undertake a particularly difficult operation, but one that he has no doubt of his own competence to perform successfully. He had pledged himself to his client that he would not handle the case in such a way as to throw suspicion, to their own danger, upon either of her own relatives, and had obtained her promise that she would rely upon him for that, leaving him a free hand as to the manner in which her instructions were carried out, even though he might appear to walk on a narrow edge.

He had to bring the witness to an easier mood, and to lead him to an admission which must have its subtle effect on the jurors' minds—particularly of any who might be disposed to favour the accused woman. He was not aiming to obtain any admission of guilt. It might be said that he would not ask the witness to pass through, but merely to look at an open door. He began: "You have told us, Mr. Merritt, that your memory is not very exact as to the time of your call upon Mr. Marks. I am not going to ask you to make any effort, at this distance of time, to correct the evidence you have already given. From what we have heard already, we may conclude, may we not, that when you made your way to Razor Street you were an angry and indignant—perhaps most people would say a justly angry and indignant man?"

William Merritt's answer was no more than the simple "Yes" that the question required, but it had stirred him to sufficient memory of his wrongs, as he had felt them then before this nightmare of murder had fallen, like a blacker confusing shadow, across the sombre prospect of his previous troubles, and a faint note of recovered manhood was in the monosyllabic reply.

"You had been released only a few hours before from a debtors' prison, into which you had been cast at the instance of Abel Marks?"

"Yes."

"And you had arrived home to find that your daughter had married the man, with no other motive than to secure your release?"

"Yes."

"And you went at once to the place which, to your knowledge, was not only his place of business, but also his home, where you expected to find him and your daughter together."

"Yes. I expected I might. It was the only place I knew where they were likely to be."

"Naturally. But, in fact, your daughter returned home, for whatever purpose, after you had left, so that you missed her at both places?"

"Yes. She went back to get some things she needed."

"I have no doubt that she did. But you went, in this mood of double indignation, at your own imprisonment and your daughter's marriage, thinking to find them together. You went as quickly as you could?"

"Yes, I didn't lose any time."

"By what means—by what vehicle—did you travel? It is a matter of two or three miles, is it not, between your own place of business and Razor Street?"

"Yes. About three miles. I walked part of the way, and went part by bus."

"And when a man is in a mood of strong indignation, his feet are apt to move rather fast than slow?"

Sir Hugh Wrexham was on his feet in protest before any answer came. "I haven't wished to interfere with my learned friend's efforts to persuade this man that his memory is even worse than he was himself aware, but I must submit that that is a matter on which the witness's opinion is of no value, and cannot properly be——"

Mr. Justice Sumners concurred, without obliging him to complete his argument. "It is a matter on which I cannot accept Mr. Merritt as an expert witness. But if you put it rather differently, Sir Henry…? He may, of course, speak to a matter of fact, from his own experience."

"My lord, I am content to leave it." Sir Henry smiled at the smiling judge. The point was made in the question, to which each juror could reply in his own mind. And William Merritt's answers were becoming rather longer, rather more readily given. Sir Henry felt that he was moving ahead on the right road. He went on: "In fact, you got there about as fast as you could?"

"Yes. I didn't know how soon they might be going away."

"And you had no special reason to notice the time?"

"No. I never gave it a thought. I didn't know it would matter then."

"Naturally not. And when you found Abel Marks alone, you told him what you thought of what he had done?"

"Yes, I said—" Mr. Merritt stopped and looked round the court as though asking them to believe that he had made a less abject figure than he now was. He finished lamely: "I'd got a bit worked up."

"That is easy to understand. And you remember what you said a good deal better than how long it took you to say?"

"Yes. I didn't give a thought to the time."

"Naturally not. And after that you went straight to Clanranald Mansions, and waited there till Miss Barman returned?"

"Yes. I'd nowhere else to go. I didn't want to go home alone."

"And I expect you found it a long while to wait before Miss Barman appeared?"

"It seemed more than a bit."

"And will you tell the court in your own way what you talked about when Miss Barman came?"

"Well, first of all, Carol got me a meal, and then we talked about my Carol's marriage, and what Abel had done, and she showed me the money he'd paid her back—I mean what was left after she'd paid the furniture firm."

"And then you rang up Razor Street to see whether your daughter was there? Who proposed doing that? Was it Miss Barman or you?"

"I thought I'd like to have a word with her if she was there."

"Very well. It was your proposal. And when you heard that Marks was dead, you said you'd go to her, and Miss Barman went with you. Did you ask her to do that, or did she offer to come?"

"I asked her to come along."

"And was she willing to do so?"

"Yes, of course. She was quite ready to come."

"Very well. I think we've got the course of events clearly now.... And now, Mr. Merritt, I want to ask you to give me your careful attention while I put a hypothetical case—an absolutely hypothetical case—so that we may see what really might have been involved in this question of your memory—or of you having made a statement without sufficient care as to what your memory was—

concerning the time when you called at Razor Street, and of how long you remained.

"Suppose that when Miss Barman had arrived at Razor Street she had found Abel Marks lying dead, as your daughter found him afterwards. Suppose that she had taken this money—money that was morally, if not legally, hers—from the open safe, and quietly withdrawn. Suppose that when she returned to her flat and found you there, and you told her over the meal that you had just come from giving Abel a father's curse—I think that is the expression you used in the statement which you made subsequently to the police—suppose she had concluded, quite wrongly, of course, that it was your hand that had dealt the blow—"

"Wait a moment, Sir Henry, if you please." Mr. Justice Sumners had been listening to this lengthened list of suppositions with a frowning intentness which now broke sharply across the imaginary picture which the learned counsel was building up amid the silence of the breathless court.

"I should like to know, Sir Henry," the judge continued, "before you question the witness further, whether that is the defence with which we shall have to deal."

"Not at all, my lord. I was putting an absolutely suppositious case."

Mr. Justice Sumners turned to the witness to say: "Before you reply, I think you should understand that there is no question of any charge being brought against yourself, and also that you are under no obligation to answer any question which may be put in such a form that it would tend to incriminate you to do so.... I can, I am sure, Sir Henry, rely upon your discretion in the line of cross-examination which you pursue."

"Yes, my lord.... I do not think there has ever been any ambiguity about Miss Barman's defence to the charge which has been brought against her. She made an immediate statement to the police. She contends that that statement is true, and that she knows nothing further concerning the matter. Her account of her interview with Abel Marks has never deviated from first to last, as the Attorney-General very fairly observed."

"Very well, Sir Henry. Pray proceed."

Sir Henry Blackett turned to the witness again. He felt that, after so considerable a diversion, it was improbable that Merritt would have a very clear recollection of the series of suppositions which he had been invited to entertain. But he did not think it well to repeat them, in view of the attitude which Mr. Justice Sumners had assumed. He came to his point at once with the direct question: "Had that been what occurred—had that terrible doubt been in Miss Barman's mind—had she from that mistaken motive decided to continue the assertion, at whatever cost to herself, that she had found, and therefore left, Abel Marks alive, do you not recognise that a careless statement concerning a time which, I suggest, you did not really remember at all, and which I suggest was materially earlier than that which was your too-careless guess, might have confirmed her in the belief that it was your hand that had struck the blow, and might have prevented enquiries being made by others through which the actual criminal might have been traced and the truth discovered?"

It is vain to do more than guess at what reply, if any, William Merritt might have been led to make, had the whole question been presented to him without the interlude that had occurred, and the warning from the judge that his obligation to answer was not without qualifications. As it was, he looked at the examining counsel in a moment of blank and puzzled silence, which was almost immediately broken by the voice of the judge interposing a second time.

"Before I direct the witness to answer that question, Sir Henry, I should like to be clearer than I now am as to its bearing upon the case that we have to try."

"It is intended to assist him to realise the importance of accuracy in what he says."

"Then," the judge replied dryly, "while I have never wished to limit the legitimate license of counsel for the defence, and especially so in a case of this gravity, I must say that the point might have been put in a simpler form."

"In view of your lordship's expression of that opinion," Sir Henry replied very cheerfully, "I will withdraw the question entirely."

He sat down as he spoke, having put an idea into the minds of the jury which he could have introduced in no other way and having been quick to perceive that the fact of the question being left unanswered might be of more advantage to him than any answer that William Merritt would have been likely to give. No man can be required to incriminate himself. Well, William Merritt had not done so. He had had the protection of the court. He had not answered at all.

What would be the legal implication of that? Nothing whatever. But in the minds of jurors to whom legal subtleties did not appeal? Who were only anxious that they should not wrongfully convict the prisoner in the dock? To them, it might be no less than the straw that will turn the scale.

Considering the instructions he had received, he might say to himself that he had done well. He had walked with some success on that narrow edge. It was true that Miss Barman did not look pleased. But his obligation was not to please her, but to set her free.

His attention, though not his eyes, turned to the Attorney-General, and he observed that that hard-fighting lawyer was in a divided mind, such as he would rarely show, as to whether to continue the examination, or let a witness go who had been of no advantage to him.

William Merritt, standing in bewildered uncertainty in the box, while the legal thunders of which he was the unworthy centre rumbled around, had felt the usher's touch on his arm, and was turning to leave the box, when Sir Hugh Wrexham rose, with a peremptory: "Wait a moment, Mr. Merritt," and twitched his gown on his left shoulder, which was a well-known trick of manner he had when confronted by a position of unexpected difficulty.

"Now, Mr. Merritt," he said, in a tone which was usually reserved for opposing witnesses, "we quite understand that your memory of these events is not what you would like it to be. But just tell me this: we have heard that when you left Razor Street you went to Miss Barman's flat at Clanranald Mansions, and waited there—I am not going to ask you how long—till she appeared. When she came in, you have told us already that you first discussed your daughter's marriage, and Abel Marks' conduct to you, and the money that Miss Barman had brought away from Razor Street—"

"I think." Mr. Justice Sumners interposed, "he said that she first got him a meal."

"Yes, my lord, that is so.... Your sister-in-law first got you a meal, and then you began to talk about what was most of all on your mind—the fact that your daughter had married a man whom you had no cause to approve?"

William Merritt, finding that he was at last expected to join in the conversation, replied with a vague "Yes."

"You did not, the moment you saw Miss Barman approaching, commence to tell her that you had come from calling upon Abel Marks? The fact that you had been for the last ten days in Brixton gaol, and the fact of your daughter's marriage, would be more to the front of your mind when you saw her first?"

The witness, who was as bewildered in his recollection of the chronology of that conversation as he was incapable of seeing the drift of this re-examination, replied with another "Yes," as vague as before.

"Yes, of course you would! And during that time, while you hadn't mentioned that you had even been in the neighbourhood of Razor Street that morning, did Miss Barman make any mention of having found a dead man in Rosenbaum's offices?"

Mr. Merritt, now thoroughly confused, but with an underlying conviction that he was being bullied into admitting that his sister-in-law had confessed to the murder, hesitated with a half-open mouth, and just as Mr. Justice Sumners (who was beginning to feel that the refereeing of this contest was becoming more difficult than he had had any reason to anticipate) was about to interpose again, he brought out the most emphatic negative that his examination had yet produced. "No, indeed. She didn't say anyone was dead. How could he have been when he'd just paid her what he owed?"

His voice trembled with a weak indignation, and the next moment he found that the baiting had ceased, and that the legal gentlemen were both willing to let him go. He left the box amid the bustle of general movement, for with the conclusion of his examination the court rose for the day.

Sir Hugh Wrexham had got that at which he aimed—an admission that Carol Barman had made no mention of a dead man, at a time when she could have had no reason—or at least no other reason—for concluding that he had been at Razor Street since he had been released from Brixton Prison that morning. So far so good. But when he thought it over, and reviewed the legal skirmish as a whole, he saw that he might have less reason for satisfaction, for if it had been a fact that William Merritt had struck the blow, was it a necessary, or indeed a reasonable, conclusion that he would have been truthful in telling the court what had passed between himself and his sister-in-law, when they had met with an equal knowledge of what lay on the floor of that Razor Street office? Might he not have replied with muddled impromptu lies to a line of cross-examination he had not expected to meet? Or might he not have agreed with his sister-in-law what they should say, even before their first interview with Inspector Combridge?

The Attorney-General did not entertain these ideas as actual possibilities, for he had a settled mind that the criminal already stood in the dock, but he saw them as obstacles upon which the foot of justice might stumble, if he were not wary to guide it well. Like Mr. Justice Sumners, he saw the case to be one which might require more delicate handling than he had previously anticipated, though his confidence did not therefore decline.

Inspector Combridge had listened to William Merritt's confused and reluctant evidence with somewhat different feelings. He was jealous of the credit of his department, and he knew that, to the public, if not to his superior officers, his own reputation was largely involved in the issue of the present trial. Should it result in a conviction, it would be a particularly spectacular addition to the list of the crimes which he had successfully investigated. Should it fail, it would be one over which a discreet biographer (if he should ever have one) would pass with a rapid pen.

But he knew the fact to be that the decision to prosecute, even the advice to do so, had not been his. He had been strongly disposed to think that Carol Barman had struck the blow, and to that opinion he still inclined. But he had always been less than sure, and, if he had allowed personal inclination to deflect his judgment, he would have preferred to regard her as an innocent woman. The friendly atmosphere of the impromptu evening meal, and the apparent frankness of the account which she had given—an account which, so far as it was capable of confirmation, was still unshaken—was a continuing influence on his mind. Had he possessed the power of controlling a past event, he would no doubt have chosen for the role of murderer the ignoble figure that had just drifted hesitantly down the stream of people leaving the court, to look round vacantly in the main corridor, until it was seen by Carol Marks (released from the witnesses' room) and steered resolutely away. He did not exactly hope, nor did he go so far as to think, that a mistake had been made, but he was aware of a larger doubt than he would usually permit himself to feel after the police decision had been made, and the prosecution commenced. And if a mistake *had* been made, inclination, duty and self-interest were in the same scale any remaining credit which could come to himself would be gained by being the first to perceive the truth, and to put it before those who—at first, if not later—would not be very willing to hear.

There may have been an additional cause for this mental disquietude that he was experiencing in the fact that Mr. Jellipot had undertaken Carol Barman's defence. He told himself, with evident truth, that the solicitor could not transform a murderess into an innocent woman by the mere fact that he had undertaken her cause, nor had he any magic power which could prevail against the weight of evidence, the eloquence of the Attorney-General, and the acute impartiality of a judge whose summings-up were notorious for lucidity and soundness of legal wit. But the feeling remained, as did the fact that he had been in opposition to Mr. Jellipot on two previous occasions, neither of which he could recall with entire satisfaction, though (in the Hamilton case, at least) he had acted with a discretion which had avoided the pit of error into which he so nearly fell. Finally—and worst of all—Mr. Jellipot looked pleased.

The brief exchanges which had taken place between them on a previous and somewhat similar occasion did not encourage a repetition of the experiment, but it was still true that they were acquaintances—even friends, he might say—of long standing, and it was owing to his own gift of pertinacity rather than any brilliance of deductive reasoning that he had gained the position which he now held. As he left the court, an idea came to his mind. The procedure would be unusual, unorthodox, perhaps unprecedented. But Mr. Jellipot was one who would not misunderstand his motive, and whose word and discretion would be equally reliable He waited for a time at the exit which the solicitor would be most likely to use, and as he did so he observed Mr. Merritt and his daughter cross the street and enter the tea-shop on the opposite corner. At that sight, he signalled to a plain-clothes officer, and instructed him to place himself as near to them as possible, and to endeavour to overhear whatever conversation might pass between them at the meal which they were evidently-intending to take together.

Shortly afterwards, Mr. Jellipot came out, in company with Sir Henry Blackett and Mr. Ridwell, the junior counsel for the defence.

He watched Sir Henry enter his waiting car, while Mr. Ridwell took the short way on foot to his Temple chambers, and Mr. Jellipot raised his umbrella to signal a taxi from the nearby stand.

Waiting only a couple of minutes, the inspector called the next vehicle from the rank, and followed Mr. Jellipot to his Basinghall Street offices.

CHAPTER XXI.

A QUESTION FOR MR. JELLIPOT

MR. JELLIPOT received the inspector with his usual quiet cordiality. He had, after much hesitation, come to a conclusion in his own mind as to what had happened on the afternoon that had cut short the existence of Abel Marks. It was an opinion to which he had been inclining for some time, and which had hardened to conviction as he had listened to William Merritt's halting and reluctant testimony.

It did not lead him to despair of procuring a verdict which would secure his client's release, but it warned him that he must be wary of every step. It gave him no clue to the purpose of the inspector's call, but it inclined him to receive him with satisfaction, below which was a determination to probe his visitor's mind rather than to expose his own. He therefore waited in silence, after the exchange of a few words of preliminary courtesy, for Inspector Combridge to begin, which he did not appear to find it easy to do.

He said at last: "We've known each other a good while, Mr. Jellipot, and it needn't make us any worse friends if we happen to be on different sides."

"Not at all," Mr. Jellipot conceded readily. "Such a consequence would show one or both of us to be, shall I say, rather weak in the head."

"And I think we know each other well enough to trust each other's words, even under such circumstances?"

Mr. Jellipot considered this rather more seriously. But in the end he agreed. "Yes," he said, with his usual careful deliberation. "I think we may say that."

"If you knew that Carol Barman were guilty, you wouldn't tell me, and I shouldn't ask you to do so."

"No. It would be a highly improper question."

"But there must be many such cases in which the defending solicitor is not sure—perhaps no more than anyone else—of what really occurred."

"Yes. As an abstract proposition, having no bearing upon the present case, we may accept that as certainly true."

The inspector became silent again. After these preliminary points of accord, it was evident that the main proposition was still to come.

He said at length: "I'm not going to suggest that we've made a mistake in this case. I don't think we have. And it isn't usual to go on making enquiries about anyone else, after we've put someone into the dock, as though we hadn't made up our minds."

"I can believe that."

"I want you to understand that I've no authority for anything that I say now. It's entirely off my own bat."

"That will be quite understood."

"If I ask you a question, can it be understood that it will be regarded as absolutely confidential, as I will treat the answer in the same way?"

"Yes. You need have no doubt about that. It must also be understood that I am under no obligation to make any reply."

"Yes, of course. That's for you to decide."

"Very well. What is the question you wish to ask?"

"I want to say that, though I have thought, and still do, that we've put the right one in the dock, I'm not quite as certain in my own mind as I like to be.... If you could tell me, as man to man, that you are convinced that Carol Barman is an innocent woman, I don't know anyone, quite apart from the fact that you are acting for her, and any special knowledge that you may have, whose opinion would influence me more. I can't say what difference it would make, because as you know, it rests now with those who are higher up than I am ever likely to be. But if I thought we hadn't got the right end of the stick, I shouldn't rest day or night, things being as they are now, till I could feel sure that we had."

"That," Mr. Jellipot said, "is how I should expect you to feel." But, having said this, which obviously fell short of a full reply to the proposition which had been put before him, it was his turn to fall into a condition of silent gravity.

He saw that, if he should decline to reply, he would confirm the inspector's present hesitating conviction of his client's guilt. That was inevitable, even though it might be repudiated on both sides. On the other hand, he was offered much. If he could speak with confident certainty of his client's innocence, the inspector would be disposed to accept his judgment, and would at once commence an energetic search for another criminal. He could not tell how far, beyond that, it was in the power of Inspector Combridge to influence the course of the prosecution, or how far he might attempt to do so. But he foresaw a time when he might come to him again, and say, not unreasonably: "It was on your assurance that the prosecution of Carol Barman was abandoned. In return for that good deed, by which my own reputation has suffered, will you help me now by telling me what your own theory of the murder is?" That might be a position which it would not be easy to meet.

He felt some disposition to expostulate against the unfairness of being faced by such a question, but he considered that the mere utterance of whatever protest might be taken as going far toward an admission of his client's guilt, which he had no intention of making.

He recognised also that the inspector was prompted by a generous desire that justice should be done, neither more nor less, and that the proposition conveyed a confidence in his own integrity at which it would be difficult to take offence.

When he spoke, it was to answer the question with his usual deliberate precision. "It is unusual, Inspector, as I am sure you will recognise, for a solicitor to be asked to assert a genuine, as distinct from a merely perfunctory profession of the innocence of a client whose case is still *sub judice*. But I will say that I am of the decided opinion that, if Miss Barman be convicted of the murder of Abel Marks, a grave error of justice will result."

Inspector Combridge considered this statement as coming from one who was accustomed to choosing his words with care. He asked: "What about manslaughter?"

"I should still be of the same opinion."

"In that case—"

"I don't think you must ask me to say more."

"Well, I can't press it. I must thank you for taking it in the right way."

Inspector Combridge got up to go. He felt that he was in the same doubt as before. The reply he had received, carelessly heard, might appear to be no less than an assertion of Carol Barman's innocence, and yet—why not say it in plain, unequivocal words?

Considering this at a later hour, he observed that, if Mr Jellipot had received confidential information that the crime had been committed, say by Carol Marks, or John Colvin, he might have hesitated, on the instructions he had received, to give a reply which would turn the attention of the law toward the actual culprit. Well, he could do no more than keep an open, alert mind, and watch how the trial would go in the course of the coming day.

CHAPTER XXII.

SERGEANT SOLOMON OVERHEARS

SERGEANT SOLOMON was a very competent officer, quick-witted, loyal to his employment, and unscrupulous in what he did. It was supposed by his superior officers that he could be made to resemble a gentleman by clothing him in a dress suit, or, at least, that description of "gentleman" who is attracted by night-clubs of the baser sort.

Garbed in that manner, he would worm his way into these resorts, where greed preys on the simplicity of its fellows, and betray without scruple the confidences which he won, even committing the mysterious legal crime of drinking intoxicants "after hours" with the comfortable knowledge that prosecution would pass him by.

He was a man of acute physical senses, and when he saw William Merritt and his daughter select a table which was only suitable for two persons, having the wall on its further side, and being separated by an electric stove from the nearest vacant seat, he was not disconcerted. To sit nearer might be to draw attention upon himself, and he had no doubt that, even across the space which the stove occupied, he would be able to overhear. Even if there should be no conversation of a momentous character between the two in that crowded place, he did not doubt that his trained faculty of observation would enable him to gather some illuminating detail that Inspector Combridge would be interested to hear.

Sitting sideways to the two, with Carol Marks in the further seat, he observed that the girl looked worried and pale. She did not look as though she had suffered only from the ordeal of waiting in the witnesses' room, not knowing when she might be called to the witness-box, and to see her aunt in the dock. She looked as though she had suffered from a prolonged strain, against which even her youthful vitality could put up no more than a losing fight. But William Merritt, whatever thoughts or feelings he may have had, showed no physical sign of anything beyond the moderate total of his years, and the moderate worries that they had brought. Neither did it appear that his appetite failed as the result of his pitiable public exhibition during the afternoon. His daughter, questioning him as to his requirements; and ordering for both, was held up by his hesitation between the attractions of a steak-and-kidney pudding and a plate of cold ham. When he had been brought by the growing impatience of the waitress to a decision in favour of the latter delicacy, his daughter completed the order with a pot of tea (yes, for two, please. And could it be made rather strong? Anything for herself to eat? No, nothing, thank you).... The waitress came on to Sergeant Solomon's table, and was dismissed with a quick order for tea and toast.

During the next twenty minutes (for Mr. Merritt ate in a leisurely manner) Sergeant Solomon turned over an *Evening News* which he had bought as he entered the shop, and listened to a conversation which consisted mainly of attempts by the man to describe or discuss the events of the afternoon, and of the girl to check him, in evident nervousness lest his remarks might be overheard.

This could not in itself be regarded as an attitude which should arouse suspicion. It might be no more than a natural sensitiveness regarding a matter which had exposed their family troubles to a general publicity, and which provided the most prominent headlines for the paper which Sergeant Solomon was pretending to read. But William Merritt appeared to be oblivious of such consideration.

It was characteristic that he should tend to forget that his daughter, as a witness, who had not yet been called, had not been allowed to enter the court, and should speak of what there had been to hear and see as though they had shared a common experience, so that she replied, more than once: "You forget, Dad, that I wasn't there." Characteristic also, that even in the witness-box, when it had seemed that his wits were hopelessly overwhelmed, he had had a mind for the observation of trivial things. He had not learnt Mr. Ridwell's name, nor was he aware that he was one of the counsel engaged in Carol Barman's defence, but he had observed a large stone in a ring which he wore on the little finger of his left hand. "I don't think," he said, "that it was a genuine stone. I could have made sure, if I hadn't left the right glasses at home." He described the ring in some detail. Valued it on the assumption that it was genuine, and again on the assumption that it was not. Lamented his failing sight.... Sergeant Solomon observed that Mrs. Marks encouraged him when he wandered thus.

As he listened, the detective asked himself the question that was troubling Inspector Combridge's mind. Was Carol Barman innocent of any greater crime than conspiring, perhaps with the equal knowledge of the younger woman, to protect the man from the penalty of a deed of sudden violence such as may be an outbreak of weakness when goaded by many wrongs?

Or did the pale anxiety of the younger woman conceal the knowledge of her own guilt, of which she would speak no word (if she ever would) while there might be a chance that her aunt would be declared innocent of the crime?

Or was she, perhaps, herself in a doubt which she feared to probe, of whether aunt or father had struck the blow?

Like Inspector Combridge, he wished he knew. But it seemed that there was little more that he would learn now, for Carol Marks had taken up her handbag, as though preparing to rise, and the waitress was at her side, making out the check. At the same moment, there was a movement of people rising from an adjacent table. There was a moment during which they obstructed both view and hearing. As they cleared away, the girl was saying, with a note of weary impatience in her voice: "Will you come now? We shan't have very much time, if we're to be there as soon as John—"

Her father interrupted her, as though disturbed from a wandering thought. "I didn't like to see your aunt sitting there," he said querulously. "It didn't seem right. And those lawyers trying to get me to say that I knew she'd done it!"

"You didn't say that, did you?" The question came clearly and sharply. For a moment it seemed that fear of her father's folly had made her oblivious of where they sat.

He got up as he replied: "No, I was rather too much for them." He spoke complaisantly, as one who looked back on a bout that he bravely won. They were leaving the table, and passing close to Sergeant Solomon as he added: "I suppose they'll try what they can get out of you tomorrow. I hope you won't—"

If she were oblivious before, she had become conscious of her surroundings again. She said quickly: "Dad, you're not going without your coat?" at which his sentence broke off abruptly, and he turned aside to the coat-pegs with an assurance, somewhat at variance with the direction he had been taking, that he had been already in the act of getting it.

Feeling confident that he had not been observed, the pertinacious detective resolved to continue pursuit, thinking that the chances of street or bus-top might be even better than that which the tea-shop had given; but when he had settled his own bill, and followed them to the pavement, he was disconcerted to see the girl signal a passing taxi, and the two drive away beyond the range of his further spying.

Later that evening he reported his observations to Inspector Combridge, and repeated, with singular accuracy, the fragments of conversation he had overheard. He added: "You can take it that Carol Barman told the truth when she said that she found Marks alive when she went in. Anyhow, Merritt didn't kill him. He hasn't the guts."

"We don't think he did," the inspector replied, "or we shouldn't have put Carol Barman where she is now. But as to not having the guts, I should say it's his sort more often than not that lets out in that sudden way. When they get worked up, they haven't got the control over their nerves that you find with a stronger man."

Sergeant Solomon did not dispute this. But he said it was something different that he had meant. William Merritt might have been led to strike down his enemy in a fit of passion beyond control; but, had he done so, he could not have maintained his present attitude, which, the detective was convinced, was genuine, not assumed.

He was troubled in an ever-wandering mind by his sister-in-law's predicament. He might take for granted that she was guilty, or he might be in a nervous doubt lest his own daughter should have been in her place in the dock. Just possibly, he might know that the murder had been committed by the younger woman. But his mind was not troubled by any memory of his own guilt.

That, at least, was Sergeant Solomon's explicit conclusion, as a result of watching him in the witness-box, and subsequently at his tea-shop meal. It was an opinion with which Inspector Combridge was disposed to agree. That it had emerged so definitely gave support to the Attorney-General's opinion, both as to the identity of the culprit and that her trial would tend to expose the truth, regarding the two other suspects.

Well, Carol Marks remained, and her demeanour in the witness-box would be demonstrated tomorrow. There was some satisfaction in that, even though it is a fact well known to all who are concerned either in civil litigations or the operation of criminal law that a woman witness is more dangerous and less reliable than a man. She may be truthful as many are, but if she elect to lie, her mendacity will be bolder, subtler, and more sustained.

CHAPTER XXIII.

THE RECOGNITION OF MR. JOHN COLVIN

CAROL MARKS, having been told that she would be required to go into the witness-box at the commencement of the second day, found that she had to wait till the morning was more than half over, for a conference among the legal gentlemen engaged for the prosecution had resulted in the granting of a request by Inspector Combridge that Richard Skimmer should first be called.

It was a procedure which gave some abortive mental exercise to Miss Barman's legal advisers, who, having no clue to the actual reason, were led to much ingenuity of vain imagining; but the fact was that the inspector had observed John Colvin enter the court, and wished to give Richard Skimmer an opportunity of identifying him if he were able to do so. It was no more than a random chance, and it was an evidence both of the patient thoroughness of the inspector's methods and of the fact that his mind was still less than at ease, that he should have seen and seized the opportunity that Mr. Colvin's presence gave.

He had in fact been in court during the whole of the previous day, but the procedure of criminal trials does not allow of the presence of witnesses whose evidence has not been heard, and when the court rose the inspector's mind had been busy with other things. Now, as Dick Skimmer was about to be called, he said to him: "You've got nothing to worry about in the box, if you stick to what you've said all along, and don't let them badger you into saying anything that you don't mean. But I want you to look at a man, a young man who's second from the left on the top row of the public seats, and tell me whether you've ever seen him before."

Dick Skimmer agreed to that, and went into court, at the usher's summons, with a cheerful confidence that his wits would be equal to any that he was likely to meet.

He had, in fact, an easier time than either he or the prosecution's legal luminaries had anticipated. Sir Henry Blackett had considered his evidence carefully, as it had been given unchallenged in the lower court, and had decided that it was only open to effective attack at one point, with which a single question he had in readiness should be equal to deal. The interval which he had put between the calls of William Merritt and Carol Barman was not long, and it was possible that sufficient pressure would have resulted in some slight extension, but the objection to that would be that the longer that interval became, the shorter time remained for that more vital one between the going of Carol Barman and the coming of Carol Marks—the interval on which he had no evidence to give.

At the end, therefore, of his evidence-in-chief, Sir Henry Blackett rose to ask: "You have said that you were absent from your stand for about ten minutes. Is that your usual time?"

"Yes. About that."

"You go to a tea-shop about three minutes' walk away?"

"Scarcely that."

"And you sometimes meet friends there with whom you have conversation over the meal?"

"Yes. But not on Saturdays."

The distinction was unexpected, disconcerting, and might be true. It took much of the point out of the question that was to come.

"Should you be surprised to know that you have been timed on three occasions, on which you were absent sixteen and one-half, twenty-one, and twenty-five minutes respectively?"

"I daresay I have. I wasn't that afternoon though. I got back rather quick."

Sir Henry Blackett left it at that. Even this point was of no great importance in view of the time at which Carol Marks herself said that she had arrived, and the indisputable moment at which P.C. Decker had been called on to the scene. The trouble was that the whole time was so short. Nothing could alter that. When the time for the final speeches should come, the possibility of the unknown murderer who had entered and left in five minutes' space must be urged upon the jury with all the eloquence that is required by an issue of life and death, though it might be no more than wasted effort when the cold, impartial logic of the summing-up had been directed upon it. At present, it may have been accepted as the only real question by almost everyone in that crowded court—which of the three relatives—by marriage—of the murdered man had been responsible for his death? And now the name of Carol Marks was called aloud, and there was a stir of expectation, a straining of necks and eyes, as the slim, pale figure of the three hours' bride, not in the mourning which would have been a mockery, but very quietly dressed, entered the dock.

The reporters' pencils raced while she was taking the oath and answering the inevitable preliminary questions, that they might have finished description, and be ready when her evidence should become of a vital kind. "Mrs. Carol Marks, wearing a hat of—" "The widow of the murdered man, looking pale but composed—"

But Carol Marks was oblivious of the interest which her coming caused. Her eyes, as she took the oath, were on the aunt whom she had not seen since she had told, in the magistrate's court, the tale which she was now asked to repeat. Their glances met. Carol Barman was not likely to repeat the outburst which had startled the court on the previous afternoon, but she strove in that silent exchange to give fortitude and encouragement to the younger woman. She saw that her niece's expression was tenser, paler, than she had appeared at the previous hearing. It was as though she, rather than Carol Barman, had suffered from the strain of the five weeks, which had intervened between the committal and the present hour.... Carol Marks regained her composure. She turned her eyes from the prisoner. They moved rapidly over the court, met the keen but not unkindly glance of Mr. Justice Sumners for one passing instant, moved along the double row of observant jurors, dwelt for a longer second upon the nearer group of the wigged and gowned fraternity of the law, and fell upon the fingers with which she had grasped the rail of the witness-box, after the Bible had left her hand But she had not raised them to meet those which John Colvin; sitting at the back of the court, and showing less composure of manner than that which had annoyed Inspector Combridge a few weeks before, had fixed earnestly upon her.

Inspector Combridge had intended to watch this witness, her every gesture and word, in his search for the truth which he was not yet sure had been guessed aright, but he was the one man in court by whom this point was unobserved. In the back of the court, sheltered from the sight of judge or usher, he was holding a low-voiced conversation with Richard Skimmer.

"Know '*im*?" said the news-vendor. "I should say I do. He's in Razor Street every week. Sundays mostly, and Saturday afternoons quite as often as not. Why, I remember now, he bought a paper from me that afternoon."

"Why didn't you tell me this before?"

"Why should I? How should I guess as you'd want to know? You didn't ask me to tell you about every customer that I had."

Inspector Combridge saw the justice of this reply. He said: "No, of course. You mean he didn't go into No. 33, so you didn't see that he'd be of any interest to me more than anyone else?"

"No. At least, not as I saw."

"Did you see him go in there at any other time?"

"No. I wouldn't say as I did."

"Do you know where he did go in Razor Street?"

The man hesitated, as the inspector was disposed to think, in a genuine ignorance to which he was reluctant to own

"No," he said at last. "I can't say I do. It wasn't Rosenbaum's. It was further up. He goes further up on the other side."

"Well, we'll have another talk about this."

Inspector Combridge recalled himself to the present scene that he must not miss. He went back to his previous post of observation.

CHAPTER XXIV.

THE SURPRISING STATEMENT OF CAROL MARKS

ON regaining a position from which he could look round the crowded court, it was perhaps natural that Inspector Combridge should first glance upward at the man who had been the subject of his conversation of the previous moment, and concerning whom he had just learnt a surprising, and perhaps sinister fact. The glance was casual, and would have passed on more quickly to the drama that was developing in the well of the court, had he not observed a difference in Mr. Colvin's demeanour from the impassive attitude of the previous day. He judged the traveller in ladies' handbags to have an exceptional measure both of assurance and self-control, and this added to the significance of the fact that he had the look of a deeply troubled and worried man. Was it wonderful that the inspector was disposed to attribute this aspect to the fact that he had become aware that he had been recognised by Richard Skimmer, that he had been conscious of the news-vendor's eyes being fixed upon him, and that he had realised that his presence in Razor Street on the afternoon of the murder, with all that it might imply, would no longer be hidden from the police? The greater the agitation that this discovery should produce, the greater also became the probability that his visit there had not been of an innocent character. Inspector Combridge, not free from his own sense of worry at the successive complications with which he dealt, had some satisfaction in the thought that the case must continue into another day. He saw opportunity for enquiry, for consultation with his superiors, before the fatal moment when the verdict would be brought in. But, for the moment, even this problem must be put aside, to observe the immediate drama that was being enacted before him.

The examination of Carol Marks had been undertaken by Mr. Rodney Westwood, under an etiquette of procedure which will usually allot to a junior counsel the examination of some of the witnesses for the prosecution—usually such as are likely to give their testimony in a simple and straightforward manner.

When Sir Hugh Wrexham had said: "You'll take on Mrs. Marks tomorrow, won't you, Westwood?" he had felt that he was being both generous and discreet. He had given his junior one of the principal witnesses, and certainly the one most likely to excite popular interest and sympathy among the rather poor team that the prosecution had been able to call together.

But her examination-in-chief, being no more than a repetition of the tale that she had told to the police, and again in the lower court, did not appear likely to develop any complicating feature. Her own ordeal, and the critical issue of the case, would come (he thought), if at all, in the event of her veracity being seriously challenged in cross-examination, in which event there would be time for him to resume the reins.

Besides this, he knew Mr. Westwood's manner to be particularly well adapted to guide a timid or reluctant witness along the narrative path that she was required to tread.

Mr. Robert Westwood was a tall, thin man, with a gentle, persuasive voice, and a sympathetic manner, which was of a genuine rather than forensic character. He was an exceptionally sound and able criminal lawyer, and his advice in chambers would be seriously regarded by those who had a far higher reputation at the bar, or in public report. But he was temperamentally incapable of the emotional exhibitions which will sway a jury, or the tenacity of argument which may outwear a judge. His defect in advocacy was that he would not willingly, and could not convincingly, go beyond the bounds of his own belief.

Now he was questioning a witness who did not raise her eyes in reply, and whose words were so low that they were not easy to hear, even in the tense silence of the listening court.

But she was giving no difficulty. Her monosyllables of assent were all that the prosecution required. If the jury should judge her to be a reluctant witness, was not the value of her testimony actually increased by that attitude? It was so natural, so significant, when it was against her aunt that she was required to speak.

"And when you arrived," Mr. Westwood went on, in his clear, gentle, yet definite manner, "you found that the door was locked?"

"Yes."

"And you unlocked it, and went upstairs?"

"Yes."

The reply came even less audibly than before. The judge leaned forward. "If you could speak a little louder, Mrs. Marks," he suggested, kindly enough, but with authority in his voice.

She raised her eyes at that, and looked round the court again, as though rousing herself to a recollection of where she was, but again without looking up to the higher seats from which John Colvin watched.

"I am sorry," she said more audibly. "I didn't know I couldn't be heard."

The judge noticed the pallor of the freckled face. He said: "You can sit down if you like."

"No," she said, "thank you. It doesn't matter. I'd rather stand.... I haven't much more to say."

Mr. Westwood resumed. "Although the door was locked, you expected to find that your husband was waiting for you in the upper room?"

"Yes. That was what he had said. I was to use the key he had given me if I should find the street-door closed, and he would be waiting for me upstairs."

"And you did, in fact, go up, and wait for some time in the rear room on the first floor?"

"Yes."

Mr. Justice Sumners intervened. The brevity of her replies might be all that the prosecution required, but they were less satisfactory to him. "Just a moment, Mrs. Marks," he said. "Tell me, did you call your husband during that time, or make any effort to attract his attention?"

"No."

The judge's face gave no sign of his thoughts, but the question, coming from him, had had a deadlier force, a deeper significance, than had it been from the lips of a hostile counsel; and few could have heard that monosyllable of reply without recognising its inadequacy.

Patiently and quietly, Mr. Justice Sumners continued his intervention. "Had he told you to wait for him in that particular room?"

"Yes. It was where I had expected to find him. I had been there before."

Mr. Westwood rose. "I think, my lord, that the witness means that she was already aware that the front room was used as a business office, and the back one for domestic purposes, so that she naturally expected to find Mr. Marks there."

Mr. Justice Sumners considered this. He made a slight gesture with his hand, as though letting the point pass, for that moment at least.

"Well, Mr. Westwood," he said, "if that seems a sufficient explanation to you!" And then, as though altering his mind, he turned to the witness again.

"Mrs. Marks," he said, leaning toward her with a kindly gravity, "I should like you to have a further opportunity of assisting the court on this point. You say that when you entered the building you had expected to find your husband there. When you went upstairs and entered the back room and found it vacant, wouldn't it have been a more natural thing to look into the front room at once?"

The witness did not appear to be confused by this question, but she became silent for a moment, as though offered a problem she could not instantly solve, and in the pause, a newspaper, pushed by a moving elbow, rustled loudly in the silence of the waiting court.

"No," she said at last, "feeling as I did, I don't think it would."

"Tell the court how you were feeling."

"I'd made up my mind not to go through with it. I wasn't in any hurry to meet him. I wanted more time to think."

"But after a time—?" Quietly the judge's voice led her on.

"I got frightened. It was so quiet. I felt I must know if he was there."

Mr. Justice Sumners leaned back again, resuming the comfort of his customary position. "Thank you, Mrs. Marks," he said. "Pray go on, Mr. Westwood."

Sir Hugh Wrexham, watching this interposition, smiled visible satisfaction. The judge had taken into his own hands the point which he had himself felt that it would be too perilous to probe, and to which he had most feared that, if the defence should decide to challenge the credibility of the witness, they would direct their attack. And the thin ice had been safely crossed! More than that, the value of the witness's evidence had been largely increased, perhaps to the extent of a fatal weight in the scale of Carol Barman's condemnation, for few who heard would doubt that she spoke from a memory of how she had mounted those silent stairs, and sat fearfully in the vacant room.

Sir Henry Blackett inclined to the same opinion. He scribbled: "I'd made up my mind not to go through with it," on the broad margin of his brief. He saw that to be the essential point in the self-revelation that she had made. But what use would it be to him?

He leaned over to Mr. Jellipot, sitting in the row before him, to say: "We can take it that that's the truth," and Mr. Jellipot, seeing their client's case to be nowise improved thereby, nodded gravely in response.

But now Mr. Westwood had risen again. "So you went at last, Mrs. Marks, into the front room. Will you tell the court, in your own words, what you saw when you entered there?"

Carol Marks raised her eyes again. She looked at the prisoner, who gave her a glance of encouragement. Had Miss Barman not been restrained by memory of her outburst of the previous day, it is likely that she would have spoken some word of assurance or warning to the younger woman. But the witness's eyes fell again to her hands, which now clutched their support so firmly that their knuckles whitened upon the rail. There was a long minute of silence, puzzling to those who watched. For though the sight which had come to her as she had entered that office-room might be an unpleasant memory to recall, it was not easy to understand why she should find so much difficulty in putting it into words, especially if it were remembered that she had already narrated the particulars for which she was now asked, with no evidence of extreme reluctance, in the lower court.

Puzzled but patient, Mr. Westwood repeated the question: "If you would just say, in a few words, Mrs. Marks, what you saw when you entered the room?"

"I expected he would be very angry. I didn't know what he would do."

Mr. Westwood persisted quietly. "If you had decided that you could not fulfil the marriage vows which you had undertaken that morning, such feelings are easy to understand. But will you please try to put out of your mind whatever fears or doubts you may have had while you waited in the back room, and tell the jury what you found in the front office when you looked for Mr. Marks there?"

She raised her head and answered in a firmer voice, as though having overcome whatever fear or hesitation had kept her silent before. "I didn't see anything particular," she said. "Mr. Marks was sitting at the desk as I went in."

Breaking the silence of utter astonishment which had fallen upon the court, Mr. Justice Sumners was the first to speak. "Do I understand you to say, Mrs. Marks, that your husband was alive and uninjured when you entered the room?"

"Yes."

"And a few minutes afterwards he was dead?"

"Yes."

"Do you realise the inevitable implication of these two statements?"

"Yes."

"And that the tale you are now telling is directly contrary to that which you have sworn before?"

"Yes."

"Do you wish to make any statement—you are under no obligation to do so—as to how the injury occurred by which your husband was killed?"

"I was frightened when he got up. I didn't know that it would do him any great harm. You don't think when you feel like that."

"You mean that you wish the court to understand that it was by your hand that Abel Marks died?"

"That's what I said."

"Not exactly, though you had implied it.... Mr. Attorney-General, I think that it may be well to adjourn at this point. I daresay you will like an opportunity of considering the position which has arisen."

Sir Hugh Wrexham half-rose, as he answered: "Yes, my lord. It would be a convenient course to adopt." But Sir Henry Blackett, who had been listening to a few hurried and urgent words from the prisoner, was already upon his feet.

"With your permission, my lord," he said, "if I could ask the witness one or two questions before we adjourn, I think it might clarify the position so far as the defence is concerned."

Mr. Justice Sumners hesitated. "I am not sure," he said, "that I should do right to allow—"

"If your lordship will permit me to explain. My instructions are to challenge the evidence which Mrs. Marks has now given, and to suggest that she told the truth in her first statement to the police."

"You mean that the witness is confessing to a crime which she did not commit, rather than give evidence which would tend to incriminate your client?"

"I do not, of course, agree that her previous evidence incriminated Miss Barman. I shall be prepared to submit to the jury in due course that Abel Marks was murdered by some person unknown, who has so far eluded the pursuit of justice. But I do suggest that the witness has been actuated by the motive—the mistaken motive—that your lordship mentions."

Mr. Justice Sumners turned to the Attorney-General: "Possibly," he asked, "your examination of the witness is not concluded?"

"With your lordship's permission, I should prefer to consider the question further before deciding."

"That being so, I am afraid, Sir Henry, that I cannot permit you to question her at this stage."

Sir Henry Blackett saw that it would be of no avail to urge his application further, nor, of his own judgment, was he eager to do so. He had done that which Miss Barman had pressed upon him, by making it clear that the defence did not rely upon, but were disposed rather to resist strenuously, the self-confession which Carol Marks had now made. He said: "As your lordship pleases," and sat down, probably as content as were his learned friends on the other side, at the adjournment which Mr. Justice Sumners had enforced upon them.

The time was then 12:25 P.M. The judge said briefly: "Two o'clock, if you please, gentlemen." He said rather sternly to the witness: "Mrs. Marks, you understand that you must remain?"

She felt bewildered that she was not arrested. She had supposed that she would be taken into custody and Miss Barman released immediately that her confession was made. But if they should all combine to say that it was not true—!

She was already leaving the witness-box, and the bustle of withdrawal had commenced in the crowded court, when the usher's voice called loudly for silence, and she turned to see that the judge had not vacated his seat. The stir of departure ceased and there was a general pause in the moving crowd. They turned to observe what scene of this drama of death they had been near to miss.

Mr. Justice Sumners had found the necessity of making prompt decision in a contest which was becoming unexpectedly difficult to referee. He saw that it might prove to be one by which his own reputation as a criminal judge would be as severely tried as that of Carol Barman as a private citizen.

He said: "Wait a moment, Mrs. Marks, if you please." The request was politely expressed, but was not in a tone, or from a direction, which she was likely to disregard. John Colvin, pushing his way down the gangway to join her against the current of those who were moving to leave the court, must pause also, with an added fear in his heart of what might be likely to follow that restraining word.

The judge said to the usher: "I think I noticed Inspector Combridge in court a moment ago.... Yes. I should like a word with him." He bent over to speak to the associate beneath his seat, discussing something with him in a voice too low even for those who were nearest to hear.

A minute later, when Inspector Combridge appeared, Mr. Justice Sumners turned to him to say: "Inspector, will you kindly make it your business to see that the witness is not approached during the luncheon interval, either by the prosecution or the defence. It will be best that she shall not discuss the evidence that she has already given with anyone until her examination has been completed."

Inspector Combridge said: "Yes, my lord," with no pleasure in the task which had been put upon him. He had thought that he would have enough to do in the next hour without that. He wondered whether the judge's instructions could be interpreted with a freedom which would allow him to discuss the subject with Mrs. Marks while guarding her from the attentions of less impartial or less intelligent minds. But he regretfully concluded that it would be a course of procedure less likely to win the approval of the court than to bring a public censure upon himself, which he would prefer to avoid.

He noticed with some satisfaction that the man who had been particularly in his mind was not leaving the court, but had the same objective as himself. Carol Marks stood at the foot of the witness-box, the judge's words having apparently deprived her of the power of further motion, and John Colvin, now that the judge had left his seat, was again making rapid progress towards her. The inspector was doing his best to the same purpose, but it was a race that Mr. Colvin was certain to win.

"Well," Inspector Combridge thought philosophically, "if I can hear what they say as I come up!" He shared the common doubt as to whether Carol Marks had made true confession or false accusation against herself, and with an additional reason of which others were unaware. He wondered whether it were not merely to save her aunt, but to avert a suspicion against her lover, that this confession, whether true or not, had been made. Had she really been alone in that upstairs room? Yes, he thought that she had told the truth about that. But how had that silence really been broken? Suppose John Colvin had been the next to come up the stairs, seeking her, and finding her there? Suppose that they had broken in upon Abel Marks together, and that, marriage, or no marriage, John Colvin had expressed his determination to take Carol away from the man who had won her in such a manner? There would be material enough for fierce quarrel there, and for act of violence to result. And now that he knew that John Colvin had been in Razor Street during the afternoon, such a theory had a very plausible sound.

Thought is swift, and these reflections occurred during the moment in which he made his way across the front of the reporters' table to the opposite side of the court. As he reached the two, Carol Marks was speaking with an urgency that took no notice of him.

"Please, John," she said. "*Please*. If you will only leave it to me. I've made up my mind. It will only make things worse if you interfere. Please don't let us quarrel again!"

She might disregard the inspector's presence, but John Colvin was more observant, and appeared to check something which he had been about to say in reply.

"I am afraid," Inspector Combridge said, duty conquering inclination, for there were few things that he would have liked better than to stand by while that conversation continued, "that I must ask you not to discuss matters with Mrs. Marks."

"She's not under arrest, is she?"

"No. She's not under arrest. But witnesses are under the authority of the judge in his own court."

Inspector Combridge thought he had improvised that definition of the position rather neatly. Technically, she was not under arrest. There was a subtle distinction, but it was one that made little difference to her.

Mr. Colvin stood his ground. "If I can't talk to a lady to whom I'm engaged, and who isn't under arrest, I suppose I can talk to you."

The temptation was too strong for the inspector to resist, even had there been more objection than he could see. "Yes," he said. "There's no reason against that."

"Well, I want to give evidence for the prosecution this afternoon."

"That's not for me to say. If you know anything, you should—"

He was interrupted by Carol Marks. "John, I'll never forgive you! If Aunt Carol—" She checked herself sharply, and he said:

"It's no use, Mrs. Marks. You can't stop this now. The truth always comes out in the end. You can't do better than keep quiet now, as the judge said."

He looked over to the solicitors' row of seats, where Mr. Thrilburn, the prosecuting solicitor, who had delayed a moment in conversation with one of his legal colleagues, was now gathering up his papers to go.

"Mr. Thrilburn!" he called out. "There's Mr. Colvin here says he can give some useful evidence for you this afternoon."

He saw the two men approach each other at the word, like equally attracted magnets across the short dividing space in the almost emptied court. He would have liked to know what evidence John Colvin was proposing to offer, and of how much of truth or falsehood it might be compounded. But he thought that there was little matter for that. When those who are concerned in illegal acts begin to give each other away, the truth is usually not very difficult to obtain. He thought that the case would be clear enough before the afternoon would be done, though he was still in doubt what its end would be.

"I think, Mrs. Marks," he added, "we'd better get on the track of a good lunch."

"Yes," she said. "Yes, of course. You'll be wanting lunch. I don't think I could eat anything, thank you."

"Oh, but you must," he replied. "You'll feel different when you've had a good meal.... And if you'll take a word of advice from someone a bit more experienced than yourself, you'll just tell the truth this afternoon, whatever it happens to be. You'll find it saves a lot of trouble, and it's almost always best in the end."

"Yes," she said vaguely, "I dare say it is." But she did not look as though she found any comfort in the counsel that she received.

CHAPTER XXV.

THE ATTORNEY-GENERAL HAS LUNCH

THE luncheon interval which Mr. Justice Sumners had allowed might be unusually long, but it was too short for the legal gentlemen who must reconstruct their lines of attack and defence to a new position, which was itself of an enigmatic character.

The Attorney-General had the less need to lengthen conference and shorten lunch owing to the rigidity of his settled conviction that he already had the criminal in the dock, from which it followed that Mrs. Marks must, from whatever motive, have invented accusation against herself, and the need for the taking of anxious thought was further reduced by a decision to which he speedily came.

"Rodney," he said to his learned junior, as they sat down to lunch together, almost as soon as the obsequious waiter had left his side, "I don't think we'd better ask Mrs. Marks any more questions when we get back into court. We'll let Blackett have a go."

"After what she's said, he's bound to try showing her up for the liar that she certainly is, and he may have pointers for that which we haven't got. If there's anything left of her when he's done, I'll re-examine, and ask leave to treat her as a hostile witness. Sumners can't refuse that, after the way that she's let us down, and with her denying all that she swore to before."

Mr. Rodney Westwood understood that his leader was resuming the reins. He had no more cause for annoyance at that than has a first officer if his captain return hurriedly to the bridge at the sound of a rising wind. He only said: "The girl must be lying, as I suppose. She told the truth to a point, but when she came to how she found Marks, she had made up her mind not to say that she found him dead, and she didn't find it easy to do."

Sir Hugh Wrexham agreed to that. He said: "Well, we must break her down." He did not expect that to be difficult. He made a shrewd guess that she might have wasted her mental resources in debate of whether or not she could bring herself to the point of such self-confession for her aunt's relief, and had less thought to construct her tale with the care which such a lie must require. Debating whether it should be told, she might have assumed too readily that it would be easy to tell. Well, she should be the easier prey.

Mr. Westwood saw a possibility which he did not mention, seeing it to be one that would not be acceptable to the Attorney-General's mind. Granted that she was now attempting a lie, it did not follow that she had told the truth when she had called P.C. Decker in to gaze at a dead man. Suppose she had witnessed a murder she had not committed, or had surprised the murderer after the deed was done, before he had time to go? Suppose she had deliberately let him escape before rousing alarm?

Might she not, now she found that her action had brought her aunt to a peril she had not meant, feel that she must accuse herself, if she were still resolved not to betray the one who had committed the crime—it might be for love of her...? When he spoke aloud, it was to give voice to an abstract reflection only.

"It is obvious," he said, "when you consider violences of this kind in the bulk, that they must be investigated, and that there must be severe penalties for those who commit them; but if any one be considered separately, I often think that the sum of human misery is increased far less by the crime itself than by the retribution the law provides, and, taken one by one, it would be a mercy to many innocent people if the truth were not discovered, and there were no legal action whatever."

Sir Hugh Wrexham did not dispute this. It was not a practical proposition, and had little interest, therefore, for a practical mind. He said: "Well, the scoundrels should think of that before they let themselves go." He showed that his mind was still upon the immediate issue they had to face, as he repeated: "I suppose that we shall be able to break her down," and went on to discuss what he thought to be the real crisis of the position, not that the prosecution would be frustrated by her protestation of her own guilt, but that the incident must be handled in such a way as to prevent the jury's sympathies being aroused, especially to an extent which might spread from her to include her relative in the dock. They both knew how exasperatingly illogical a jury may be!

Carol Marks, he said, must be made to appear contemptible, rather than heroic or pathetic, if that could be contrived. Her crime of perjury must be brought into prominence, from which, first or last, there was no escape. Perhaps her marriage to Marks could be exposed in a repellent light. His words suggested that they must walk warily, but that his confidence in himself, or in obtaining the conviction at which they aimed, remained too deeply rooted to be disturbed. Rodney Westwood, saying little and listening well, recognised the difference of mental process which had made Sir Hugh Wrexham Attorney-General, and left himself in a lower seat, and, characteristically, he was not stirred to envy or emulation, but to an abstract doubt as to which of them was revealed thereby as the better man.

The Attorney-General, who rarely wasted mental energy on such abstract considerations, felt that he had completed the dispositions which the position required, and would have settled down, in a spirit of leisurely comfort, to the excellent lunch which it is seemly for successful barristers to consume, had not his clerk intruded upon them with a message from Mr. Thrilburn, asking for a conference before going into court, to consider fresh evidence which had just come into his hands.

The soup had been removed, and Sir Hugh paused with a frown upon his face, and the first succulent mouthful of partridge upon his fork. He preferred his midday meal to be as ample and leisurely as the length of the luncheon interval would allow, with a time for cheerful anecdotage over the wine, but he would not have come to his present place had he not put the requirements of his profession before the comforts which its liberal remuneration supplied.

"Do you know," he asked, "what it is now?"

"They've got hold of John Colvin. He'll go into the box to say that Mrs. Marks is lying to save her aunt."

"Very well. It won't take long to get that straight. Say one forty-five."

He resumed his meal with a feeling of satisfaction. He thought the case would go well during the afternoon.

"I'm inclined to think," he said, "that that young woman is about putting the rope round her aunt's neck."

Mr. Westwood protested. "You don't think they'll hang her? I should say manslaughter most likely, or else a reprieve."

"Oh, of course! I didn't mean literally. It's a five-year sentence, more or less, we've got to expect. Unless something fresh comes out, I shan't press for a conviction on the capital charge.... Only, she's rather queering the pitch for herself by sticking out that she hasn't done it at all."

CHAPTER XXVI.

THE CROSS-EXAMINATION OF CAROL MARKS

CAROL MARKS re-entered the witness-box and Mr. Justice Sumners addressed her immediately.

"Mrs. Marks," he said, "before you give further evidence, I want to be sure that you appreciate the serious position in which you stand. When you called the constable in from the street, you told him that you had found your husband dead, as he then lay. You subsequently repeated this tale in a written form, and you swore to it later in the evidence which you gave in the lower court. You swore this morning that you had found him alive, and, if that be the truth, there would be an end to the present prosecution. If that be the truth, it would be difficult to avoid the deduction that Abel Marks died either by your hand, or by that of another, whose guilt you have been resolved to conceal.

"Perjury is a serious crime, for which very serious penalties are provided. It is also a serious crime, in a case of homicidal violence, to conceal knowledge that you may have: to become an accessory after the event.

"You have had time for reflection. If the evidence you gave this morning were untrue—if you spoke from a reluctance to give testimony which might tend to incriminate one to whom you may feel a natural affection—you have an opportunity now—perhaps the last opportunity you may have to correct your error. If, however, you have previously withheld the truth, I need not say that it is your duty to speak it now, in accordance with the solemn oath you have sworn, regardless of consequences either to yourself or others.

"That, in the position in which you have placed yourself, is the best advice that I can give you; but I must add that the law does not require you to give evidence which will incriminate yourself."

Carol Marks lifted her eyes to the judge as he admonished her in this way, and their glances met. The words were solemnly and earnestly spoken, and to anyone placed as she was they could not fail to have an impressive force. But her eyes did not fall. In the interval which the adjournment had allowed she seemed to have gained assurance and self-control.

Owing to the instructions which the judge had given, she had not been molested or questioned. She had been practically alone with her own thoughts. Had she offered confidence to Inspector Combridge, or asked advice, it is possible that that zealous officer might not have had a sufficient rectitude to refuse the opportunity that Mr. Justice Sumners had thrust upon him. He might have argued that the judge's prohibition could not apply to himself, who was neither for prosecution nor defence, but seeking only the truth with an open mind. But, in fact, Mrs. Marks had not shown a disposition to tempt him to such casuistry.

She had been quiet, self-collected, and spoken only as the occasion required. It was as though those quick angry exchanges with John Colvin had fixed her intention, or braced her mind.

Now she answered the judge in words that sounded clearly to the back of the court. "Thank you, my lord. It doesn't matter about me. I want to say what happened."

Mr. Justice Sumners regarded her with a face which had become inscrutable. He said: "Very well.... Now, Mr. Westwood."

Mr. Westwood scarcely rose to reply: "I am not proposing to ask this witness any further questions, my lord."

The judge's eyes passed on to Sir Henry Blackett, and the K.C. rose with no appearance of reluctance, but feeling no gratitude for the celerity with which the witness had been handed over to him. Lunching more frugally than the Attorney-General, he had spent most of the interval in a prolonged conference with Miss Barman, the result of which had been to curse all women in his bachelor heart, and especially those (of whom he felt that he now had one before him and one behind) who think they are competent to manage their own affairs in their own way, rather than to depend upon the advice of competent men.

Indeed, he would have been inclined to tell a difficult client that she must either leave her defence to him or seek a new advocate, had he not been influenced by Mr. Jellipot's hesitant suggestion that the position contained possibilities of development which might embarrass the prosecution even more than the defence, "especially," he added, "as I hear that Mr. Colvin is offering to give evidence for them."

Sir Henry Blackett considered this view with a more flexible mind than the Attorney-General would have directed upon it. He said: "John Colvin? What can he say? The defence should not be further surprised at this stage. Can we object to him being called?"

"If you ask my advice," Mr. Jellipot replied cautiously, "I would object, and give way. The more possibilities that appear, the more the jury will be unsure. I do not say that he is wise, nor how it may end, but we are not acting for him.

"Well," Sir Henry replied, "I have to deal with two women who go their own road. Mrs. Marks, as I suppose, is advised by none, and Miss Barman will take advice if it suits that which she has already resolved. If she would be quiet, I might get her clear. You may see light ahead, but, if so, you can see better than I."

"I did not say that," Mr. Jellipot replied doubtfully. "I do not know when I had a more anxious mind."

This conversation had been no more than a few moments before, as they came into court, and now Sir Henry rose to examine a witness who had offered evidence which, if it were believed, must give his client a free passage out of the dock, and his emphatic instructions were that he must discredit her testimony by every means that legal acumen could contrive.

"You said this morning, Mrs. Marks," he began, "if I understood you rightly, that when you entered the front room you found Mr. Marks alive?"

"Yes."

"What was he doing?"

"He was sitting at his desk."

"Will you tell the court what passed between you?"

Mrs. Marks looked momentarily disconcerted by the general nature of this question, but she quickly recovered herself to answer: "we quarrelled."

Sir Henry remained silent, as though waiting for her to go on, and she confronted him passively, as though there were no more to be said. He was quick to recognise that he was engaged in a duel of silence he could not win. He asked: "Well, what then?"

She gave him a straight glance, and her voice was slightly raised as she replied: "I say Aunt Carol couldn't have killed him, because I saw him alive. I don't see why I should say more."

"You don't think any explanation is necessary? Although he was dead a few minutes later, and you were alone with him in that otherwise empty house? By the way, *were you alone?*"

The final question came with an unexpected abruptness, though the suavity of Sir Henry's voice was not otherwise varied. It brought a sudden startled look into the girl's eyes. "Was I—?" she began. "You don't mean—? Yes, of course." And then, as though the suggestion had frightened her into further detail than she had intended before: "It was when he said he wasn't going to let me go. I hit him to let me pass."

Sir Henry repeated the words slowly, as though rejecting upon them. "He said he wasn't going to let you go, and you hit him to let you pass.... Mrs. Marks, do you really ask the court to believe that?"

"Yes," she said, with a recovered coolness, "that's just how it was."

"That's just how it was! And when you had hit him, why didn't you go, as you were so anxious to do?"

"Because of the way he fell."

"How exactly did you expect him to fall?"

"I didn't mean to hurt him as badly as that."

"You intended to disable him so that he couldn't follow you out?"

"So that he would get out of my way."

"Mrs. Marks, if you would think a moment before you speak! How could he have got out of your way? Were you not nearer the door?"

"No. We—were about the same distance away. He was getting up—"

"Yes? With what weapon did you strike him?"

"With the ruler."

"From where did you get that?"

"I picked it up off the desk."

"Then will you explain how you could have done that if you were both about the same distance from the door?"

"Well, we were, anyhow.... I must have picked it up a minute before."

"You mean that you had been threatening him during the previous minute with that dangerous weapon, and he had remained quietly seated at his desk—this angry man who was so determined to prevent you leaving that you must strike him down to get free?"

"It mayn't have been that long."

"That is the best reply you can make?"

"I've only told you the truth."

"Mrs. Marks, I must put it to you plainly that the tale you have told us now is not the truth, but an absolute and rather clumsy invention, which you have made to shield either Miss Barman, or some other person unknown, who may, or may not, be as guilty as you suppose. I suggest to you that you could not have picked up that ruler without being in such a position that a man seated at the other side of the desk could not have prevented you from going out of the door, even if a man remaining so seated could have had any intention of so doing."

"You can't expect me to remember everything just as it happened. It was all over too quick."

"I don't expect you to remember at all.... Are you left-handed?"

"No. Not generally."

"With which hand did you pick up the ruler?"

The question evidently disconcerted the witness with the fear of an implication she did not follow. She hesitated before she replied: "I suppose it was with the right."

"And you would be surprised to be told that no one but a left-handed man could possibly have struck the blow from which Abel Marks died, unless he were between Abel Marks and the door?"

"I mayn't be right as to just how it was."

"You may not be right at all. You say that you told your husband that, though you had married him three hours before, you did not intend to keep your vows, but would leave him at once?"

"Yes. That was what I wanted to do."

"And you quarrelled in consequence?"

"Yes. Of course."

"And all this time, when the bride for whom he had been waiting entered the room, and during the subsequent quarrel, you were standing and he remained seated at his desk?"

"I didn't say all the time."

"Perhaps he was standing at first, and sat down as a means of preventing you from leaving the room?"

"I didn't say that."

"At what time did you form this resolution to leave your husband?"

"I'd been feeling that I could not go through with it all the time."

"While you packed the suitcase, and carried it to your husband's house?"

"I made up my mind while I was waiting in the back room."

"And you seriously ask the court to believe this improbable—I may say this impossible—story?"

"Yes. Of course."

The learned counsel shrugged his shoulders in a slight, but sufficiently expressive manner, and sat down. Mr. Justice Sumners, who had been watching the witness with an intent, but otherwise expressionless face, stirred himself to ask: "Do you wish to ask this witness further questions, Mr. Attorney-General?"

"Just one or two, my lord.... Mrs. Marks, it is a fact, is it not, that you married Abel Marks, on the day of his death?"

"Yes."

"And you took a solemn vow to be faithful to him, as a wife should?"

"Yes. It was the usual thing."

"That would be about 11:00 or 11:30 A.M.?"

"Yes."

"And at 3:00 P.M. of the same day you had been considering deserting him for some hours?"

"Yes, I only did it because—"

"Never mind why. We will agree that you may have had cause. So that if there be sufficient cause, you see no objection to breaking the most solemn vows, even while their echoes have scarcely died? Well, I won't press you to answer.... A few weeks ago you swore that when you entered that room you found your husband dead on the floor. You swore this solemnly, in the public court at which your aunt was committed for trial, largely as a result of that evidence?"

The reply came slowly, reluctantly, but was an inevitable, though almost inaudible, "Yes."

"And today you swear to an utterly different tale?"

"Yes."

"And that being how quickly you are prepared to break the most solemn vows that a woman can enter into, and how ready you are to perjure yourself when you have taken your solemn oath, what do you suppose, Mrs. Marks, that your word is worth?"

Having asked this question, the Attorney-General sat down, without waiting for a reply, and Carol Marks left the box.

It was during the momentary interval that elapsed between the withdrawal of Carol Marks from the box, and the rising of the Attorney-General, that Sir Henry Blackett leaned over to Mr. Jellipot to say: "I hope I didn't go wrong, Jellipot, about the positions of desk and door. I wasn't quite as clear as I ought to have been as to just how the door stands. But it seemed worth trying."

"Yes, you were near enough," the solicitor answered. He saw that it had been a case of the random shaft hitting the mark. But the point as to the position of anyone who had picked up the ruler had been on his own mind, and it was not one which could be considered useful for Miss Barman's defence. It suggested that the murderer had been well inside the room and facing the murdered man, so that, if he had remained seated, it must have been one whose entrance he had not resented. The point of the blow having fallen on the left temple had been debated, as he knew, between the police and the medical witnesses, but—particularly in the absence of any left-handed person among the possible suspects—had been considered too uncertain in its implications for any theory to be founded upon it. But the position in which anyone must have been when the weapon was seized—yes, he had thought of that, and had hoped that the attention of the prosecution would pass it by.... He turned his attention to Sir Hugh Wrexham, who was making his expected application in the inevitable phraseology—and then Sir Henry Blackett was protesting, and giving way in such a manner as to gain the utmost credit for the defence that the position allowed.

"We have never questioned," he said, "that Abel Marks was dead or dying, when his wife entered the house. What we say is that the tragedy must have happened before then, but after Miss Barman left."

"In view of the entire change," Mr. Justice Sumners finally ruled, "in the evidence which Mrs. Marks has given, I cannot exclude the hearing of any fresh witness bearing on her veracity, nor can it be argued reasonably that the defence will be prejudiced thereby, considering that they themselves do not rely upon, or even accept, the tale which we have heard from her today."

Sir Henry Blackett made no further protest, and Mr. John Colvin entered the witness-box.

CHAPTER XXVII.

THE EVIDENCE OF MR. JOHN COLVIN

THE general feeling of those who observed the entrance of this new and unexpected witness might be one of lively curiosity, but there were four who regarded it in more various ways.

To the Attorney-General, it meant no more than a final hammer-blow upon a nail which had been already driven in. He felt that the attempt of Carol Marks to take her husband's murder upon her own shoulders had already failed, and that it approached an act of redundancy to call John Colvin at all.

Inspector Combridge looked at it from a different angle, and with an exasperated sense that the course which the trial took was adding further confusion rather than elucidation to an event which he felt that he had not yet thoroughly understood, and increasing the risk that a miscarriage of justice might occur.

As soon as he had relieved himself of attendance upon Carol Marks, he had hastened to inform the prosecuting solicitors of the fact that Mr. Richard Skimmer was prepared to swear to having seen Mr. John Colvin in Razor Street on the afternoon during which the murder occurred, but he found it to be information which they received with obvious embarrassment, and which the Attorney-General, when it was communicated to him, put firmly aside.

John Colvin had volunteered to swear to certain conversations which had taken place between Carol Marks and himself, which were of a nature to dispose finally of the spoke which she had attempted to thrust into the grinding wheel of the law. So far, good. But to use the opportunity of putting him into the witness-box, to draw from him either an admission or a denial that he had been in Razor Street that afternoon (and a denial might be the more likely result), of what use could it be? Its only possible consequence would be to put a new weapon into the hands of the defence, a new doubt into the jurors' minds. Obviously, it could not be done. The Attorney-General dismissed the information with a curt word. He thought that there was little cause to thank Inspector Combridge, if that were all the help he could give to the official side when the battle was at its height....

Carol Barman heard that John Colvin was to be called to the witness-box with a deeper dissatisfaction, being more nearly concerned. She did not blame either her brother-in-law or her niece for the evidence they had first given, and she had had a good hope that she would have come free, had they let it stand. She saw no more than added danger for herself when Carol Marks attempted to make confession of a crime which was not hers, and when she heard the name of John Colvin called, she could make no more than a vague guess of what he would be led to say, but she saw the shadow of prison walls close round her more threateningly than before.

To Mr. Jellipot, his appearance upon the scene brought anxiety of a different kind. He did not know of Skimmer's identification that morning. So far as he was aware, the information which Mr. Colvin had given him in professional confidence, and subsequently allowed him permission to use if it should be needful for Carol Barman's defence, was still private between themselves, and unsuspected by the police. Did he himself intend to mention it now? Or had the occasion come when it would be legitimate to use the conditional permission he had received? And should he do so, what effect upon the minds of the jury would it be most likely to have? From another angle, how, if at all, would it affect the position of Carol Marks (murderess or perjuress) in the eye of the law?

Feeling that he had rarely had so difficult a decision to make, he wrote a few words on a slip of paper, turned as though to hand it to Sir Henry Blackett, and then recovered his position with the folded slip still in his hand, as the Attorney-General's examination commenced.

"I think, Mr. Colvin, I am right in saying that you have been acquainted with Mrs. Marks for a considerable period?"

"Yes."

"You were, in fact, engaged to her almost up to the time of her sudden marriage to Abel Marks?"

"Yes."

"And that engagement has subsequently been resumed?"

"Yes."

"That being so, the circumstances of the death of Abel Marks have naturally been a subject of conversation between you?"

"Yes, we have discussed the possibilities of what may have happened many times."

155

"Carol Marks has spoken to you freely and confidentially on this subject?"

"Yes."

"Has she ever at any time suggested to you that Abel Marks might have died by her hand?"

"Never."

"What has she said?"

"She has spoken of herself as being responsible for the tragedy, and of her inclination to say she had done it, if that would release her aunt from suspicion."

"Why should she have regarded herself as responsible?"

"I don't think she should. I told her that it was a morbid idea. But she knew she ought not to have married him feeling as she did, and she thought that all the trouble had come from that."

"Then she must have believed that he had died by her aunt's hand?"

It was a deadly, and seemed a natural inference, on which the Attorney-General had been quick to seize, but John Colvin whose manner in the witness-box reminded Inspector Combridge of that which he had shown to himself on an earlier day, put it coolly aside: "I neither said nor implied anything of the kind."

"Then will you explain why Mrs. Marks should feel that her conduct had been responsible, if Abel Marks had died by a stranger's hand?"

"She thought that if she had acted differently her aunt would not have been there at all."

"Nothing beyond that?"

"Nothing at all. I think she was morbidly unreasonable, but that was the feeling she confided to me."

"But it is obvious, is it not, that she would not have gone to the length of accusing herself of so grave a crime unless she had been convinced, in her own mind, that the murder had actually been committed by Carol Barman, so to speak, on her behalf?"

"Or unless she had thought that Miss Barman was in danger, through her, of being condemned for something she had not done."

"At any rate, you can swear positively that the conversations which Mrs. Marks had with you were not consistent with her husband's death having been dealt by her own hand, but showed a growing disposition to accuse herself as a means of securing her aunt's release?"

"Yes. That is the fact."

"Thank you, Mr. Colvin, that is all."

Sir Hugh Wrexham sat down, with some hope that his witness might not be further questioned. The defence had repudiated the method of relief which Carol Marks had offered, and John Colvin had done no more than give support to their own contention. Why should they not be content?

So for a moment it seemed that it might be. The Attorney-General sat down, and Sir Henry Blackett did not rise. A moment before, Mr. Jellipot had resolved his own hesitation by passing the slip of paper which had been twisted between his fingers to the hand of the K.C., and now that gentleman was leaning forward in a whispered conference with the solicitor, momentarily oblivious of the waiting court. Mr Justice Sumners observed this without allowing his dignity to take offence. With a slight motion of his hand, he had signalled to Mr. Colvin to keep his place, and had been understood without hesitation by one as coolly alert as were any of the legal gentlemen to whom the court was the constant battleground of their lively wits.

Mr. Justice Sumners, from his long experience, approved Mr. John Colvin "*a good witness*," as he had written in a small neat marginal note on his own record of the evidence of the day. Mr. Colvin was a man who could express himself with precision, and who knew what was important to say.

John Colvin waited impassively for one silent half-minute, successfully concealing the fact that he would have been glad to go. Then Sir Henry Blackett looked up. "I beg your pardon, my lord," he said. He turned to Mr. Colvin, who saw that his ordeal was not yet done.

Looking down on the slip of paper, as though reading therefrom, the learned counsel asked:

"Please tell me, Mr. Colvin, whether you believe that consideration for Miss Barman's position was the sole motive actuating Mrs. Marks in accusing herself of this murder?"

There was a moment of tensest silence while John Colvin stood evidently considering his reply. Even those who might not be able to guess where the question led, felt that it presaged some new revelation; or would lead up to the disclosure of some unexpected line of defence, such as will at times alter the fundamental issues before the court when it seems that a legal battle is nearly done. It was a feeling of dramatic climax which did not lessen when John Colvin gave his deliberate, though perhaps reluctant reply: "No. She was also quite needlessly nervous lest suspicions should be directed upon myself."

"Was there any ground for that fear?"

"None whatever."

"Then why should she think that?"

"Women are sometimes unreasonable."

"Yet there must have been some cause that seemed formidable to her own mind?"

"It was because I was in Razor Street on the afternoon of the murder. Nothing further than that."

"For which you doubtless had a sufficient reason, which you have been able to explain to the satisfaction of the police?"

"I have not explained anything to the police."

"You mean probably that you have not been asked to do so?"

"No. I mean that I have declined."

"Why should you have acted in that manner?"

"I told them that I had not murdered Abel Marks, did not know who had, and was entirely unable to assist them in investigating the crime. That being so, I had nothing further to say. Razor Street is a public thoroughfare, and the fact that I use it when I have occasion to do so does not concern the police."

"But you would agree that it is the duty of every citizen to assist the guardians of public order when a crime of this gravity is under consideration?"

"The question did not arise. The police were already misleading themselves with the idea that I might have committed it. It would have misled them further to mention that I had been in Razor Street at the time that Marks was killed."

"That was your only reason?"

"No. I can't say that exactly. I had business there which I did not wish publicly discussed at the time."

Mr. Justice Sumners interposed: "Business at Messrs. Rosenbaum's, do you mean, Mr. Colvin?"

"No, my lord. The call I made was at the farther end of the street."

Mr. Justice Sumners considered this. He said only: "Very well.... Pray go on, Sir Henry." He leaned back again, in evidence that his interposition was finished.

But Sir Henry Blackett did not go on. He felt that he had gone far enough. He might have put a further doubt into the minds of some of the jurors—a suspicion that things had happened in Razor Street that afternoon which had not been disclosed. Beyond that, there was no need to go, for he had no intention of accusing John Colvin, and, indeed, his instructions were of a directly opposite kind. And beyond that, there was the probability that, if Mr. Colvin said more, the vague suspicion might have become less. He said: "I think that is all, my lord." He sat down.

But Mr. Justice Sumners roused himself again, seeing him do that. The judge watched the manœuvres of his learned brothers for or against the prisoner, which he did not disapprove. They played by the rules of the deadly game. But it was his business to get at the truth: to have the case fairly put to the jury, free from irrelevant issues, at last. He leaned forward again to say: "Wait a moment, Mr. Colvin. Having said so much, it may be best—it may be due to yourself—that you should tell the jury what the occasion was which took you to Razor Street, on quite separate business, on this particular afternoon." He observed Sir Hugh Wrexham to be fidgeting with his gown, but was not deterred thereby, thinking that to be a sign that there might be something here which, in the cause of justice, should be made plainer than it now was. "I am sure you will agree, Mr. Attorney-General," he said, "that this point should be cleared up."

"Certainly, my lord." What else could he reply? Mr. Colvin did not look pleased, but he answered plainly enough. "I made a business call on Weinzel & Co., 117 Razor Street—the opposite end of the street from Rosenbaum's premises."

"A business call on Saturday afternoon? Would Mrs. Marks have expected you to be going there?"

"No. Not at that time; she knew nothing about it."

"Wouldn't it have been simpler and in every way better to have told the police of your being there, and of the purpose for which you called?"

"No. I don't think it would. It might have been brought out publicly, which I wished to avoid."

"Do the reasons, whatever they were, which caused you to wish to avoid publicity—do they still exist?"

"Not so much as they did then."

"But they still do to some extent?"

"It is a matter of discussing my private business affairs, which have nothing to do with the murder in any way whatever."

Mr. Justice Sumners had another moment of silence.

He thought it to be a singular thing that all these people who had no cause to love Abel Marks—William Merritt, Carol Barman, Carol Marks, John Colvin, should have come to Razor Street at, or about, the time, that he was killed; but Mr. Colvin's contention that it was a public thoroughfare was legally sound. In the absence of any evidence that he had entered No. 33, or that he had not been, as he said, in the street on quite separate business affairs, it would be improper to direct him to say more. He asked: "And there is nothing you wish to add?"

"No, my lord. I think not."

"Very well, you may go."

Mr. Colvin withdrew, and was succeeded by Mr. Gurtner, whose evidence was clearly and convincingly given, and served to bring the attention of the jury back to the direct issue they had to try. From doubts as to what William Merritt or his daughter or John Colvin might or might not have done, their eyes were directed in imagination upon Miss Barman again. They saw her come out from the building where Abel Marks was to be found dead so short a time after, and deliberately turn to shut fast a door which had stood open to let her enter. Was it the leisurely act of an innocent woman, unaware of need of concealment or any haste, and closing the door, perhaps with a little spinsterly fussiness, or just automatically, in oversight of the fact that it had not been opened to let her in? Or was it the act of a murderess, calculating and cool, who did not intend that there should be discovery of the deed until she had got safely away?

These were speculations on which Mr. Gurtner had no opinion to give. He only knew what he had seen. He could only say that Miss Barman had closed the door and walked briskly away, but at what had appeared to be no more than her usual pace.

CHAPTER XXVIII.

MISS BARMAN ADVISES HERSELF

"IT doesn't matter whether it's true or not," Miss Barman said firmly, "that is what I am determined to say." Mr. Jellipot (who was interviewing her prior to going into court, for the third day of the trial) protested mildly. "I wouldn't say that. I think it matters a good deal, and in more ways than one.... It matters, also, whether it will be believed, being a different tale from what you have told before."

"It's the first time I've given evidence."

"Yes. You've not been under oath previously, and it was natural enough to deny everything before you had been directly accused. If it's the truth, I don't say you're wrong. But, apart from that, I think you should take Sir Henry's advice before you decide such a point definitely. He might think it better for you not to go into the box at all. It's only courtesy to him to consult him first."

"I don't know about that. You think I ought to listen to what he wishes, but he wouldn't listen to me! I didn't want John Colvin examined the way he was. It seems to me that everyone else does just what they like, and I'm the only one to stay put."

"Yes," the solicitor agreed, "everyone has been running a bit wild. It isn't altogether a bad thing. It keeps the jury more or less open-minded, wondering what's going to turn up next, and a lot more likely to quarrel among themselves arguing it out.... But you see, Blackett doesn't think it's his business to please you with what he says. He thinks it's his duty to get you off."

"And someone else in, more likely than not?"

"That scarcely follows. But he might say 'One thing at a time.' Besides, someone did it. That's the case with all murders, and you can't get anyone out of the dock without clearing the way for someone else to be put in."

"Well, that's why I've made up my mind in the way I have."

"Suppose Sir Henry should decide to retire from the case?"

"I shouldn't think he'd do that."

"I can't say myself what attitude he might take."

"Well, if he's that sort, he must quit. I suppose he can't prevent me from giving evidence if I want to?"

"I'm sure he won't attempt that. He may advise you against it, but that's different. So far, it has been assumed that you will; though of course, it was to say something different from what you're talking about now."

Mr. Jellipot looked at his watch. He added: "I'd better go now, or I shan't have time to explain before we go into court.... I suppose you've made up your mind finally...? Then I'll just say that I'm not sure—I'm not *absolutely* sure—that you're wrong. But we must see what Sir Henry says."

Mr. Jellipot hurried away to the counsels' room, where he found Mr. Ridwell changing into his gown. Sir Henry Blackett had not arrived.

"Anything fresh?" Mr. Ridwell asked. "I've been going over yesterday's evidence rather carefully, and the more I think about it the less sure I am what to believe. It's common enough to have the jury fogged at this stage, and to be thinking how you can fog them a lot more, but it isn't often that those who are handling the case haven't a clear idea of the truth at the end of the second day."

"There's nothing fresh, except that Miss Barman's altered her tale during the night. She's determined to go into the box and tell the court how the man died."

"You mean that she's going to confess to the murder?"

"I don't think," Mr. Jellipot answered cautiously, "that I should put it that way quite. She doesn't admit that anyone did anything very much wrong, unless it were Marks himself.... Anyway, she won't alter. I am disposed to think," he went on reminiscently, for there had been a half-hour of earnest and abortive argument before he had recognised that her demeanour would not be changed, "that when the lady's made up her mind she could give points to a mule.... What I'm most worried about is how Sir Henry'll take it. I know he likes to handle matters his own way."

"He'll take it badly if she's made up her mind to anything that will alter his speech for the defence. He'll have thought out some good phrases by now that he won't want to waste."

Mr. Jellipot was of the same opinion, but before he had expressed it, Sir Henry Blackett hastened into the room.

"Couldn't get here earlier," he said hurriedly. "Had a consultation in chambers in the Broderick case. That's been set down for tomorrow in Wakeman's court. Damned nuisance it is. You'll have to open for me, Ridwell, if this isn't over by then."

Mr. Jellipot showed the adroitness of his legal mind by the swiftness with which he turned this information to the advantage of the position that must be disclosed.

"Then I've some good news for you," he said. "Miss Barman has resolved to unburden her soul in the witness-box in a manner which ought to bring it to a quick end."

Sir Henry stared for one astonished second, and then resumed the immobility of expression which the profession of advocacy demands. "You mean she wants to confess? She mustn't do that. The way things are going now, we might get her off more likely than not. Isn't that so, Ridwell?"

"I think," Mr. Ridwell agreed, "that we've got three of the jury on our side, and probably more. Of course, they're always liable to be pulled across by the summing-up. But I should say we've got a good chance. Wrexham showed temper once or twice yesterday, and that's always a hopeful sign."

"You'd better tell her, Jellipot," Sir Henry said definitely, "that she can't change what she's already said. It's too late for that. We haven't time to take a fresh line. Why, we're due in court in two minutes now.... If these people would only stop trying to whitewash each other! It's almost as bad to handle as when a gang start giving each other away."

Mr. Jellipot heard this decided opinion, and was slow to reply. He looked mildly obstinate.

Mr. Ridwell spoke for him. "I think Jellipot's done his best that way already. He was quite hoarse with talking when he came in."

"It isn't only that," Mr. Jellipot said slowly, "the trouble is that I'm not certain—not *absolutely* certain—she isn't right; and then there's the question of whether it's right to object, if an accused person says she'd rather tell the truth in the witness-box, than stick to a lie."

"That would be sound enough, Jellipot," Sir Henry replied, "if we'd got anything more than a poor guess what the truth is. If Miss Barman says she killed Marks, it doesn't show that she did. Rather the other way! Look at Mrs. Marks yesterday."

"Yes, I admit that. But there's another point. If she should be believed, she might get a much lighter sentence than if—"

"If she should be believed! Isn't a prisoner usually believed when he pleads guilty, which, if I understand rightly, is practically what she's proposing to do?"

"Yes, of course. But I meant if she's believed in her account of how it happened, and then— But if you'll listen to me for five minutes—"

"We can't do that," Sir Henry said firmly. "We're late now."

"If Mr. Justice Sumners should be kept waiting for five minutes, or even ten," Mr Jellipot began diffidently, "I don't suppose that—"

"You'd better go into court, Ridwell, and—" Sir Henry began, and then changed his mind. "No, stay here. If Sumners sees that we're all absent, he'll know something's up. He'll put the brake on, more likely than not, and send someone here to enquire.... We can always apologise.... Fire away, Jellipot. If we've got to be hung for a sheep, it's no use making it a whole flock."

While he spoke, Mr. Justice Sumners was in the act of bowing to the court, which had risen as he entered to take his seat, and Miss Barman, whose less voluntary presence was of at least equal importance, was taking her less comfortable seat in the dock.

Mr. Justice Sumners, gazing down upon the legal gentlemen assembled below him, observed that Sir Henry Blackett was not there. Doubtless, till he arrived, the prisoner's interests were in Mr. Ridwell's capable hands. But Mr. Ridwell also was absent. His glance moved to the solicitors' table. Doubtless Mr. Jellipot would be able to—but Mr. Jellipot was not there.

"I think," he said, "that something must be detaining Sir Henry Blackett."

Four minutes later, as Sir Henry had foretold, he gave instructions that enquiry should be made concerning the absence of Miss Barman's legal advisers, but, as he did so, they entered the court together.

CHAPTER XXIX.

MISS BARMAN GIVES EVIDENCE

SIR HENRY BLACKETT was sufficiently acquainted with the character of Mr. Justice Sumners to have expected that he would not look pleased. Personally considerate and always courteous in his attitude toward those who pleaded before him, he was rigid in the standard of respect which he exacted for the abstract dignity of the law, and he imposed a punctuality upon others which he observed with an equal exactitude.

In a civil action, the delay, short though it had been, might have had serious consequences. There was an instance in which a case had been dismissed for no greater default, and only reinstated on the list after a display of much penitent humility on the part of the dilatory advocate, and with the costs of the day to be paid by his unfortunate client. But it was obvious that Mr. Justice Sumners could not treat a criminal charge in that manner. He could not instantly condemn Miss Barman, or release her from the dock because her legal representatives were not there.

It was a public rebuke which Sir Henry Blackett had to expect, and to avoid that he must get in the first word. He therefore commenced his apologies at the earliest second he decently could, as he gained his place, and without delaying to take his seat. If he could get that first word, he had some confidence in the substance of what he would say to turn admonition aside. He ended his apology with the explanation which had been agreed before he came into court: "The fact is, my lord, that I received fresh instructions only ten minutes ago, of which I do not approve, and I had to consider seriously whether I should retire from the case."

This explanation had, at least, the first result which had been anticipated from it.

"I was sure, Sir Henry," Mr. Justice Sumners replied placably, "that you would not have been absent without serious cause, and I am glad to learn that you have felt it possible to continue the defence."

He paused upon the consideration that counsel would not even threaten to retire from a case of such gravity without serious cause, and that instructions usually come from the prisoner's solicitor. He looked at Mr. Jellipot with an expression of somewhat puzzled severity as he went on: "I may add that the accused could not desire to be represented by an abler and more experienced advocate, and that, having placed herself in your hands, she would almost certainly be wise in her own interests to be guided by your advice."

Sir Henry observed the implication upon Mr. Jellipot, and was careful that it should not remain: "I can only say, my lord, that Miss Barman's instructions are contrary to all the legal advice which she has received."

"Very well, Sir Henry. Pray go on."

"In view of the position which has arisen, I do not wish to address the court at this stage of the proceedings. I am calling Miss Barman immediately."

With a wardress at her side, as though it were absurdly feared that she might make a wild dash through the crowded court (but actually for no reason at all except the blind tyranny of routine), Miss Barman left the dock and entered the witness-box.

"Miss Barman," Sir Henry commenced, as soon as she had taken the oath, which she did in a very firm and audible voice, "you have already made a statement to the police concerning your visit to Abel Marks on the afternoon of his death, and that statement has been put in evidence here. Do you now say that that statement was correct?"

"No."

"You say that it was untrue?"

"Part of it was untrue."

"Will you tell the jury at what point you now say that it deviated from accuracy?"

"Where it said that Abel Marks agreed to pay back what he'd had from me."

"Did he refuse?"

"Yes, he did."

"And what happened then? Perhaps you had better tell the jury in your own words."

Miss Barman had a moment of silence. She stood quietly, with no trace of nervousness, or of mental stress, such as her niece had shown on the previous day, and those who watched and waited for her to speak might be in doubt as to whether she were choosing her words with care to give an accurate picture of that which memory held, or were marshalling imagination of an invented tale.

As she stood thus, Mr. Justice Sumners, who had been regarding her with a puzzled intentness, leaned forward to say: "Just listen to me a moment, Miss Barman, before you say more. It is not my business to advise you, for which purpose you have the services of a learned and most able advocate. It is my part to hold the scales fairly, and to see that justice is done.... But we have heard that you are acting against the judgment and advice of your competent legal advisers, and I wish you to understand, without possibility of misconception, in an issue of this gravity, that you are under no obligation to give evidence at all. Should you remain silent, the law requires that the charge against you should be proved—if at all—from the mouths of others.

"Should you prefer to remain silent, I shall instruct the jury that they have no legal right, from that circumstance alone, to assume your guilt.

"But should you wish to say more, you will remember that you are under oath, and that the same law which allows you to remain silent, requires you to speak truth, if you speak at all, without regard to the consequences, either to others or to yourself."

"The old josser," an irreverent juryman who sat next to the schoolmistress remarked in a whisper which fortunately did not reach the bench, "seems to think that it's a family habit to make false accusations against themselves."

"It makes it very difficult to tell what the truth is," the woman answered seriously, forgetting that she had found it necessary to snub the young electrician to silence once or twice previously, the effect of the two days' propinquity on a normally volatile disposition having been to encourage a degree of familiarity which she did not welcome.

"Oh, well," he replied, in a voice sufficiently loud to draw some admonishing glances upon him, and reduce him to a short period of abashed quietude, "I don't see why you take it so seriously. They can't make us hang her unless we like." He remembered being told by a friend who had been on a jury which had sat for ten days watching an action for infringement of patent rights, which had been fought out at enormous cost, that in the end they had been divided six to six, and after the judge had admonished them to reach a verdict if possible, to spare the parties the cost of a second trial, they had decided to spin a coin, which seemed to him a very sporting and sensible course to take, as perhaps it was. But Miss Barman was speaking now, and he gave her his attention closely enough. He meant to do his part honestly, and though he had formed an opinion at an early stage that she had committed the crime, he endeavoured to listen with a still open mind. He did not agree with the opinion of the somewhat somnolent publican that you needn't listen till the judge begins summing-up, as you'll get the fairest account from him, and a plain hint as to what verdict you ought to render.... Apart from that, had he not said to his neighbour yesterday afternoon that it was better than any play?

"I wish to tell the jury what happened, my lord." Miss Barman replied, in her clear, pleasant, rather masculine voice. And then, after a pause, she had turned her eyes directly upon the jury-box, and commenced her narrative.

"When I got there, I found the outer door open, but there was a counter across the hall. I didn't try to go past that. I touched an electric bell on the wall, and when I'd rung it twice, Abel came down. I knew him at once, but I could see he'd no idea who I was, though we'd known of each other for twenty years, more or less, and met once and again.

"I said: 'I should like a few words with you, Mr. Marks,' and he said he was busy, and perhaps I'd look in on Monday. He said: 'We're not open for business now.'

"I said: 'Well, I think you'll be open enough for mine. I'm Carol Barman.'

"He looked queer at that, as though he didn't know how to take me, or whether I'd come to quarrel or make the best of a bad job. Then he said: 'I suppose you know that Carol and I got spliced this morning?' and I said: 'Yes. I haven't come to talk about that. It's no use crying when the milk's out of the pail. I suppose you know who got her father clear of the place you'd put him into this morning?'

"He said, No, he'd been wondering who it could be, and I suppose that was the truth. Anyway, I said I'd tell him if he wouldn't keep me standing there, and I think he was curious to know, and he asked me to go upstairs.

"When we got there, he sat down at his desk, and asked me to take a chair rather at the corner, I mean not quite so far as the other side, and said he didn't want to be rude, but would I make it as short as I could, as he'd got rather a lot to do. It didn't look as though he'd been particularly busy, and I thought again that he was in a hurry to see me gone, lest Carol should come on to the scene, but I didn't mind that. It wasn't her that I'd been wanting to see. But it made me come to the point a bit more abruptly than I might otherwise have done.

"I said at once that it was I who had got William free, and told him what it had cost. I said that that was without Mr. Jellipot's charges. I didn't know what they would be, but I'd pay them myself. I didn't want anything more from him than the money he'd had from me, and I shouldn't think that he'd make a trouble of that. He'd got Carol, which was what all the trickery had been for, and I didn't suppose that he'd want to take my money as well.

"He laughed at that. He said he hadn't asked me to interfere, and he knew I hadn't done it to be any help to him. If I chose to come butting in, I mustn't squeal if I got hurt.

"After that we had some bad words. I don't say they were all on one side. I told Abel just what he was, or a bit worse, and I don't suppose it was pleasant for him to hear. And he said some things about William that don't matter, and didn't then. I might have said them myself any time, if I got riled. And he made a joke of how John Colvin and I had paid William's debts to keep him from getting the girl, and how in the end he'd got her and the money too.

"Well, I might have stood that. I don't know. But he went on to say that he didn't care for Carol a straw. He'd stopped doing that since he'd understood how she felt for him. He'd only wanted to marry her out of revenge, and so that John Colvin shouldn't. 'She's feeling sorry for herself now,' he said, grinning at me, 'but it's nothing to how she will before morning comes.'

"When he'd said that, he looked as though he'd have had it back if he could. I'd got him angry, and he'd said more that it was sensible to let out, and he saw that all the more when I answered back.

"I said: 'Abel Marks, I don't know whether or not this marriage will stand in law, but there's one thing I do, and that is that Carol's coming back with me. After what you've said, I wouldn't trust you with her for half an hour.' I didn't know where she was then, but I'd got him, and I made it clear that we were going to stick together until I got a chance to see Carol, and persuade her to come away.

"When I said that, he got mad. He said he'd give me two minutes to clear out, if I didn't wish to be thrown, and I told him it was no use talking like that, for I shouldn't stir.

"I don't know whether he could have done it, or not. He wasn't much of a man. But I saw by the look in his eyes that he meant to try, and I didn't like the idea of being mauled about, and struggling with him.

"I saw him getting up, and I picked up the first thing I could, and hit him the way I did. It wasn't quite how I meant it to be. I meant to bring it down on his head, where it mightn't have done very much harm, but he was moving as I struck, and we all know what happened.

"When I saw how he lay on the floor, I guessed I'd killed him more likely than not, and of course I had."

Miss Barman paused, as though having brought her tale to a sufficient climax, and Sir Henry Blackett saw that it rested with him to make the best he could of its legal aspects. He asked: "You struck without premeditation?"

"Yes."

"And without any intention of inflicting serious injury?"

"Yes, certainly."

"And under expectation of physical violence against yourself, which Abel Marks had threatened, and was obviously about to attempt?"

"Yes."

Mr. Justice Sumners interposed. "Tell me, Miss Barman, had there been any actual violence on the part of Abel Marks—anything beyond angry and threatening words toward yourself, before you picked up this formidable weapon, and struck the blow which had this tragic consequence?"

"No, my lord. It wasn't what he had done, it was what he was going to try to do that I had to stop if I could."

Sir Henry Blackett intervened. "He was in the act of rising, my lord, for a purpose of violent assault which he had explicitly threatened."

"Yes, Sir Henry, I appreciate that.... Tell me, Miss Barman. What did you do when you saw the man felled by your own violence, and, on your own statement, in peril of speedy death? Did you make any effort either to relieve him, or to summon help?"

"No, my lord. I was more concerned for myself."

The judge paused upon the inexpedient bluntness of this reply, but he asked no further questions. He said only: "Please go on, Sir Henry."

"There is one matter, Miss Barman, which you have not explained. That is in relation to the money, which it is admitted that you received, but which you have said that Marks refused to repay."

"Well, the fact is that, with the quarrel we had got into, and the other things that were said, it had gone clean out of my mind, and I don't suppose it had ever been of much importance to Abel, except to feel that he'd got the laugh of all of us at the last. But when I looked round, there was the safe open, and the cash drawer pulled out—I suppose he'd been doing something there when he heard me ring, and came down to see who was there—and I thought it would sound better to say that he'd paid it back pleasantly, and so I looked, and as there was plenty there, I took what was due to me."

"That would have been in accordance with the account which you have consistently given until you altered it this morning?"

"Yes."

"And why have you decided to alter it now?"

"Because other people seemed to be getting under suspicion, and Carol told that silly tale yesterday."

"So that you decided to take it upon yourself, whether you were guilty or not?"

"Oh, I did it, if you mean that!—I shouldn't call it guilty myself, but I suppose you'd all say that I'm not the best one to judge."

"Well, that is for the jury. No one has said you are guilty yet. Tell me this: had you had the remotest suspicion what the result would be, would you have struck the blow?"

"No. I don't suppose that I should."

"And I have no doubt that you deeply regret the result of that perhaps natural impulse of anger and self-defence?"

"Well, I'm sorry for all the trouble there's been, and I don't want to be here. But, if I'm honest, I don't think he was much loss."

Mr. Justice Sumners intervened again. "Miss Barman, I should like to feel that you are answering with deliberation and with due regard for the serious position in which you stand. Do you wish to give the jury the impression that you do not regret your action?"

Miss Barman remained silent for a moment, as though this question were not one to be easily answered. "My lord," she said at last, "I don't want the jury to think that, but I don't think I did more than to give a natural truthful reply. I didn't intend to kill him, and I wouldn't willingly have done such a thing to anyone living. I don't suppose most people would. Anyhow, the idea wouldn't have entered my mind, even when I knew how he'd got Carol trapped. But all the same, when I think of how he'd acted to William Merritt, and how he'd got that girl tied to him for life—well, I think it may have been all for the best, whatever trouble it means for me."

Mr. Justice Sumners had listened to this explanation with an intent gravity, but whether it would have been followed by any further question or observation upon it must remain unknown, for, as Miss Barman concluded, a spectator at the back of the court was moved to his own lawless emotions to ejaculate "hear, hear," in a very audible voice.

The judge sat up sharply. "Turn that man out of court," he said, in his sternest voice. "No. Let him stand up first."

The court became very silent, but no one rose. There was a movement of enquiring constables. A man was heard to make audible indignant denial of the accusation which a neighbour must have made against him. "Ah'm not so sure abaht you," he was heard to add, in disconcerting counterattack.

"Never mind, constables," Mr. Justice Sumners directed, seeing that the incident was acquiring an importance he did not desire. "That will do. If there be any further interruption of any kind I shall clear the court.... Go on, Sir Henry, please."

"I think that is all, my lord."

The judge's eyes moved on to the Attorney-General, who showed a moment of hesitation, exchanged a word with his learned junior, and shook his head.

Let the woman go! To gild the lily is proverbial waste of time. And after the admissions that she had made—! Not that he could not have asked her questions of damning sorts. Bad as her tale was, could she expect the jury to take it for simple truth? Is it not also proverbial that one tale has a good sound until the other side has been heard? And Abel Marks was not here! It seemed that there was no one to speak for him. Only the voices of the murderess and her family lifted against him. And to what did their accusations amount? That he had taken absolutely regular legal means to collect a debt that was legally due. And he had told a woman to leave his premises after, on her own admission, she had been grossly offensive to him, and had said that she would continue to trespass there for the explicit purpose of seducing his wife to leave him. And under these provocations he had actually attempted to get up from his seat! That was the extent of his iniquity, for which he had been struck down by this violent woman—struck down, not in the heat of conflict, but by one unprovoked, savage, relentless blow! Why, if Marks had laid hands upon her to throw her out, he would have been doing no more than the law allowed, for what right had she to remain there, in his own house, after he had told her to go?

So he had thought, and he had seen that he might have been able to put these questions with deadly effect, perhaps inducing more of those blundering uncompromising replies from one who would not even profess to be sorry for the fatal violence that she had done. But there was a risk. Her very stubbornness made it possible that she would win sympathy in the mind of some juryman or woman, where it might be difficult to dislodge. That "hear, hear" had been a warning he was too skilled an advocate to disregard. All these things could be said—certainly would be said to the jury with all the eloquence, all the plausibility at his command—when she could no longer reply, when she had withdrawn from the box, and her voice in her own defence would be silenced for evermore.

So, with these thoughts, the Attorney-General shook his head, and Miss Barman returned to the dock.

Sir Henry Blackett said that he had no other witnesses to call, and the final speeches commenced....

CHAPTER XXX.

THE JURY RETIRES

"AT 5:40 P.M.," the evening papers announced, in their stop-press columns, "the jury retired."

The speeches on either side had not been unduly long. The summing-up, somewhat longer, and taking more time proportionately, as it had been more deliberately spoken, had occupied slightly less than two hours. There had been one of those tacit understandings, so frequent in legal circles, that the trial should not be carried on into another day. The issue had, it appeared, become relatively simple. Murder or manslaughter? The Attorney-General had argued for the capital verdict, but had not urged it. Sir Henry Blackett had pleaded for an acquittal with much ingenuity, and complication of sentimental and legal issues, but to argue is not always a synonym for to hope. The judge had been impartial in tone, cautiously tentative in suggestion, and firm in legal directions, as his function required. It had been if—and if—and if—and always for the jury to judge—but still, from the carefully balanced phrases, the contingent inferences, there had emerged the idea that though he would not say that it was less than murder in strictest law, the jury yet had the final word, and manslaughter might be the one that mercy, if not the strictest legal definition, might see cause to prefer. But the responsibility was to be theirs—the responsibility of bringing in a verdict in accordance with the law as he had expounded it to them, and the facts as they might find them to be....

Mr. Rivers West, the foreman of the jury, was incidentally managing director of the well-known Thomas West Stationery Co.—but perhaps incidentally is the wrong word. To Carol Barman, to whom he was the spokesman of those who held her fate in their hands, it might seem incidental enough, but Mr. West regarded it differently. To him it was the vital fact on which his prosperity, his comfortable home in St. John's Wood, his dignity, his somewhat expensive lunches, and the existence of a little flat in Lower Compton Street, the secret of which he believed to be successfully kept, were entirely based. It was a mere incident that he was foreman of a jury at the Central Criminal Court—or so it would have appeared to him, had it not involved him in a peril which threatened that basis of all his peace. For there was no concealing the fact to his own mind that the cash deficiency was beyond hope of legitimate explanation, if it should be discovered now, as it almost certainly would if he were not back tomorrow, and it should fall to Mr. Pilson to check over the weekly statements from the various branches of the firm, and the balances which the central account should hold. By the end of the year, before the auditors would come on to the scene, he would have it straight, as he always did. But this sudden call!— Was it right that a man should be imprisoned for several days on account of a murder with which he had had nothing to do? He could not deny that he might become liable to just imprisonment for his own irregularities, if he should be clumsy enough to expose them to hostile eyes, but that did not alter the fact that the law was hitting below the belt when it held him here.

To Mr. West, more than to any other member of the imprisoned jury, it was a pleasant relief to see the trial hastening toward its close. And they would be able to bring in the verdict almost without leaving the box!

Of course, if he had been inclined to stick out for the severer verdict, it might mean that there would be longer talk, but he had sounded one or two already whom he had thought inclined to the harder view, and found that they were not so implacable toward the old girl that they would risk not being home for the evening meal for any pleasure that it would be to them to hear her sentenced to be hanged by the neck. No, manslaughter it should be, and a verdict rendered in half an hour, or a bit less....

Mr. Justice Sumners gave instructions that the prisoner should be taken below. He instructed the usher to inform him at once when the jury should be agreed. He retired to his own room. He felt, with a long experience for his guide, that he could forecast what the verdict would be. Should he pronounce sentence tonight, or defer it until tomorrow? It was really a question of whether he should make it three years or five.

He was willing to believe that the thing had happened more or less as the woman said, though he was much less than sure. She certainly wasn't the common criminal type. There wouldn't be one chance in fifty thousand that she would repeat the offence, even though she were let loose tomorrow. The primary aim of punishment in such cases must be to deter others from similar violences—and, of course, to uphold the dignity of the law. Perhaps three years would do. But before exercising such leniency it was always best to defer sentence, giving the effect of such mercy being exercised in an exceptional manner.... Besides, if the sentence were for no more than three years, there would be less probability of appeal, and Sir Henry Blackett had a reputation of finding ingenious points of procedure or law on which an appeal could be successfully based. He did not confess this argument to his own mind, yet it may have had some, even a decisive weight, for he hated appeals that challenged his summings-up. He had the best record of any judge in the King's Bench Division for his decisions remaining unchallenged, or sustained on appeal. It was a distinction he valued, and which he knew depended mainly upon the infrequency of such appeals being set down. The pitcher that goes often to the well—yes, three years it should be.....

He finished a frugal tea. He read the last chapters of *The Murder in Finches Dene*, which he had been obliged to put aside unfinished since yesterday, for the sake of the summing-up. He looked at the clock. More than an hour! Why, he would be late for dinner now, at the best. He touched a bell. "Ask Reid to enquire whether the jury are ready. If not, tell him to come to me."

A few minutes later the usher appeared. Mr. Justice Sumners heard him, and looked surprised, and then stroked his chin. He had experienced the perversity of juries before now, and the worst of it was that you had to take them patiently, as long as they were respectful to you.

"Can't agree?" he exclaimed. "That's absurd! Of course, they've got to agree. Ask them if I can be of any further assistance to them. If they say yes, I'll have them back into court at once. If not, give them ten minutes more, and I'll have them in court whether or not. I suppose they don't want to be locked up for another night!"

Fifteen minutes later he took his seat in a court which was no less crowded than before. It had been the general opinion, both of public and bar, that the verdict would be promptly given, and few places had been vacated.

Mr. Justice Sumners glanced at the empty dock. He gave instructions for Miss Barman to be brought up at once. It is the etiquette of such occasions that nothing shall be done except in the presence of the accused, even though his legal advisers may be there.

Miss Barman, her mind braced to hear verdict given and sentence pronounced, found that it was a case of ordeal deferred. She had scarcely been told that she might sit, before Sir Henry Blackett leaned over the dock-rail to whisper: "They say that the jury can't agree. There's not much to fear about that, nor to hope. They're almost bound to agree on manslaughter now, which is the best we've ever had much cause to expect. We may get a recommendation, of course."

Miss Barman merely nodded. He did not think she would make a scene, even though it should be murder on which they should finally agree, which he did not expect to hear. He turned quickly to scan their faces, and hear what the judge was saying to them.

"I am told," Mr. Justice Sumners began, "that you are finding some difficulty in coming to a unanimous verdict. The case, on the evidence which you have heard, and with the assistance that you have had, not only from myself, but from the learned counsel on either side, does not appear to me to be one that should present any prolonged difficulty. The verdict, as I have instructed you already, must be yours, and must be unanimously rendered. But if there should be any point in particular, any point of law on which I can be of further assistance to you, I shall be pleased to hear it."

"I am afraid, my lord," Mr. West answered, as boldly as he was able in that still formidably unfamiliar atmosphere, "that there is no hope that we shall come to an agreement at all."

If he had spoken with the anticipation that they would be discharged immediately as a result of that definite statement, he must have been disappointed by the judge's reply.

"I am afraid I cannot accept that, Mr. Foreman," he said, with some severity in his tone. "It is a case in which you should make a most earnest effort to arrive at a verdict, which should present no insuperable difficulty."

"I am afraid there's no hope of that, my lord. I may say we're eleven to one, but that one's as obstinate as a pi—mule."

"I must still direct you to make a further effort. If I can be of any assistance to you by going over the evidence, or any part of it, once again, or if you would like it read over to you—"

Mr. Justice Sumners, before he spoke, had observed a slip of paper that had been passing from hand to hand in the jury-box, and was now in the foreman's hands. He broke off in mid-speech, to say: "If that is something which is intended for me, perhaps I had better see it."

The usher passed the folded slip up to him, and Mr. Justice Sumners looked down and read: "Ask him if we're bound to believe Miss Barman's account of what happened."

Even his long experience of the vagaries of English juries had not prepared him for this. His eyebrows met for a moment in a frown of irritation, which he had smoothed out next moment to reply with the patience that the occasion required.

He passed the slip of paper down for the inspection of the learned counsel concerned, and then turned to the jury to say: "You ask me whether you are obliged to accept Miss Barman's evidence. The answer is that you are not bound to accept the evidence of any witness. You must use your own judgments, as you would do in your own business affairs. I need scarcely tell you that no evidence must be rejected merely through perversity or caprice, but in every instance you should try to weigh its credibility in impartial minds, considering how far it may be supported by the testimony of others, or the inherent probabilities of the case. The demeanour of a witness may also be taken into account. With regard to Carol Barman's evidence, you may be disposed to consider that an accused person will naturally be disposed to put his or her actions in the best light, and especially so when narrating that which no other living person is in a position to contradict, but you will also consider that she was on oath, and that she is as much entitled as any other person of good character to be believed, if there be no independent refutation of what she says.

"You should therefore scrutinise her testimony with the most scrupulous care. But you will bear in mind that, if you are not bound to accept it in every detail, neither are you entitled to base your verdict upon a mere supposition of what might have happened, which would go beyond necessary deduction from the evidence which has been placed before you."

The concluding words were uttered with the emphatic gravity of admonition, after which he added, in a lighter tone: "I feel assured that these considerations will enable you to overcome whatever difficulties have obstructed your deliberations." He turned his eyes from the jury-box to the legal gentlemen before him, as he concluded: "I regret that it should have become necessary to adjourn this case until tomorrow."

If there were one member of the jury who was standing out obstinately for the extreme verdict, it would be better, the judge considered, to give him time for reflection during the night, rather than press for an immediate decision, which might only accentuate the existing deadlock. And it was already late. Feeling that he had handled an exasperating position with sufficient wisdom, Mr. Justice Sumners rose from the bench.

CHAPTER XXXI.

IN THE JURY-ROOM

INSPECTOR COMBRIDGE found Mr. Jellipot at his side as they came out of the court, and felt that the time had come when he could discuss the case with the friendly freedom which had been impossible during recent weeks. They might still be on opposite sides, but the fight was done. Even in the remote contingency of the jury persisting in disagreement, and of a new trial becoming necessary, Miss Barman's confession had left no occasion for further investigation by the police, or for reticence on the part of the defending solicitor. It would be a case for no more than repeated evidence, and legal argument and exhortations before—it might be hoped—a jury of more pliable minds.

So Inspector Combridge looked at the case. He was disposed to talk, and found Mr. Jellipot in a mood to listen.

"I haven't often been more relieved," he said frankly, "than when I heard Miss Barman own up. I've never felt absolutely sure of where the truth was, and when I found out this morning that Colvin had been on the spot—well, I wished I'd known it a week ago."

"Which, I can assure you, would have made no difference whatever."

"No. I see that now."

"What you are really telling me," Mr. Jellipot went on, as though thinking aloud, "is that you never felt really sure that Miss Barman killed Marks until today, and now, because she said it, you feel that the doubt's gone?"

The inspector stared. "You're not going to tell me that I'm wrong there?"

"No.... No.... I'm not going to suggest that. I'm sorry that it seems so obvious to you, but it wouldn't serve any useful purpose to explain why.... I think that Miss Barman is naturally a truthful woman. I was only trying to follow the processes of a detective's mind."

"Of course," the inspector allowed. "I don't say we've heard all the truth now. I'd still give something to know how John Colvin spent the afternoon."

"Well, he might tell you that now, if you should ask him when he's feeling inclined for a chat. But I don't think it would help you much."

"I was a bit surprised at first," Inspector Combridge went on, "that you let her give herself away as she did. But I soon saw what you were at. If she'd gone on denying it, she mightn't have been believed, and she'd have risked being convicted of murder, and there'd have been no opening for saying anything for her by explaining how it really occurred. You're sure of nothing worse than manslaughter now, and may get a light sentence for that. Sumners isn't so bad."

"You think it's sure to be manslaughter now?"

"Yes. You can't call it murder when it happens on a sudden like that, and wasn't meant in the least. Blackett was right there."

"Yes?" Mr. Jellipot queried doubtfully, as though still thinking aloud. "I thought Blackett put it very cleverly, as I knew he would, but I don't think I could have gone quite so far. You know the law doesn't accept any violence of language as excuse for a fatal blow, and Marks hadn't even raised a hand, if I understood what Miss Barman said.... And she was trespassing at the time. She'd been told to go. You see the legal difference there. It's a narrow point."

"I wonder you let her go into the box, if you thought like that."

"I didn't let her. She settled that for herself, and didn't ask any advice. But if you're sure that the verdict will be manslaughter, it seems that she didn't do quite as badly for herself as it might have been feared she would. By the way, I wonder why you feel sure of that?"

"I don't see that there can be any doubt, after the question the jury asked, and what the judge said. He almost told them to agree on the milder verdict. Wrexham certainly took it that way. I've just heard that he told Westwood that he can't get into court tomorrow, and that he should be ready to reply to any plea for mitigation of sentence, if he feels that it goes too far."

"Did he really?" Mr. Jellipot answered with interest. "I doubt whether Sumners would hear him on that. But Wrexham never knows when to stop worrying a bone. After all, it's got him where he is now.... But I see what you mean. You're most likely right, as you mostly are. The only doubt I had was whether the judge understood what the jury's difficulty really was."

Inspector Combridge looked puzzled at this, but Mr. Jellipot only added: "Well, it doesn't matter. I'm quite likely wrong."

He turned away to speak to Carol Marks, who was leaving the court with John Colvin at her side. "I shouldn't be too despondent, my dear," he said, with what might be no more than professional cheerfulness, as he saw the misery in her face. "The years soon pass, and it might have gone much worse than everyone says it has.... Anyway, you did all you could, though I'm not going to say it was very wise."

"No," she answered, declining comfort. "Everything I do makes things worse than they were before. You feel sure that—"

"No," he answered the unspoken question. "I don't think you need have any fear at all."

He spoke confidently to her, but he was too experienced a lawyer to feel assurance of what any jury might do. And his opinion of this particular one was not high. Besides, it is difficult for one of a naturally diffident temperament to hold an opinion which is so clearly separate from anything which is in the minds of his experienced professional colleagues. He went on, looking thoughtful and rather worried, as though, whatever Inspector Combridge might feel, the problems of the case were not over for him. He had spoken of Miss Barman as an exceptionally truthful woman. So he thought her to be. He had observed more than once before in the course of his varied legal experiences, that few can tell a lie as convincingly as a habitually truthful woman. He did not doubt that he had listened to an illustration of this truism in the witness-box a few hours before....

While these conversations were taking place in the corridor of the court, the jury were being herded firmly back to a room which they would have preferred to leave.

"His lordship's orders," the usher replied to the protesting voices of those who would have chosen to be taken to the comfortable hotel where they had been incarcerated during the two previous nights. The last instructions that Mr. Justice Sumners had given, before departing for the moderate luxury of his own home, had been that they should be conducted back to the jury-room for a further hour, or such shorter period as might elapse before the foreman could announce that they had reached a unanimous decision. For the next hour, if they should continue to disagree, they must remain without the distractions of food, or the literature and amusements that they were permitted to share, that they might again unite in unhindered consideration of the problem of Carol Barman's guilt, with the advantage of the admonitory advice which they had heard from the mouth of the learned judge.

"Well, ladies and gentlemen, here we are again," the foreman commenced, as they seated themselves round the dingy table of a singularly comfortless room. He spoke with the difficult geniality of a much worried man, who must still endeavour to exercise self-control, through which control of a desperate situation may yet be won.

He had had some practice at taking the chair at business meetings, and others of more convivial character, and he thought (with some truth) that he was adroit at steering disputation toward a harmonious end.

Two or three hours before, he had sat there listening to the growing acrimony with which two men of obviously antipathetic temperaments had disputed as to whether the judge had meant them to understand that murder or manslaughter was the extent of Miss Barman's guilt, while the other members of the jury—six men and three women—had listened in comparative silence, and he had interposed the suggestion that a ballot should be taken.

He knew that opinions are more readily surrendered in this form than by verbal recantation, and when the minority had seen how much they were outnumbered—well, a few friendly arguments, and another ballot might see the hopeless difference disappear!—And they would get away before their home circles had ceased expecting them for the night.

To a point, his diplomacy had been justified by its results. The declaration of the first ballot had shown:

For Murder…3
For Manslaughter…8
For Acquittal…1

He had read out the one vote for acquittal, written in an obviously feminine hand, with a smiling shake of the head and a remark: "I'm afraid, ladies and gentlemen, we can't possibly say that, much as we should all like it. Not after what we heard this morning from the poor woman herself. We've got a public duty to do. Unpleasant, of course. But there it is, all the same."

After that he had turned the conversation to what he had felt to be the real issue—murder or manslaughter? No doubt, left to itself, the one foolish sentimental plea for acquittal would silently disappear. For the moment it was actually an advantage, as suggesting to those who had voted for the most merciless verdict that they would be compromising rather than surrendering when they came, as they obviously must, into the majority camp.

So they had talked for a time, and when he thought that a propitious moment had come, he had said genially: "Well, friends, I think it's about time to send the hat round again. I suppose we all want to get home tonight"; and when he had watched the bookmaker toss his slip in with a sulky grunt, which made plain that he was hauling down a reluctant flag, he had anticipated that the last of the extreme party had given way.

So it had proved to be. There had been eleven votes for manslaughter, but the one for acquittal was still silently there. Evidently the policy of ignoring it would not succeed.

Directly challenged, the schoolmistress, Mrs. Woolcott (for she surprisingly gave a married name) had readily admitted that the vote was hers. "I have been listening to you," she said to her fellow-jurors, "thinking that you might have arguments which would show me that I am wrong, but I am sorry to say that you have only convinced me the more of the soundness of my own opinion."

"But, Mrs. Woolcott"—Mr. West's voice had been gently persuasive—"I am sure that you will not wish to stand out against an opinion which is otherwise unanimous?"

"I'm not going to say a woman's guilty when I'm not sure, if you mean that."

"But, Mrs. Woolcott! I won't only ask you to consider the evidence. Consider that it is a compromise verdict on which we are otherwise agreed! How can we ask those who honestly think that murder is the right word to apply to give way in the generous manner that they have, if you stand out on the other side?"

"I haven't asked them to give way. Honestly, I don't think they should, unless you have convinced them that they are wrong."

So the conversation had been proceeding when the usher had unlocked the door to enquire whether they were prepared to render their verdict, and the foreman had accepted the position of hopeless disagreement, in the mistaken expectation that the judge would discharge them forthwith, if he should state it with sufficient finality.

And now he sat down at the head of the narrow table again, and tried to speak more confidently than he felt as he addressed the recalcitrant member: "I suppose there's no doubt that that question came from you, Mrs. Woolcott, and now that the judge has answered it, perhaps we're not hoping too much—"

He paused on the word, and the lady replied without requiring him to repeat the obvious query.

"I'm afraid," she said quietly, "I didn't word it very well, and I can't complain if the judge made me look rather a fool. Of course, I didn't want to know whether we were bound to believe that everything happened just as Miss Barman said, but whether we were obliged to take her word for having done it at all. I thought, if he answered that as I supposed that he would, that there might be a chance that we should be able to agree that it wasn't proved."

"But, my dear madam! When she admits it herself! Even if there hadn't been enough proof without that! You may be sure that it was only because she saw there wasn't a chance that she'd get clear that she made up the tale she did.... Or else her lawyers made it up for her, more likely than not. They're as artful as monkeys in finding ways for these wretches to dodge the rope. If you ask me what I really think, I should say that she meant to kill him, and get the money, and get clear away without being noticed at all. It was only Mrs. Marks coming on the scene as she did, and her being seen by the chap at the paper-stall, and that Gurtner, that put the salt on her tail.

"But we're all agreed now to take the more merciful view. Where there's a doubt, as the judge said—I suppose most of us aren't overkeen on sending any woman to swing.... Well, we've agreed to give her the benefit of the doubt. You can't ask us to do more than that."

"If you didn't believe Carol Marks, I don't see why you should believe her."

A slim man, neatly dressed, who had said little until now, and who had voted for manslaughter from the first, interposed a remark here. He was a University tutor, casually acquainted with the schoolmistress, and was perhaps the most likely one there to be able to influence her to give way.

"I think, Mrs. Woolcott," he said, "if you will consider—perhaps I should say if you will contrast—the evidence of the two women fairly, you will recognise that their narratives can hardly be put on the same plane. That of Mrs. Marks, even before we had heard the admissions of the older woman, was singularly unconvincing to me. It lacked circumstance. I think the general feeling throughout the court was that she was making a generous but rather clumsy effort to save her aunt."

"I'm not sure that you are wrong about that, Mr. Clayton," Mrs. Woolcott answered. "I had the same feeling myself. But we might be wrong. And if Mrs. Marks lied, it doesn't follow that Miss Barman was telling the truth. Besides, a good guess isn't proof, and when we are asked to send a woman to jail for I don't know how many years we want something more than a good guess. All I ask for is what Mr. West said a few minutes ago. Give her the benefit of the doubt where we can't be sure."

"You're doing that, ma'am," the bookmaker broke in, "when you call it manslaughter, while it's about as bad a case of murder as ever I've heard tell. The poor fellow never lifting a finger before he's—well, you might call it pole-axed at his own desk, just because he tells her to go. I'd like to know why I'm to give way, if there's not the same sauce for you."

Quietly obstinate still, Mrs. Woolcott turned to her latest assailant. "I don't think you should, Mr. Gadgett. If that's what you think, it's only right for you to stick to it. I've always understood that no one ought to be convicted unless twelve people agree. It's not really agreeing to say we'll give way so that we can get home.... But perhaps, if we can't agree, the fairest thing is to let her go. You can't *want* to see the poor woman sentenced to be kept like a beast in a pen—you'd want to be very, very sure before you'd feel willing for that."

"Some of us," other voices broke in, "have some respect for order and law, Mrs. Woolcott."—"You can't be sloppy about such matters as this."—"And some of us don't approve of honest men being knocked on the head in their own offices."

Mr. West, seeing that the discussion was taking an angry tone, interposed with: "Gentlemen, gentlemen, please! I'm sure we all appreciate Mrs. Woolcott's feelings. They're very natural, and they do her credit. There's no harm in a soft heart, and we always bless the ladies for being that way inclined. But there are two others here, and they seem to have been able to look at things rather differently. They haven't either of them said much so far. Suppose we ask them to tell us how they've been able to come to the same conclusion as us."

Mr. Clayton, studying the scene with more detachment than he, perhaps, ought to have felt, and giving as much attention to the foreman's defects of grammar as to the larger question with which they dealt, looked at the two ladies, and doubted the wisdom of this appeal. He compared the managing director of the Thomas West Stationery Co. to a bowler who has been hit off his length, and sends down a short ball through sheer despair of succeeding with those of a better sort.

Mrs. Culpepper, a broad-faced woman, with a distinctly Hebrew cast of features, and a figure which might be described as falling abroad, who would retire to the supervision of a ladies' second-hand dress warehouse in Poland Street at the close of this unexpected interlude, was the first to answer. "Did it?" she exclaimed. "Of course she did it! We've got ears, haven't we? A bare-faced woman I call her. I don't hold with such goings-on, and I don't see how anyone what ud call herself a lady could.

"I've said manslaughter from the first. She slaughtered the man, didn't she? Then what more would you have? I don't hold with hanging women, but if it wasn't murder, what else was it but manslaughter, I'd like to know?"

Mr. Clayton's quiet, cultured voice, with a hint of sarcasm too delicate for most of the jury to observe, answered with another question. "You've heard of justifiable homicide, haven't you, Mrs. Culpepper?"

"Heard of it?" she retorted, with cheerful energy. "I should say I have! You can't read the Sunday papers these days without hearing of worse than that. But I don't hold with such goings-on. Those who've been brought up proper don't go into prisons for debts and knocking men on the head, if you ask me. I call it a dirty tale."

"And you, Mrs. Fitchett?" the foreman asked of a small ineffectual elderly woman, clothed in shabby black, with a sagging mouth, who had so far uttered no more than the minimum of unavoidable words.

"I don't understand law very well," she answered weakly, when she had realised that she was expected to speak, and that all eyes were directed upon her. "I didn't want to come here at all. But if you gentlemen say it, I've no doubt that's what it was."

Mr. West said: "Thank you, Mrs. Fitchett," rather blankly. He could not feel that the two ladies had offered Mrs. Woolcott convincing words.

Mr. Clayton suggested: "Suppose we have another ballot now, Mr. Foreman?"

Mr. West looked dubious. "If you think any useful purpose will be served?" he said hesitantly.

"I think it might tend to clarify the position."

"Very well, if you think that."

Once more the voting slips were prepared and the hat went round. The foreman opened and read them out one by one.

"Manslaughter—manslaughter," he said. Seven times. So far, good. There was hope while that word recurred. Then the eighth—"Not guilty"—showed that no progress had been made. It showed more than that to the eyes that were upon it, for the writing was not that of the schoolmistress. Her slip came next—"Not guilty" again. Then two more of the expected words, and a third unexpected "Not guilty" to end the count.

That was how the position had been clarified by a further ballot. It was nine for manslaughter and three for acquittal now.

"Well, ladies and gentlemen," the foreman said, not unreasonably, "I'll ask those who've changed to speak up, and let us know where we are now."

Mr. Clayton was the first to answer. "I've come to the conclusion," he said coolly, "that there's more reason in what Mrs. Woolcott says than we've heard from some on the other side. She has put a small doubt in my mind. I won't say that it's more than that—but if there's a doubt at all, the accused is entitled to an acquittal. There's no doubt that's the law, so I've voted the only way that I can."

He asked himself, even while he spoke, how far that was the truth Had he really an honest doubt? Or had he been moved by no more logical impulse than distaste for the mental quality of some of those by whom Carol Barman had been condemned. Was Mrs Woolcott's opinion to be taken as of less weight than that of the two other women who had been invited to state their reasons for sending a fellow-woman to the horrors of penal servitude or a lonely cell? Perhaps that was it, joined to a natural disgust of seeing at close quarters what a jury's "unanimous" verdict so often means. Right or wrong, he felt he gave his support to the better side.

As he finished speaking, there came the voice of the young man who had sat next to Mrs. Woolcott for the last three days. Had she been as ready to talk to him as he had been to her, he would have known her views before the first ballot was taken, and the votes for acquittal would not have been less than two.

He had supposed previously that he was doing no more than the obvious, necessary thing when he had voted for the manslaughter verdict—that the choice between that and murder was all that he had to make. He saw differently now.

"I hadn't thought it out properly," he said, "when I voted first. I daresay we were all a bit rushed. But I say, if she did it the way she says it wasn't such a terrible thing. Marks mayn't have got more than he deserved. And as we're not all that sure we can't do better than let her go back to her own folk."

While he spoke there had been the sound of a turned key in the lock. Now the usher appeared. "Ladies and gentlemen, if you please, the cars are waiting to take you to the hotel. I expect you all feel like a good dinner."

The jury rose with alacrity. They had had nothing since lunch. Mr. West led the way, with a jest on his lips, and anxiety giving actual pain in his heart. He thought of the dock, where he had watched Carol Barman sit, rather grimly quiet, for the last three days; but the figure that he saw there was intolerably, impossibly his. And there was still a chance—if he could only get back to his office before midday! He could write—in this maddening confinement he was permitted to write. He could say definitely that he would be back, and give directions of what was to be left for himself to deal with. If he could only be sure that the judge would be prompt to discharge the jury if they should still not agree!

He asked the usher about that and got a disconcerting reply. If the judge heard that they were still divided, he might quite possibly commence the hearing of another case, and get that over—the next one on the list would not take more than three or four hours—before calling them into court. He would wish to spare both the State and the prisoner the cost and anxiety of a second trial, and if a few hours further solitude might bring the jury to a reasonable unanimity— well, there was no knowing what course he might take. But one thing was certain. The judge thought it to be a case in which agreement ought to be reached.

As he was driven with his fellow jurors to the Old Packhorse Hotel, he considered desperate expedients. He considered being taken ill in the night. But suppose he should fail to simulate illness in a convincing manner? Or suppose he should do it too well, and be removed to a hospital from which he could not make escape with sufficient promptitude? And then to be at his business desk through-out tomorrow would be difficult to reconcile with such a pro-gramme.... No, he must think of something better than that!

CHAPTER XXXII.

THE VERDICT

AS Miss Barman dressed herself next morning, in the solitude of her prison cell, to the music of rain that beat upon the narrow window in gusty squalls, the rather grim half-smile which had been frequent upon her lips since that fatal Saturday of sudden marriage and sudden death, came again as she wondered how distant the day might be when she would be allowed to handle those clothes again. She did not seriously think that she would hang, even though a verdict of murder should be brought in, which she was prepared to hear. She knew that the extreme penalty is rarely inflicted in the case of women ("not," as she considered impartially, "that there's much reason in that"), especially when the crime is one of sudden violence, rather than secret deliberate craft. No, she would be reprieved. That was sure enough. And as to listening to the rigmarole about being hanged by the neck, and the Lord's mercy coming into play where human mercy was proving inadequate to the occasion—well, she would take it quietly, for the pointless mummery that it would be! It was the sort of thing that men enjoyed doing with solemnity, even though everyone in the court might know that the sentence would never be carried out.... It was because men never really grow up. It had been a favourite saying with her that there were only women and children to make the world—the men all coming under the less responsible designation. Perhaps, on that argument, it was not women but men to whom the freer mercy should be extended when violence was uncontrolled.

And how credulous they could be! How easily they had accepted her account of how Marks had died! "Like milk," she said to herself, with the grim smile lurking again, "it was like milk that they lapped it up." Except, perhaps, the judge. She respected him. His questions had a probing quality, which she had recognised before she had had occasion to fence with, perhaps to foil them, herself.

And Mr. Jellipot. She felt that he had made a good guess from the first, though it had been unspoken on either side.

No, she did not fear that she would hang. But it might be a reprieve, which would mean a life-sentence. That would really be fifteen years, so she was told. It would be best to expect that! Then, if there were a manslaughter verdict, and she got less, it would be all to the good! It would make it a good day of her life. One on which she had been liable to fifteen years imprisonment when she waked, but from which many years had been taken during the day.... But the dress she wore would be of little value when the time of release should come. Fashions change! She would tell Carol to sell the rest of her wardrobe for the best price she could get.... And she would have no expenses while she lived on the hospitality of the state. The money would accumulate in the hands of her trustees. Or, had she not heard somewhere that, in cases of felony, it was forfeited to the State? But probably such a law would not be enforced in these merciful days. She comforted herself from that sudden fear by reminding herself that she had read, not long ago, the details of a murderer's will. No, it would surely accumulate, perhaps more than filling the hole which had been made by that £500 which had passed into the lawyer's pockets. She would be able to live much as before. She would not be so very old, even then.... If only Carol wouldn't take it so tragically! Carol had got John Colvin now; she had got financial freedom as well. She told herself, in almost the words that Mr. Jellipot (less immediately concerned) had used so cheerfully to her niece the evening before, that the years pass. She quoted to herself from the only poet she really loved:

> The mind is in its own place, and of itself
> Can make a Heaven of Hell, a Hell of Heaven.

Well, she would have opportunities enough to test the wisdom of that!

She recognised that she had experienced little of active oppression, or intended rudeness, and some evidences of sympathetic consideration from the wardresses in whose charge she had been. She had not much ground for complaint against them. But over all, like a foul black shadow, had been the cold brutality of the system which was preparing her for being treated as a number, not as a name. They were doubtless more careful here of the needs of the physical body than would have been the keeper of a medieval jail, but they were also so much more active to take away whatever of freedom, of individuality, may still be possible to one who is confined to a prison cell. She would be kept, she knew, like a beast—like a well-kept beast in a pen. But with less freedom to sleep or wake. "There nothing is but thinking makes it so." Well, she would have opportunity of proving that too....

It was ten-thirty when she stood in the dock again. Presumably, the jury had found it possible to agree during the night. She was not sure that that was of good omen for her, but she still felt some satisfaction that the battle would not be fought again. She had had enough of that dock. Better to know the worst, and to know that the long sentence would be shortening with every hour!

The jury had not yet come in.... She noticed that the judge had a sterner expression than she had observed previously. He did not meet her eyes, though she looked straightly at him. She supposed that the black cap would be near his hand.... The jury was filing in now. She looked straightly at them. She remembered reading somewhere that if a jury were convicting anyone of a capital offence, it could be told from their sombre faces without need to wait for the spoken word. Well, there was no assurance in that. They did not look at her. They looked rather as though they were doing something of which they were ashamed, or for which they expected rebuke. Her heart paused at the sight. Was she going to make a weak feminine scene, after all the resolutions that she had formed? Had she not prepared herself for the worst, or was that no more than the self-delusion of a mind which had persuaded itself that the ordeal of the capital sentence would not be hers?

Someone—not the judge—was questioning the jury now. Did they find her guilty of murder? *Not guilty*, the foreman said. Her heart leapt. But there was really no more in that than her reason had told her that she would be most likely to hear. There was still the ordeal of condemnation, of the long sentence, to come. The question of how many years. She scarcely regarded the fact that the jury were being questioned again. It was hardly worth listening to the answer to that. Was she guilty of manslaughter? What else could they say now? But it was *Not guilty*, the foreman said.

A murmur, half astonishment, half relief, like a sudden gasping of breath, went through the court. Carol Barman stood dazed.

The judge's head gave a little jerk. He said sharply: "What was that?" The associate, already entering the verdict, looked up in reply: "Not guilty, my lord."

The judge's glance travelled along the two rows of jurors, his eyes stern, his lips slightly contemptuous, but he did not speak. He looked at Carol Barman at last. He had it on his lips to say: "You may consider yourself a very fortunate woman," but the habit of restrained speech prevailed. He said coldly: "Let the prisoner go." He spoke a stern word to restrain the excitement that stirred the court, and the conduct of the prisoner's friends who were pushing toward the now-opening dock. It was one of those moments at which he was accustomed to allow a little momentary relaxation of the decorum the law requires. A little—but not much.

In his mind, the question of the jury remained. Certainly he would not empanel them for another case, but he would punish them, if he could, for a verdict which had disgraced the administration of justice, and the court over which it was his honour to preside. Fortunately for them, he had little power. But they need not be told that he would not use them again.

"Usher," he said, "you will understand that this jury is not released. They will remain till the court rises at the end of the day." He repeated this instruction to the jury direct, so that no man might fail to hear.

CHAPTER XXXIII.

INSPECTOR COMBRIDGE IS ASKED TO LUNCH

IT was not Carol Barman alone to whom the jury's verdict came as a bewildering shock. Inspector Combridge felt almost as dazed as she. Whatever might be the truth, he had assumed, after hearing the written question which had come from the jury-box, and Mr. Justice Sumners' reply thereto, that the jury would come to agreement upon a verdict of man-slaughter, and that, as far as the police were concerned, the case was over. Continued disagreement among the jury, of an obstinacy which would require a second trial, was still a possibility, but it was one too remote to be considered by a practical mind.

He had left the court on the previous evening with the feeling that Miss Barman's confession had justified both his own conduct of the investigation, and the decision of his superiors thereon. It would be one more to add to the long list of his successes, with the feeling which he valued even more than public or departmental credit—the feeling that substantial justice was done.

He was not without sympathy for Miss Barman, and, had it rested with him, it is likely that her conviction would not have been followed by a very onerous penalty, but he could not be expected to vex his mind concerning matters on which he had no responsibility, and over which he had no control.

Now, in a moment, by the jury's verdict, he saw the case opened again. It came as an astonishment of a most unwelcome kind, but he was less ready to condemn it as perverse owing to the lurking doubt that had never been entirely expelled from his own mind.

But whether they had judged wisely or foolishly, he knew that they were officially right. The law had declared that Carol Barman, in spite of her own confession, was not the victim that it required. Tomorrow he would be expected to resume investigations which would aim at supplying another occupant for the dock. There would be Carol Marks to consider. On her own evidence alone, he would be justified in applying for a warrant for her arrest. But there was no room for a second mistake. Even if Carol Barman had not been as innocent as the verdict declared, it did not follow that there was no other guilty person to be discovered. And because Carol Barman's confession had been rejected, it did not follow that that of Carol Marks was of greater veracity. Curiosity revived in his mind as to what had taken John Colvin to Razor Street that afternoon, and still more as to what his occupation had been while he was there. If Carol Marks had known that not only her aunt but her lover also would be in jeopardy if the truth were bared, it would give a stronger reason for the sentimental folly which had attempted to draw the legal lightning upon her own head.

Such thoughts moved in his mind as he stood in the corridor of the court, and observed a group consisting of Carol Barman and her friends, with Mr. Jellipot among them, who moved uncertainly, as though inclining to go, but being unresolved as to the destination to which they should direct their steps. The sight of the solicitor reminded him of two cryptic remarks of which he might ask the explanation now; and though he felt no certainty that Mr. Jellipot would gratify his curiosity, he saw that there must be significance, even in refusal to do so. Would it not imply that there was still danger for one or more of the little group of those who were talking and laughing around him now, which would be augmented by such replies being given?

Yes, a talk with Mr. Jellipot must be one of his earliest occupations. But the present moment would be obviously inappropriate, even indecent, for intrusion upon him. Of course, if he should separate himself from his clients—but while the inspector hesitated, Mr. Jellipot observed him, and raised his umbrella in a gesture of invitation.

With some reluctance, but reminding himself that opportunities of obtaining information must not be lost, Inspector Combridge accepted the signal.

He greeted Mr. Jellipot, and then extended a hand to Miss Barman, in some natural doubt of how it would be received.

"I hope you bear no malice, Miss Barman," he said. "You know I did no more than my duty was, and that isn't always pleasant to do. We all make mistakes at times, and it's a good thing when we've got an English jury to set us right."

Miss Barman showed no reluctance to accept the offered hand. She had been fortified during the last few minutes by Mr. Jellipot's assurance that no one can be put on trial a second time for the same offence. She said: "If you ask me, I think they must have been weak in the head."

Having expressed this uncompromising, and ungrateful opinion, Miss Barman appeared to consider the subject completely dealt with, and the conversation closed; and the inspector, who would have had no objection to chatting with her, but was more reserved in his attitude toward the other members of the group, made a motion of withdrawal. Miss Barman was like an inoculated person among those under suspicion of foul disease. She was officially certified as immune, and there could be no complication arising from contact with her. But from the others, whom her immunity made more suspect, he would prefer to hold some distance away—at least until the attitude of the police had been officially decided.

Mr. Jellipot observed his hesitation. He said, in his most genial manner: "I had just asked our friends here whether they would do me the honour of lunching with me. The hour is somewhat earlier than is usual, but there are, perhaps, worse troubles in life than that, and if you could see your way to come with us, it would, 1 am sure, add greatly to the pleasure of all concerned."

"It's very kind of you to say that, Mr. Jellipot," he began, with more distance in his manner than in his words, "but we mustn't forget that this case isn't over, and I can't think—"

"It was for that very reason that I asked you to come with us. I think that a frank discussion of the position may be in the interests of all concerned."

The inspector looked unconvinced. He remembered a previous occasion when Mr. Jellipot had persuaded him into a position which had gone near to requiring his resignation from the C.I.D. Frankness from these people must be at their own peril now, and it was not reasonable to suppose that their conviviality would be increased by a caution in the usual formula. On the other hand, he was resolved to keep clear of any sympathetic or confidential entanglement, such as had come near to casting him down before.

Mr. Jellipot surveyed his indecision with understanding eyes. "If I give you my assurance," he asked, "that, if you accept my invitation, you will have no occasion either for personal or official regrets?"

"It's very good of you, Mr. Jellipot. But I still think I'd rather see you another time, if you don't mind."

Mr. Jellipot had no intention of bidding higher than the occasion required, but he was resolved to prevail. "My advice to my clients," he said, "will be to talk with absolute frankness, and so long as they do so, it is, I am sure, to their own advantage that you should hear what is said. I am not suggesting that it will be widely different from what you have heard already."

"You are asking me to come to hear a new version of the murder of Abel Marks?"

"Revised," Mr. Jellipot replied, with his usual precision, "might be the more accurate adjective."

"Well, we'll say a revised version. And it will be understood that I am neither bound to believe it, nor to treat it as privileged in any way? May we say now that anything which is said will be put afterwards into formal statement by those concerned?"

Mr. Jellipot avoided a direct answer to that. He said: "It will be understood that you are invited to join us strictly and solely as Inspector Combridge of the Criminal Investigation Department of New Scotland Yard, with all the implications attached thereto, and that you have cautioned, or will caution anyone whom you may now, or at any later moment may have cause to suspect of the murder of Abel Marks, or of complicity therewith, with all the formality that the police regulations require."

Inspector Combridge could not avoid smiling at this comprehensive certificate of moral immunity. He said: "Well, if you put it like that, I suppose I can't ask for more! And it's not my business to make objections to hearing any confession that comes my way."

Seeing that he was of a disposition to yield, the whole party commenced to move toward the main gateway, but though he made no further objection, the influence of past experience still gave him a doubtful mind which was not relieved by Mr. Jellipot's reply: "I don't know that confession is quite the right word to use, but if I said that it was rather early for lunch when we began to talk, it's a bit later now, so perhaps we'd better be getting on."

The Inspector observed that the little group of suspects around him had listened to this conversation, the subject of which concerned them so nearly, with a lack of seriousness which he felt to be inappropriate to the position in which they stood. They looked and laughed as people might whose troubles were suddenly, unexpectedly, almost miraculously done.... He still could not resist the idea that the lawyer sought to catch his feet in some cunning trap. He followed with the wariness of a wild elephant doubtfully lured by tamed females of its kind toward the perils of human paths.

CHAPTER XXXIV.

THE TRUTH

"THE occasion," Mr. Jellipot observed, "is, perhaps, one which will excuse a little more than the ordinary cost and conviviality of a midday meal, and is also one for which a private room is explicitly indicated. Suppose we try the Savoy?"

No one raising any objection to this, he signalled with his umbrella for a taxi, and then for a second, to leave the rank. "As," he said, "we are too numerous a party to be inserted with comfort in a single vehicle, and especially so on a day that is far from dry, it will, perhaps, be most conducive to the satisfaction of all concerned, if our friends take the first, and you and I, Inspector, enter the second vehicle."

Inspector Combridge, still watchfully suspicious of hidden purpose in all that Mr. Jellipot did, was yet not unwilling to have an opportunity of a few words apart from the presence of his possibly criminal clients. He made no protest, therefore, against this division, and after watching William Merritt, John Colvin, Carol Barman, and her younger namesake, enter the one vehicle, he joined Mr. Jellipot in the other.

"I wish I knew how you do it," he said, as soon as they were seated. "I know Blackett put up a good fight. I heard it said that his speech was about the best that he's ever made. But I didn't think you were even aiming at anything better than a manslaughter verdict. I haven't often seen anyone more disgusted than the old judge, and even the lady herself seemed to have rather a shock."

"I'm afraid," Mr. Jellipot replied modestly, "that you mustn't give me any credit for that. As a matter of fact, it didn't go quite as I thought it would. There was something going on in the jury-room that I couldn't follow, though I thought the judge was taking it the wrong way, which it was very natural for him to do, because we all have a tendency to think that other people have the same type of

197

mind as ourselves, and Mr. Justice Sumners is an exceptionally sensible man. But, as I have said, there was something going on among the jury that I couldn't understand, and that I can fathom now even less than I thought I could yesterday.

"But, apart from that, you may say that Miss Barman won the game off her own bat, and by what I am afraid I must describe as an unorthodox stroke."

"You don't really mean to tell me that she made up the whole tale?"

"I am not aware that I have said anything from which that deduction can be logically derived."

"But you told me once that her conviction would be a miscarriage of justice."

"Did I say that? Or more probably something of a rather similar sound. It is improbable that I should have said anything which I did not mean.... But we seem to be nearing our destination, and, with your permission, I must be ready to alight promptly, so that I may discharge my debt to the taxi which I see is still somewhat in front, lest I should be forestalled by my guests."

There was, in fact, still a queue of vehicles and a red light between them and the Savoy when the conversation came to this point, but Inspector Combridge understood clearly enough that Mr. Jellipot intended to enlighten him at his own time, if at all, and he had sufficient discretion to accept the statement without reply.

It was not until a private room had been engaged, and a good lunch not only ordered, but advanced to its more substantial courses, that Mr. Jellipot led the conversation, which up to that point had been of a particularly reserved and tentative character, directly to the circumstance of that abrupt decrease with which the mind of Inspector Combridge was most concerned.

"I am going," he said, "to invite you to give some explanations to Inspector Combridge, which may save a good deal of trouble to himself, and, for all I know, to some of you also. As I have watched the development of this enquiry, and the prosecution which was very properly instituted, I have thought that the inspector acted with the perspicuity, both in what he did and what he avoided doing, which I should have expected from personal knowledge, and also from the public reputation which he already had."

Inspector Combridge received this somewhat unexpected compliment with a silent reminder to himself that he had resolved not to be won over by any honey of words, and with an inclination to say that it was not by his advice that Miss Barman had been arrested at all, which he suppressed from loyalty to his superior officers, by whom that prosecution had been ordered.

He therefore remained silently unresponsive, while Mr. Jellipot, apparently oblivious of his reaction, went placidly on.

"So far as Mr. Merritt is concerned, I have never seen reason to doubt the substantial accuracy of the account he gave of his last interview with his old-time colleague, and somewhat uncompromising creditor of more recent years. I do not think that there is anything which I need ask him either to alter or add.

"But I think that both Miss Barman and Mrs. Marks may be willing to either add or subtract something from the accounts which they have given under legal exigencies which may explain, if they do not excuse, some deviation from the path of verbal rectitude that the law demands.

"Mr. Colvin also, though in a different position, and open to criticism, if at all, for a severe economy of confidence, rather than any lack of veracity in the evidence which he gave, may also think that the time and occasion have come when he may oblige Inspector Combridge with the fuller information which he is, I think, entitled to have."

"Of course, I'll hear anything anyone likes to say," Inspector Combridge interposed, "but it's understood that it's at their own risk."

"The question, Inspector, really does not arise.... Perhaps, if Miss Barman will speak first, with the frankness permitted by the legal immunity which she has so perilously acquired, the remaining explanations will be more easily and entirely believed."

"What I can't understand," Miss Barman said, in response to this invitation, "is how you tumbled to it as quick as you did. I've always felt that you knew about as much as though you'd been in the room at the time."

Mr. Jellipot looked actually embarrassed by this testimonial to his penetration, which he disclaimed with modest sincerity. "I am sorry," he said, "if I gave such an impression, which it was certainly not my business to do, and which goes far beyond the accuracy of any guess that I was able to make.

"I was, in fact, extremely puzzled, until I heard you give the explanation in the witness-box which supplied the missing motive for what you did.

"What had puzzled me until then was why you should have killed him at all, and even then I could not accept the account you gave, because, among other equally cogent reasons, I was certain that you are not the type of woman who would have reacted so violently to a verbal threat, even had Marks been the type who would have tried to resolve the difficulty by a physical struggle.

"I had no doubt that you had deliberately struck to kill, but I sought vainly for any motive which would appear adequate to one of your character for such a deed."

"Well," Miss Barman replied, "there doesn't really seem to be any need for me to speak at all. But if Inspector Combridge would like to have it from me, now that it can't make any more trouble, I'll say that you're right as to how it happened and why.

"I couldn't have supposed that anything would have made me look at a man and decide that he shouldn't go on living, and I would have stood almost anything else from him without such a thought coming into my mind, but when he boasted of the hell that he was going to make of Carol's life, it was just the last straw in the scale.

"He'd hardly said that she would be sorrier before morning came—it wasn't only the words, it was the look with which they were said—before the thought came that if I'd strength in my hand to kill him, he shouldn't live. There was a second during which our eyes met, and I think he knew what I meant—and then I saw that metal rod. I didn't know what it was for, but it seemed the right thing to me.

"He didn't get up to attack me, unless I'm wrong. He tried to get up to bolt. But I snatched the bar in my left hand, and that gained a second, besides being what he didn't expect, so that I caught him on the side of the head as he rose, and when he fell I saw I'd done enough harm, without striking a second blow.

"Anyhow, I don't know that I should have struck him again. I felt differently after I'd done it. But I don't mean that I had any re-grets.... No, I'm not sorry. I'm glad. The old judge tried to get me to say that I wished I hadn't, and I went as near as I could. I wasn't anxious to get hanged. But I've been glad all the time.... I was more glad than before when I heard how Carol felt as she went up his beastly stairs."

Inspector Combridge heard, and believed. The final words had a quality which brought conviction to his experienced mind. Cer-tainly, if this were true, it reduced the importance of any explana-tions that he had yet to hear.

He asked: "So all the rest that you told us was true?"

"Yes," she replied. "I didn't lie more than was needed to save myself. It was all true, except that I wasn't frightened, and didn't strike him in self-defence. He didn't threaten to throw me down-stairs either. There wasn't time. And I don't think he'd have had the pluck."

"And you were wise enough to wipe the rod before leaving?"

"No, I didn't. Women sometimes wear gloves."

"But you were not wearing them when you saw me later in the afternoon?"

"That was because women aren't always absolute fools."

"I see. You're a cool hand, Miss Barman." The inspector looked at her with feelings in which some respect, even some liking, were confused with official reprobation of one who had broken and foiled the law, besides the more personal offence of making fools of the C.I.D. He took his last point as he added: "I didn't know you were left-handed, or we might have got home."

"Well, I'm not. I'm what you call ambidextrous. I suppose I was naturally left-handed, but persistence in making me use the right hand when I was young left it a drawn game. In a moment like that I should use whichever hand happened to be nearer."

"Inspector Combridge," Mr. Jellipot remarked, "has probably been looking all the time for a left-handed person he could suspect. But he preferred to keep his eyes open, and his mouth shut, and it was no use raising a point that didn't apply. I may say that the defence considered the same point—the difficulty of seeing how the blow would have fallen as it did from the right hand of anyone in a position to pick up the rod, and strike suddenly—but it was too vague to introduce while we were contending that Miss Barman left Marks alive, and after that its importance was gone."

"And I suppose you, Mrs. Marks," Inspector Combridge enquired, "are going to tell me that your first statement was true, and the evidence you gave afterwards was concocted to save your aunt?"

"Yes," she replied, "everyone seems to have guessed that, almost at once. I'm afraid I wasn't very good at making it up."

"You couldn't surely have thought that she would let you take it on to yourself?"

"Not if she'd done it. But I wasn't sure that she had."

"Well, even so, it was more than most nieces would try."

"But it was all my fault from the first! If I hadn't quarrelled with John, and then married Abel like a silly fool, it wouldn't have happened at all. And besides," she added honestly, a slow blush spreading over her freckled face, "you mustn't think too much of that. I don't think I really expected to be believed—not so that I should really get hanged. I only thought that if I said I'd done it too, I might muddle the jury's minds."

"Which only shows," Mr. Jellipot commented kindly, "that you had more wit, and less folly, than most people supposed. I may confess now that I had the same idea when I urged Sir Henry to acquiesce in Miss Barman's determination to tell her own tale in the witness-box. I didn't think she was going to tell the truth, though she might have decided to go nearer to it than she had done previously, but I thought that we should get nothing worse than a manslaughter verdict—which we must expect, at the best, if she didn't give evidence at all. Beyond that, I thought that she might get some sympathy, and just possibly enough to divide the jury, or even get them to admit the doubt of who was telling the truth which Sir Henry was to make the leading plea of his speech, as you know how ably he did."

Inspector Combridge digested this with some difficulty. His own doubts had been that the prosecution might be directed against an innocent woman. Now he must face the fact that his scruples been misdirected, and that justice had been foiled by what he felt to be no more than an elaboration of successful deceits.

"Of course," he began, "if you thought it right as an officer of the court, Mr. Jellipot—"

The solicitor took the point before it was made. "You will remember that Mrs. Marks was your witness, not ours. We were emphatic that we did not believe her. And Miss Barman went into the witness-box to tell the tale she did against Sir Henry's or my advice, as he was careful to tell the court."

"Oh, I've no doubt you were right! That's the devil of it. You were right, as you always are. And we were right too. You can't deny that. But we're the ones to get left in the soup. And you say now that you guessed all along that it was murder and nothing less. Yet you told me that it would be a miscarriage of justice if we got the verdict we wanted. I should like to know how you explain that."

"I made a similar remark," Mr. Jellipot replied equably, "to the junior counsel for the prosecution about two hours ago, when we heard what the verdict was. Mr. Westwood replied that if he spoke as a lawyer he must deplore the jury's perversity, but, as a man, that the point of view which I had expressed was one for which much could be said.

"To marry a girl, not for love but revenge, and with the intention of abusing the intimacies of marriage, is not an offence which (in the absence of conspiracy) can be easily reached by the law, but it appears to me to be one beside which murder may, under some circumstances, be an almost trivial crime."

"Well," Inspector Combridge replied, "the law doesn't recognise reasons for private murder, and I don't suppose that it ever will. But you win all the same. I shall have to call off the dogs. We agree that Miss Barman did it, and she's not guilty by English law. But there's one thing I should still like to know—out of curiosity, nothing else. You haven't told me why Mr. Colvin was in Razor Street at the time."

"I don't think Mr. Colvin will refuse that, if you still want to know "

John Colvin turned to the inspector with a friendlier regard than he had shown at their first meeting in Mrs. Nichols's dining-room. "I'm afraid, Inspector, I was rather rude when you called on me in Thurlow Road. You'll find the explanation rather an anticlimax if you've been thinking of me as hiding behind the doors, or sliding down the rain-spouts at Rosenbaum's, but I don't see what more I could have said to you at the time

"The fact is that a cousin of mine, Tom Colvin, died about twelve months ago, and left me executor of his will. He'd had a little business at the other end of Razor Street—Weinzel & Co. it's called—that imports Sicilian corals and shell, and as it provides the only income there is for a widow and two children, I've been trying to keep it on, going there on Sunday mornings, and Saturday afternoons more often than not.

"I hadn't told Miss Merritt about it because—well, it was foolish not to, but I'd been finding some money for it, and it was partly that which rendered me less able to help Mr. Merritt's business than I'd talked of doing at first. And I hadn't told my own firm, because, though I was doing no wrong to them, I wasn't sure how they'd take it, and I couldn't risk losing the only sure income I had. And not having told them would have made it worse if they'd first read of it as being brought out in court.

"And if you'd been more uncertain about Miss Barman because you were in a fog about me, I can't say that I should have minded that. Miss Barman's one of the best, and if anyone blames her for saving Miss Merritt from that filthy cad—well, you can't expect that I shall agree."

His glance turned from the detective as he concluded to Carol Marks, and Inspector Combridge, seeing the happiness in her meeting eyes, could not fail to observe that Abel Marks would have been even more trouble alive than he had been from the time of his too-sudden death. "No," he said, "I can't expect you to look at it like that."

CHAPTER XXXV.

MRS. WOOLCOTT EXPLAINS

INSPECTOR COMBRIDGE got up to go. He had heard enough, and he could not suppose that his prolonged presence would be particularly desired by those whom he had brought under so dark a shadow of the criminal law.

He excused himself, and shook hands with the cordiality of one who could accept defeat in a generous mood. He considered, as he walked away, that things might have been worse. Certainly worse for him. The miscarriage of justice, as he must still consider it to be, was one for which the lawyers, rather than his department, must take the blame, and his mind would be freed from the necessity of hunting for a culprit who did not exist, which was the too-frequent sequel of such a verdict being obtained. Certainly Mr. Jellipot had done him (as well as others) a good turn, when he had invited him to hear those explanations of convincing frankness.

But the jury's verdict was still a puzzle he could not solve. "He's clever," he said to himself. "Damned clever. But how could he have made out to himself that they'd take that view?"

His reflections were interrupted by P.C. Decker, who was coming away from the court, and halted before him.

"I thought you might be interested to know, sir, that the foreman of the Barman jury has just snuffed it. It'll be in the papers in half an hour."

The long-necked constable, whose discretion had once earned the praise of Superintendent Davis, spoke no more than the truth, being, among living men, the one most directly responsible for Mr. West's untimely decease.

Mr. West, after much gradual manoeuvring, which he had supposed to be unobserved, had made a dash for the street, and P.C. Decker, who had been given the duty of seeing that the Barman jury did not leave the precincts of the court, and who had been following his movements with suspicious eyes, started his long legs in much swifter pursuit.

At the grip of the constable's detaining hand, Mr. West lost his head. He struggled so fiercely that he actually broke away. He tried to board a rapidly passing bus, from the step of which he slipped to the street. Caught again, he struggled for a moment, and then collapsed.

"He was dead in five minutes," P.C. Decker said, with complaisance, as though the fact added virtue to his energetic vigilance. "Too flabby for that sort of game. Bad heart they'll be most likely to bring it in. Shaking with excitement like a leaf he was, when I caught him first. Like a leaf. Just like a leaf."

Inspector Combridge accepted the reiterated simile without comment, and thanked the constable for the information "Queer," he said to himself, "but still I don't see—"

He did not see very much more, even when a quite innocent man was arrested (and promptly discharged) in connexion with a large deficiency in the bank account of the Thomas West Stationery Co., and it was nearly a year later that a lady called upon Mr. Jellipot, whose face he faintly remembered as having been on the Barman jury.

She introduced herself as Mrs. Woolcott, and explained that she was a widow, having a teaching appointment which she was unwilling to resign. She had been offered marriage by a Mr. Osbert Clayton, and she desired legal advice as to whether a second marriage would jeopardise her position.

"I will advise you freely," Mr. Jellipot replied, "on the point you raise, if you will put me under an at least equal obligation by telling me how a jury which was resolved upon a manslaughter verdict became unanimous for acquittal during the night, an event for which I have received a degree of credit which I am confident that I do not deserve."

"Do you think I ought to disclose that?"

"Do you think it really necessary to ask me that question?"

"I am afraid it was rather gauche," she replied, smiling. "The fact was that I was the only one for acquittal at first, and I'm not sure now how much I had a real doubt, and how much I sympathised. But if you'd heard some of the reasons that some of them gave! You felt you'd simply got to say something sane on the other side. I was alone at first, but before we parted that night I'd got two of the men to come over to me.

"After that, we were separated—two other women and myself being put up at the hotel apart from the men. The two women were of no account. They'd both agree to anything the rest said rather than be kept there.

"I didn't see what happened after that, but I've been told. The foreman must have been in a desperate hurry to get away, as he showed by the way he acted afterwards. I suppose he saw that I wouldn't budge, and the only way was to come over to my side.

"Anyway, he bribed a waiter to take a lot of extra drinks in, and he persuaded the other men—six it would be that he'd have to talk over—that it would be better to let her go than to be kept longer themselves, and—well, I suppose that's what does happen on most juries, more or less."

"We must hope," Mr. Jellipot replied cautiously, "that it's most often better than that.... And now let's see what we can do for you."

ABOUT THE AUTHOR

SYDNEY FOWLER WRIGHT (1874-1965) penned over seventy volumes of science fiction, fantasy, classic mysteries, historical novels, poetry, and non-fiction, many of them being published by the Borgo Press Imprint of Wildside Press.

Printed in Great Britain
by Amazon